PRAISE FOR *DAUGHTERS OF THE LAKE*

"Simultaneously melancholy and sweet at its core."

—*Kirkus Reviews*

"Well-delineated characters and a suspenseful plot make this a winner."

—*Publishers Weekly*

"*Daughters of the Lake* has everything you could want in a spellbinding read: unexpected family secrets, ghosts, tragic love stories, intertwined fates."

—Refinery29

"Perfect for anyone who loves a good ghost story that bleeds into the present day."

—*Health*

"*Daughters of the Lake* is gothic to its core, a story of ghostly revenge, of wronged parties setting history right."

—*Star Tribune*

"*Daughters of the Lake* provides an immersive reading experience to those who love ghostly mysteries, time travel, and lovely descriptions."

—*New York Journal of Books*

"*Daughters of the Lake* is an alchemical blend of romance, intrigue, ancestry, and the supernatural."

-Bookreporter

THE
HAUNTING
OF
BRYNN
WILDER

OTHER BOOKS BY WENDY WEBB

THE
HAUNTING
OF

A NOVEL

BRYNN
WILDER

WENDY WEBB

LAKE UNION
PUBLISHING

Published by Lake Union Publishing, Seattle

www.apub.com

Amazon, the Amazon logo, and Lake Union Publishing are trademarks of Amazon.com, Inc., or its affiliates.

ISBN-13: 9781542020121
ISBN-10: 1542020123

Cover design by Damon Freeman

Printed in the United States of America

For the Illustrated Man,
who brought laughter back into my life.

PROLOGUE

Everyone is haunted by something. A road not taken. A hurt, carried deep inside. Harsh words that echo long after the sting of them is carried away on the wind.

Some of us are haunted more literally. We've seen and felt and heard what simply cannot be, but is. A low moan coming from the corner of a darkened room. A glimpse of an ethereal shape. A tangible encounter with . . . something. A passer-through.

My haunting is like that—strange, magical, unexplainable—but at the same time, it's real enough to touch and feel and wrap my whole self around. Real enough to inhabit my dreams and sit like a stone on my heart as I carry it with me day after day.

Memories of other parts of my life over the years—love, loss, the mundane minutiae of living—might be hazy around the edges, dream-like, as I look back on them now. But when I think of him, the one who haunts me still, the images are crystal clear. Even after all these years, I can taste him on my lips. Hear his voice, low and deep, in my ear. I love him with every cell in my body, even now.

As I sit alone with my thoughts in this empty house, in the dark, a fire crackling in the fireplace and snow falling outside, it all comes back to me. And I'll let it come. God help me, I will let it come.

CHAPTER ONE

Driving north from my home in Minneapolis, I was trying not to look into the rearview mirror at what I was leaving behind. *Focus on what you're heading toward,* I told myself. I was driving to Wharton, a tourist town on the shores of Lake Superior. It would be my home for the summer while I pushed the reset button on my life. Had I known what I was driving into, would I have turned around? I ask myself this question often.

But all I knew then was that my next three months would be about kayaking around a glorious chain of islands and letting the big water deliver the kind of peace that only it can give me. The native peoples in this area thought of this lake as a deity, and as far as I was concerned, they weren't wrong about that. Lake Superior had a way of dropping my blood pressure as I listened to the waves lap, lap, lapping at the rocky shoreline. I needed that, after the three nightmarish years I had just been through. A shudder ran through me, but I pushed those thoughts out of my mind and took in what was coming into view as I rounded the corner and began to descend into town.

In Wharton, there was nothing other than the discreet Wi-Fi signs in most establishments to betray the fact that the town had, indeed, entered the modern age. Instead, you'd find block after block of Victorian homes with widow's walks and balconies overlooking the most temperamental of the Great Lakes, whose mood could change from calm to deadly in an instant. No department stores or chain hotels, no fast food, no buildings more than three stories tall, no bustling nightlife. Only mom-and-pop markets, locally owned restaurants, small banks, stores with local artisans' work on display, apparel shops, and pharmacies. That was Wharton. It was like going back in time, but with all the modern conveniences. People flocked there, especially during the summer and fall, just to get a taste of what it felt like to time travel.

I was here at the urging of my friend Kate, whose family was from Wharton going back generations. Their home was now one of the town's most magnificent inns, Harrison's House, a stunning Victorian masterpiece on the hill overlooking the water.

I'd be spending time with her during my visit, but I would not be staying at the inn that she, her cousin Simon, and his husband, Jonathan, ran. Even with the discount they were prepared to give me, it was out of my financial reach to take up residence in that grand home for the summer. And I didn't want to take away the revenue they could get during high tourist season, which was just about to begin. So, they found me a place at LuAnn's, a century-old restaurant that had been a boardinghouse back in the day, with upstairs rooms rented by the week, the month, or the summer at prices that seemed to be taken from a simpler time.

This was what was rolling through my mind as I drove down the hill, watching the town, and the lake, laid out before me. Sailboats, their spinnakers unfurled, decorated the water, and ferries chugged in and out of the harbor on their way to the islands that dotted this area of the lake. One, Ile de Colette, was inhabited; the rest were wild. Boats were docked at the slip, and I saw people working on them, readying for the coming season. It was the week before Memorial Day, so tourists had not yet descended en masse, but a few people were strolling around the streets and wandering into the shops and restaurants, which were all open for business. I drove by Harrison's House and told myself to call Kate when I got settled, then made my way to LuAnn's, where I'd be living for the summer.

It was a three-story building with deep-red wooden siding and four-paned windows that looked as old as time. A neon sign proclaiming the establishment "Open" hung above the front door. I pulled into the parking lot.

A woman I assumed was LuAnn herself came outside to welcome me, leopard-print leggings, oversize glasses, bling around her neck and all. I put her at about seventy-five years old, maybe older?

"You must be Brynn," she said, squinting at me as I got out of the car.

"I am. You're LuAnn?"

She smiled a broad smile. "The one and only. Welcome, honey." She threaded an arm around mine. "Let me show you around. We can deal with your bags later."

We walked through the door, and I saw a restaurant that could have been plucked out of the 1950s. It was an odd disconnect. The building itself had a much older feel to it, as though the century-ago happenings inside of it still hung in the air, just out of reach. And yet I was standing in what looked like an old-fashioned diner.

Several round red-pleather barstools bellied up to a long linoleum-topped bar that was backed by what clearly had once been a soda fountain, now converted to dispense beer. A jukebox stood in one corner. Tables with a mishmash of chairs around them were scattered in two oak-paneled rooms. The tables themselves were a mix of styles, too—wooden, linoleum, tile topped, round, square, whatever.

Framed news clippings with historic headlines about D-Day, the moon walk, the Kennedy assassination, Watergate, Barack Obama's election, and other life-altering events in this country lined the walls, reflecting a time line of American life over the course of a century. I looked closer at one of them, a photo of a handsome young man standing at the front door of LuAnn's.

"Is that John F. Kennedy Junior?" I asked her.

"Adorable kid," she said, shaking her head. "He came here with a group of friends to kayak around the islands. Damn shame what happened."

I nodded in agreement. It was a damn shame.

"This place was built in the 1800s, originally as a boardinghouse." She gestured around the room. "Been remodeled a few times since then, obviously. We're open all day. Breakfast, lunch, and dinner. You get one meal a day with your stay, and you get half off if you choose to eat your other meals here, too. Alcohol is extra, but you can just run a tab and pay for it at the end of the month with your rent."

I nodded, looking around.

"Happy hour's at three every day except weekends," she said. "It's a good way to get to know people in town, if that's what you want. Everyone comes here."

"Okay," I said, taking it in.

She leaned over the front desk and fished an old-fashioned skeleton key off one of the hooks. "Let's go upstairs," she said. "I'll show you your digs. You'll like the room. It's one of my favorites."

I followed her through the dining room to a narrow door, which she opened, revealing a long and narrow staircase. We walked up the uneven stairs and entered a hallway with alcoves jutting out on either side. There weren't many rooms, just a handful. Mine was at the end, on the corner, next to a door with a large window that opened out onto a shared deck.

As we made our way down the hall, I shivered, just a little.

LuAnn opened my door to reveal a spacious room with light-yellow walls and big double-hung windows on two sides, each with sheer white curtains billowing in the breeze. The age of this room radiated out into my bones. A century of souls inhabiting a place will leave an imprint that lingers long after they're gone, and it lingered here. Not in a bad way. It felt well lived in.

A queen bed with a white down comforter and an antique wooden headboard sat on one wall. The dresser, complete with a curved mirror and a seat, looked to be from the same era. I caught a glimpse of myself in that mirror and wondered how many women, from how many time periods, had done the same. A rocking chair with a wide leather seat was perched near one of the windows, and a couple of comfy armchairs sat on either side of an end table that held an antique lamp with a rose-colored etched-glass shade.

A small fridge stood outside the bathroom next to a darling antique hutch, where a French press coffee maker was waiting for the morning along with two cups. A flat-screen TV hung on the wall, propelling the room into the present.

"Now, you're not going to want to be eating all of your meals out," LuAnn chattered on. "That gets spendy. There's a grocery store just a block up the hill. What most residents do is stock up on things like yogurt, cheese, fruit. Feel free to grab dishes, silverware, glasses, whatever you need, from the kitchen, and just return them when you're finished. You'll see the tubs where we put the restaurant's dirty dishes before they get loaded into the dishwasher. Gary or Aaron will take care of the washing up."

"Good to know."

I peeked into the bathroom. Just a toilet and a sink.

"Two showers and one bathtub are down here," she said, leading me through the hallway and opening one door, then another to reveal two tiled single shower rooms. A third held a deep claw-foot tub.

"You're sharing these with just one other summer lodger. There are six rooms total, and the suite—occupied all summer long by a couple—has a full bath, so they don't use these showers or the tub. That leaves two rooms for renters, who come and go."

I nodded.

"You'll find people are pretty courteous," LuAnn continued. "Nobody's taking long showers. You get in, you get out. Shampoo, conditioner, and bodywash are in containers on the wall in each shower. Baths are another story. People like to soak, and so be it. I find the tub isn't used too often, so if you like baths, bring a glass of wine and a good book, and don't worry about a backlog."

"Got it," I said, knowing I'd do exactly that.

"We've got towels, too, but there's no guarantee you'll find one when you'll need one, so Mickey's down the block has everything you need—towels, comfy robes, flip-flops, puffs. If you want your own shampoo and bodywash and other bath accessories, you can find them there, too. Most are locally made."

We walked past another stairway going up to a third level of the house. "You can go up there if you like," she said, waving an arm in an upward direction. "That's our bunk room. Had been a ballroom back in the day. Sometimes the staff stays after closing time and has a few drinks. Sometimes more than a few. I've got five bunks up there for people to crash in, so they don't drink and drive. Safety first, with no judgment from me."

All of a sudden, something didn't make sense. "Wait," I said, doing the math. "You said I'm sharing the showers with one summer lodger and the other has an en suite bath. That's three rooms. Two for renters, that's five. I thought there were six?"

LuAnn's face grew serious. "That's right. I've got one of the rooms shut up for now."

I was going to ask her why but didn't get the chance. Someone called for her from the restaurant, and she excused herself to attend to whatever it was.

I figured this would be a good time to unpack, so I traipsed back out to the car, hauled my suitcases upstairs, and set about organizing my things.

With that handled . . . *What next?* I wondered. I sank into one of the armchairs and gazed out the window. It had been so long since I'd had nothing to do, nobody to care for, no errands to run, no calls to make, no one depending on me for anything, that I wasn't sure what to do.

A vague sense of guilt pricked at my skin as I looked up and down the street. Was I forgetting something? Some important job that needed doing? My mind raced for a moment, but then I realized. No. It was truly over. I wished with all my soul it wasn't, but it was.

I plucked a tissue from the box on the bedside table, dabbed at my eyes, and pushed myself out of the chair. I scooped up my purse, remembering to grab the old skeleton key that LuAnn had set on the dresser, and locked the door on my way out.

CHAPTER TWO

I didn't get far. As I walked down the hallway, I noticed the door at the opposite end from my room was open. Inside, at a scrubbed wooden table facing the door, sat a handsome man who I assumed was in his late sixties. I caught his eye.

His face broke into a devilish grin, and he ran his hand through his thick white hair. "Hi!" he said. I couldn't help smiling back. That grin was infectious.

"I'm Brynn Wilder," I said. "Are you the other summer lodger?"

"One of them." He hopped to his feet and came out to greet me, extending his hand. "Jason Lord," he said, a positive energy radiating around him. "My husband, Gil, and I have been coming here every summer for . . . oh, let's see"—he looked off for a moment—"at least five years. Maybe six."

"I'm in the last room by the deck." I nodded down the hallway.

"Ah, the Yellow Lady." He smiled. "It's a lovely room. LuAnn told us you were arriving today. We've been looking forward to meeting you."

I peeked around him. "Wow," I said. "This is a suite?"

He gestured into the room. "Come in! Have a look around."

The two-level suite was enormous compared to my single room, and the vibe was totally different. It was like my room and this suite existed in two different moments in time. It had the same feel as the dining room in a way—plucked from elsewhere in time and set into the four walls of this seemingly timeless boardinghouse.

My room was vintage Victorian, but this suite was more like a Northwoods lodge. Warm wooden paneling lined the walls. The ceiling was open to the second-story hallway, which had a black wrought-iron railing. A stone fireplace reached all the way to the roof. A flat-screen TV sat on the hearth, which looked to be an entire tree trunk halved and polished so the wood shone. It faced a leather couch and love seat in the middle of the room. A small kitchen with a fridge, stove, sink, and some cherrywood cabinets was tucked into a corner, a marble-topped center island between it and the living room. On the far end of the room, french doors opened onto a private deck.

"We've got two bedrooms, two baths," Jason said. "It's really perfect for us. Much more homey than staying in a hotel all summer, plus, we like having the extra bedroom. Family always comes to visit, and this way, we can offer them a place to stay without the hassle of renting a house."

We stood in silence for a moment, smiling at each other. "Hey, it's five o'clock somewhere." He grinned. "How about a glass of wine?"

I had planned to head up to the grocery store, but it could wait. "I'd love that."

"It's a beautiful day," he said, opening the fridge and grabbing a bottle. "Why don't we sit on the deck and chat for a while?" He gestured toward the french doors. "You go make yourself at home, and I'll be right there."

Outside, I settled into an Adirondack chair and took in the view of the town's shops, restaurants, and inns that were up the rather steep hill from the lake. Jason popped outside a moment later carrying two glasses filled with white wine, then handed one to me.

"So, the question we summer people always get is: 'Oh, you're spending the *whole* summer?'" he said, sinking into his chair. "Be prepared for it, because everyone is going to ask. They all want to know if you're retired or taking time off or whatever. We're a nosy bunch here in Wharton."

I managed a chuckle, but nosy people were the last thing I wanted to deal with.

"You don't have to tell them anything, or you don't have to tell them the truth," Jason said, as if reading my thoughts. "But you should have an answer ready, especially if you're coming to happy hour today."

"I've heard about this happy hour." I sipped my wine, stalling for time. "LuAnn says it's quite popular. Everybody wants to know everybody's business, huh?"

Jason laughed. "This is a small town."

Since I'd be asked to offer some sort of explanation for why I was here, I thought I might as well practice my spiel. "An old friend of mine from college lives here," I began. "She suggested I come for the summer after a rather"—my words trailed off into a sigh—"a rather difficult few years."

He nodded. "I get it. Taking a break from the rest of the world?"

"Something like that," I said, tears pricking at the backs of my eyes. "I'm a college professor and was on sabbatical last year. I'm gearing up to go back to work in the fall, and I just wanted to take the summer to recharge."

Jason reached over and squeezed my arm. "This is a very good place to do that," he said, his voice impossibly kind.

I rested my head on the back of the chair and gave him a sidelong glance. "Thank you."

"Who's your friend?" he asked. "The one here in Wharton?"

"Kate Granger. Now it's Stone, I guess. She got married last year."

"Oh! We know her! Kate's cousin Simon is the reason we started coming here years ago. He and Gil go way back. They went to school together."

What a small world. Coincidences like this seemed to happen to me regularly. Some would argue they were not coincidences at all. I hadn't been close with Kate over these past few years—more than a few—but I knew she had gone through a divorce and an upheaval of her life. I had been too busy with my own problems to be present for hers, a situation I regretted. The fact she had reached out when she heard I needed some help made me regret it even more.

"So, our story." He cleared his throat and began. "After being a Realtor for many years, I now own a gaggle of rental properties, and Gil's a high school teacher. I can manage what I have to manage from anywhere—I've got a guy who handles any maintenance issues that come up. Gil's got the summers off, of course, so we like to take advantage of that, unplug from the world, and come here. It's sort of our 'life's too short' philosophy. Our boat is docked at the town pier, and we like to putter around from island to island—you'll have to join us sometime soon—and we're big kayakers, too. We've both been drawn to this lake as long as we can remember."

"It sounds lovely," I said. "What a nice way to live."

Jason sighed and ran a hand through his hair. A shiver ran through me, but I wasn't quite sure why.

"There's something different about this summer, though, something you really should be aware of, since you'll be living here," he said.

But he didn't get a chance to tell me what it was, because a man I presumed to be Gil poked his head around one of the french doors.

"Oh!" he said, looking at me, first with surprise, then with a grin. "Hello."

"You're back!" Jason said. "Honey, this is Brynn. She'll be in the Yellow Lady this summer. Brynn, my husband, Gil Tanaka."

Gil extended his hand. "Welcome," he said, his dark-brown eyes holding mine in their gaze. "I'd heard we were getting another summer lodger. You have hit on the best-kept secret in Wharton. I'd never stay anywhere else." He turned to Jason. "I don't want to be rude to our new neighbor, but we have that conference call in a couple of minutes. Remember?"

Jason glanced down at his watch. "Is it that time already?" He let out a theatrical groan and pushed himself up from his chair. "Brynn, please excuse us. This can't wait." He extended his hand to me and helped me up.

"Of course," I said. We walked back into the main room, toward the door, both sipping the last of our wine.

"It was so delightful to meet you," Jason said. "We'll see you at happy hour?"

"I'll be there."

As Jason was closing the door behind me, I caught a concerned look on Gil's face as the two men exchanged a glance. It made the hairs on the back of my neck stand up, and I wondered what was going on, if this call was about the "something different" about this summer that Jason had alluded to. But then I shooed those thoughts out of my mind. I wasn't going to be one of Wharton's busybodies. Their business was theirs. Not mine.

Groceries gathered, the cold stuff assembled in my fridge, and the shelf-stable items lined neatly on top of it, I was wondering what to do next when my phone rang.

"So, you made it." I recognized Kate's voice on the other end of the line. "Settling in?"

I nodded, as though she could see it. "It's great," I said. "The place has everything I need."

"LuAnn's a trip! You met her?"

I chuckled. "Leopard-print leggings and all. She seems really nice. And I met a couple of the other summer lodgers today, too."

"Jason and Gil?" she asked. "You'll love them. They've been friends of Simon's for a long time." Kate was silent for a moment, and then continued. "How are you holding up?"

I knew the question was coming, but my whole body stiffened when I heard it. "I'm doing okay."

"Yeah." Kate's voice was soft. "I'm so glad you agreed to come here. This will be just what you need. A summer of nothing but enjoying yourself. Getting back on your feet. The peace of this place will smooth out the rough edges and put life back into perspective again. I would know."

Kate had come to Wharton to stay with her cousin when her own life had fallen apart—a nasty divorce and the loss of her job in the process—and had found love and a new life here. I didn't know if I was ready for all of that, but the fact that she had found her feet again here in Wharton gave me hope that I might, too.

"I was planning to let you settle in and then come over for happy hour," Kate said. "But I've got a meeting with a bride—and her mother, God help me. The wedding is in our ballroom in the fall, and they're here to pick out the menu, sample some cakes, and go over the details."

She dragged the word *details* out so it had several extra syllables. I could hear the groan in her voice, and it made me chuckle.

"I can already tell meeting with brides is your favorite part of the job," I said.

She laughed. "You have no idea. We had one mother of the bride who asked if we could take the paneling out of the ballroom and paint the walls green to match their color scheme."

"No!"

"True! Simon and Jonathan have helpfully put me in charge of all things wedding because, after a few bridezillas—and momzillas—they 'couldn't even.'" She chuckled. "Anyway," she went on, "I probably won't be able to get there today unless—"

I cut her off. "Don't rush over here just for me," I said. "It's okay. Like you said, I'm settling in, and I'm pretty beat after the drive and . . . everything."

"Okay," she said. "Let's do lunch tomorrow or the next day to catch up."

"Sounds good to me." *I could use the time alone tonight,* I thought to myself.

After we hung up, I glanced at the clock to see I had plenty of time until the much-ballyhooed happy hour. Time enough to freshen up and rinse the travel out of my hair.

My stomach knotted a bit. I had made these arrangements in a hurry and didn't realize I'd be sharing a shower with strangers. I hadn't done that since my college dorm days, but when I thought about it for a bit, I remembered the drill. I had picked up a fluffy chenille robe, a couple of towels, and flip-flop sandals at a shop a few doors down. I got undressed, pulled my robe tightly around me, grabbed a big thirsty towel, and hurried down the hall, hoping nobody would be there.

I saw one shower room was occupied, but the other was free, so I quickly slipped into it and locked the door behind me. The white subway tile was pristine. There were the products, as LuAnn promised. Shampoo, conditioner, and bodywash in containers affixed to the wall. I hung my robe and towel on one of the hooks on the back of the door and turned on the taps, waiting a few moments until the water came up to temperature.

I stepped into the stream and turned my face to the water, letting it wash over me. I closed my eyes, and then the tears came, as they always did. The shower had been the place for me to cry for some time now. I tried not to utter a sound, not knowing how thick or thin the walls were. I imagined the water was washing away all the sadness that bubbled to the surface when I was vulnerable and unguarded, and I wondered how long it would take for all of it to be gone, when I could take a shower again without crying.

And then came a loud knock. My eyes shot open. I pulled my face from the stream and listened. Was somebody at the door? No, that was silly. It couldn't have been a knock. Maybe a hot-water pipe acting up? I shampooed my hair, rinsed, and then conditioned. And there it was again. Knocking. Bang, bang, bang. But it wasn't coming from the door. It was coming from the wall that the shower shared with another guest room.

A shiver ran through me. The banging continued as I hurried to rinse my hair, shut down the water, dry off, and pull my robe around me. I turbaned my hair with a towel, and only then did the banging stop. Now I was getting annoyed. The only explanation was another guest, deliberately banging on the shower wall. Why would they do that? How rude. I would have a talk with LuAnn about this.

I pulled open the door just as the occupant of the other shower room opened his door. My throat nearly seized up at the sight of him.

He was about six feet tall, a dark robe pulled around his massive chest, slippers on his feet. I could see tattoos peeking through the front slit of his robe, and on his wrists and legs. Strange religious symbols, animals, mystical shapes. I didn't look too long. I couldn't.

"Did you hear that?" he asked me, a slight southern accent making music of his words. His voice was the lowest and deepest and smoothest I had ever heard. "That banging?"

I just stared at him, my mouth open. What was I, thirteen years old? I managed to nod.

"You look like you've seen a ghost," he said to me, breaking into a wide movie-star grin. His mouth was perfect—the full lips, those startlingly white teeth. I couldn't take my eyes off his face. I couldn't respond. I was mesmerized, as though I were in the thrall of a cobra.

"Don't worry," he said with that voice again, humor buoying it. "It's just somebody messing with us, considering what they say about this place."

"What do they say?" I managed to squeak out, wishing he would just keep talking.

He laughed. "Don't you know? It's haunted."

I truly don't remember how I left him, or how I got back to my room. I only know that I somehow managed to pull myself together, get dressed, and dry my hair. I made my way downstairs to happy hour, determined to find out who this man was and if what he was saying was true.

CHAPTER THREE

The bar was packed with people. Laughter and conversation filled the air, and more than one head turned when I walked into the room. I was the new girl in town, and everyone already knew it. I spotted Jason and Gil, who both put up a hand in greeting. I smiled into a sea of curious, if friendly, faces on my way over to join them.

Jason took a glass of white wine from the bartender and handed it to me. "This is Gary," he said to me, nodding his head toward the man. "He's ground zero for everything around here. Gare, meet Brynn. She's in Wharton for the summer."

Bartender Gary was a grizzled sixty or so, his heavily lined face witness to a life hard lived.

"Welcome," he said to me, his smile warm. "Anything you need, you just come to me. I'm here all the time—too much!" He let out a throaty, whiskey-soaked laugh. "Seriously, though, whatever you need, I'll be here."

"Thank you." I smiled at him.

He held my gaze longer than I was comfortable with. Was he trying to say something to me?

I sipped my wine and turned to Jason and Gil, who led me a few steps away.

"So! Are you getting settled in?" Gil asked.

"I'm all unpacked, and I had the most interesting—"

I was going to tell them about my encounter with the other summer lodger, but just then, LuAnn circled by carrying a tray of meats and cheeses.

"Hi, honey," she chirped at me. "I see you've met these two ne'er-do-wells." She nodded her head at Jason and Gil and gave them a wink. "Everybody that's here right now I call the usual suspects. People who own or work at the inns in town, restaurant owners, people with summer places here."

I looked around at the crowd of about twenty people.

"Don't worry, you'll get to know faces and names in time," she said, brandishing her tray. "Now have some snacks, all of you, before the vultures descend."

A dark-haired woman, whose back had been to me, turned around toward LuAnn. "Who're you calling a vulture?" She took slices of cheese and salami and popped them into her mouth.

"Brynn, meet Beth St. John," LuAnn said to me. "She owns the bookstore down the street."

Beth was a woman of about fifty, with a round, kind face and big, dark eyes.

"I was glad to see Wharton had a bookstore," I said, smiling at her. "Haven't had too much time for reading lately, but I'm hoping to change that this summer."

"Heard you were here for the duration," she said. "What brings you here?"

Jason caught my eye and grinned. "I'm just enjoying the summer recharging," I said, repeating the line I had said to him earlier.

"This is a good place to do that," Beth said, giving me a look that I couldn't quite define.

"Beth is a true local," LuAnn told me. "Most of us have come from other places, but she grew up just down the road."

"Oh?" I asked.

"On the rez just outside of town," Beth said, taking a sip of her drink. "I tried to move to other places, but Lake Superior kept calling to me."

"I can understand that," I said. "It's beautiful here."

She smiled. "Peaceful, too. C'mon over to the bookstore anytime. If only to get away from this old biddy for a minute."

At this, LuAnn squealed. "Biddy, my ass," she laughed. "Now, if you want to call me a cougar, that's a title I'll take." She lowered her voice to a conspiratorial whisper and raised her eyebrows. "Especially with the new guy in town."

Beth gave her a mock scowl. "I think it's against some sort of hotelier bylaw to hit on guests half your age."

"Hey, that's the best perk of the job!" LuAnn chortled.

Laughter then, all around. LuAnn circled off with her tray, and Beth excused herself, though not before squeezing my arm and offering another welcome to town, leaving Jason, Gil, and me to ourselves.

"I think I met him today," I said to them. "The man LuAnn and Beth were talking about."

"Oh?" Jason said, raising his eyebrows.

"We came out of the shower rooms at the same time."

Jason and Gil exchanged a glance. "The Illustrated Man?" Jason said. "Do tell!"

I couldn't help smiling. "Why do you call him that?"

"Didn't you notice?" Jason lowered his voice to a whisper. "He's covered in tattoos!"

I could feel my face heat up. "I did notice but didn't see much," I said. "I didn't want to look too long."

Gil let out a hoot. "I know! You want to figure out exactly what the symbols are, but you don't want to stare like a crazy person."

The three of us shared a laugh.

"So, what's his story?" I asked. "Who is he?"

Jason leaned in and took a sip of his wine. "We don't really know," he said. "LuAnn has been uncharacteristically tight-lipped about him. He got here a week or so ago. We haven't met him properly. He comes and goes at all hours. All we know is that the man is ungodly handsome."

"The smile," Gil added.

"The smile!" I could feel myself blushing. "He smiled at me, and it was like I was paralyzed. I felt like I was back in middle school."

They both laughed at that.

"He never socializes," Gil said. "He hasn't been to happy hour since he got here. I don't know if he's met—" Gil's words were stopped short by the Illustrated Man himself walking into the room.

He was wearing a long-sleeved black T-shirt, tight enough to outline his muscled physique, and faded jeans with black boots on his feet. The three of us fell silent as he walked through the room toward us. I noticed others watching him, too. All of us held our breath as he drew closer, and I realized he was walking toward me.

"We didn't get a chance to be properly introduced earlier," he said to me, his eyes twinkling with humor.

Had I ever seen that before? Did eyes really twinkle? Yet that was what it seemed to me, at the time. He held out his hand, and I took it. Electricity shot through me when skin met skin.

"I'm Brynn Wilder," I said, glad I remembered my own name even as my words were stumbling over each other. "I'm here for the summer. I just arrived."

"Hello, Brynn Wilder," the Illustrated Man said. Gil shot Jason a look. "I'm here for the summer, too, depending on a few things. I'm Dominic James."

I just stood there for a moment, holding this man's large, strong hand, staring into his impossibly handsome face. I could not come up with any words with which to respond. Thank goodness Jason jumped to my rescue.

"Jason Lord," he said, extending his hand to Dominic, who squeezed mine and gave me a wink before taking Jason's hand in his. Jason went on. "All of us summer residents should know each other. This is my husband, Gil."

"Hello!" Gil smiled at Dominic, his next words coming out in one long, quick stream. "We've seen you coming and going from time to time but just haven't had the chance to meet. We're in the suite at the end of the hall."

Dominic nodded. "Oh, yes," he said. "LuAnn told me about you. Glad we're finally getting a chance to meet. I've been busy tying up some loose ends before the summer really gets going and haven't been too sociable. I'm sorry about that."

Jason and Gil both went through a chorus of "Don't be silly!" and "Think nothing of it!" before Dominic broke in.

"It looks like I'm the only one without something to drink," he said, turning that electric smile at Gary.

Jason pulled a face at me behind Dominic's back, and we started giggling silently like children in church. Gil pinched Jason's arm and gave him a mock scowl, quieting us down before Dominic turned back around toward us, holding a beer. He raised it slightly at the three of us.

"To the beginning of summer," he said, his voice so deep and low it sounded like velvet. I clinked glasses with him and wondered exactly what this summer might hold.

CHAPTER FOUR

After happy hour wound down and people trickled off to their shops, restaurants, and homes, Dominic excused himself to make a phone call. Jason, Gil, and I found ourselves alone at the bar, finishing up the appetizers.

"Okay, so that was interesting," Jason said, raising his eyebrows. "He was really nice, don't you think?"

"Who?" Gil asked, brushing an unseen piece of lint off his shoulder.

Jason threw a piece of salami at him. "Who."

The three of us shared a laugh.

"I don't want to be Captain Obvious here, but wow, that is one handsome man," I said.

"Tell me about it," Gil said. "He's unsettling."

I took a sip of wine. "Has anyone asked him *the* question?"

"The 'Why are you in Wharton all summer?' question?" Jason asked. "No, I haven't. This is the first time we've talked to him."

Gary emerged from the kitchen and poured a drink for himself. He popped some cheese into his mouth. "I'm all prepped for the dinner rush," he said, "but I don't think we're going to have much of one tonight. Too early in the season yet."

Jason narrowed his eyes at him. "Do you and LuAnn know why Dominic is in Wharton?"

Gary smiled. "I plead the Fifth," he said. "Listen, my policy is a guest's business is their business. I don't get involved."

"I've never seen him before, so I'm assuming he's new to Wharton," Jason pressed.

"Fifth," Gary said, calmly taking a sip of his drink.

"He had to have heard about LuAnn's from someone. It's not exactly on the map."

"*F-I-F-T* and *H*."

Jason shook his head and took a sip of wine, scowling at Gary. "Remind me to use you if I ever need an alibi."

Although I wanted to know more about Dominic, I appreciated Gary's level of discretion. There was clearly no use in asking any more questions.

Gil glanced down at his watch, tapped it, and gave Jason a look.

"Oh!" Jason said, pushing himself off his barstool. "We've got dinner plans." He leaned down and gave me a quick peck on the cheek. "Brynn, you are lovely. I'm so glad you'll be here with us for the summer. See you tomorrow?"

"I'll be around," I said as they hurried out the door.

For the second time in one day, I wasn't sure what to do with myself. Go back to my room? Wander around town? Neither sounded like great options.

"Want some dinner, doll?" Gary asked me.

Doll. Nobody had ever called me that. It was so 1950s that it made me smile. I liked it.

"Whatcha got?" I asked him.

He leaned over the counter. "Everything on the menu is good here, because I make it myself when those kids who call themselves my cooks aren't around. But for the special tonight, I've been roasting a pork shoulder all day with Mexican spices, and it smells like heaven. It would make a mean burrito if you're wanting one."

"Ooh, that's tempting."

"LuAnn herself likes a concoction she calls a taco salad burrito," he went on. "It's basically a taco salad, with the pork, lettuce dressed with chipotle ranch, tomatoes, and onions, along with refried beans and melted cheese, wrapped in a tortilla. Sour cream, guac, and salsa on the side."

That was all I needed to hear. "Yes, please," I said, not remembering the last time I had eaten anything that decadent.

"You go sit at that four-top by the windows, and I'll whip it up for you," Gary said, disappearing into the kitchen.

I did as I was told. Sitting there on my own, with nobody to talk to, nobody to take care of, nothing to worry about, I gazed out the window and let my mind simply exist in, and appreciate, the present. I was here in a beautiful little town for the summer. This boardinghouse was filled with nice strangers who might become friends as we got to know each other. I exhaled, realizing I was at peace for the first time in a very long time.

Gary emerged from the kitchen with my plate and set it in front of me.

"This burrito is as big as my head." I smiled up at him.

He laughed. "That's how we do it here. Enjoy, doll."

I noticed some other patrons coming through the door. The dinner rush was starting, and Gary was back on the clock.

I dove into the rather large slice of heaven on my plate and watched the streetscape as I ate, people coming and going up and down the block, everyone laughing and having a good time. There was a positive vibe here. I was glad to be part of it.

Later, after polishing off that enormous burrito, I thought about taking a walk, but in the end, I made my way back up to my room, snuggled into bed, and flipped on the television. I made a mental note to stop in at the bookstore the next day. Reading for pleasure with nothing more important to do. What a delicious idea.

One day down in my Wharton summer. *I can do this,* I said to myself, exhaling. *I can do this.*

I awoke to find my room bathed in moonlight. I hadn't pulled the shades when I had finally turned off the TV and gone to sleep, preferring to lie in my bed and look up at the sky full of stars through the window. I sat up, took a sip from the glass of water on my nightstand, and settled back under the covers.

"Hellooo?"

It was a voice as thin as tissue paper. I shot up, looking around my room. The moonlight shone in through the windows—there was the dresser, my closet, the door to the hallway (latched, I could see from my bed). I shook my head, not sure I had heard anything at all. Maybe it was the remnant of a dream.

"Hello? Is anybody here?" There it was again, scratchy and thin, as though it were coming from another time.

I slipped out of bed and grabbed my robe from a hook inside my closet door. I drew it tightly around me and padded up to my door to listen. The knob turned and rattled, first tentatively, slowly. Somebody was trying the door.

"Will you let me in?" the singsongy voice said. "Please, won't you let me in?"

Would I let her in? Oh, hell no! I was frozen, staring at the door. Is this what Dominic was talking about earlier when I had met him at the showers? Was this the haunting? I watched as my doorknob turned back and forth, back and forth. Click, clock, click, clock.

Someone was trying to get into my room.

Then, a scuffling out in the hallway. Urgent voices, in whispers. Jason? I couldn't be sure who it was, and I certainly wasn't opening the door to find out. I listened as the voices seemed to make their way down the hall, fading until they disappeared.

I stood there for a good long time, my ear to the door. All was quiet. Wasn't it? I let out a breath I wasn't even aware I had been holding.

I had the urge to open the door to ensure the hallway was really empty, but I thought better of it. That's what they did—monsters, ghosts, the undead—they waited quietly until you decided to check if they were gone. I'd seen enough movies to know that. I chuckled a bit at this silly thought and slipped back into bed, my robe still belted tightly around me.

But I lay there, my eyes wide open, my pulse racing. It took a while for my breathing to slow and my eyes to feel heavy once again.

As I was drifting off, not quite asleep yet, a dream came bubbling out of wherever they come from. It was one of those lucid dreams—I have them often—in which I commented to myself, almost like I was the narrator, about what was happening in the dream.

A woman I didn't know, a lovely blonde older woman, reed thin, dressed in cream-colored slacks and a sweater set, was standing in front of the house where I grew up, a 1950s split-level home on a wooded lot not far from a meandering creek in the suburbs of Minneapolis. She was smiling at me, beckoning me to come closer.

"Hello," she said. "I have something to show you." She gestured to the door of my house. "Go on in."

I walked through the door. The foyer was just as I remembered it, a short set of stairs on the right, living room on the left, kitchen straight ahead. I took a few steps into the living room—the rust-colored shag carpet looked new, as did the sofa and armchair with big rust-colored flowers that my mother had bought when I was a kid. I hadn't thought of those in years.

I looked out the front window and saw all my neighborhood friends, children as they were decades earlier, playing. Some were running through the front yards, others were riding their bikes in lazy circles on the street. I glanced back at the new carpet and sofa, and out again to the kids outside. The year was somewhere in the late 1970s.

Two little girls were standing on the bridge that spanned the creek. I watched as they dropped sticks over the side and ran across the street to the bridge on the other side, peering down at the water. Pooh Sticks, we used to call it. Whoever's stick drifted under the bridge the fastest won.

The girls on the bridge looked over at me, seeing me peering at them from our front window, and waved. And that's when I saw it. One of them was my best friend, Jane, who lived across the street. She had a pixie cut, and she looked like one, too—blonde, blue-eyed, beautiful.

The other girl was me. I actually remembered the pants my little dream self was wearing. White denim jeans with colorful flowers embroidered on them. I had a pair like those when I was in the fourth grade. *Look at that*, I said to myself. *I haven't thought of those pants in decades.*

The girls ran off the bridge and down the riverbank toward the water—an act strictly forbidden by our parents—and I knew they were going to make a game of walking across the creek under the bridge on a beam that ran the length of the creek bed, maybe seeing some crayfish or bullheads along the way. The idea was to get all the way across without slipping and falling into the water. I hurried to the door and poked my head out.

"Watch out for the turtle!" I called to them.

When I was a kid, the entire neighborhood of children took a collective breath when the enormous ancient snapping turtle who lived somewhere under that bridge decided to walk across the road from one side to the other. It was a living, breathing reminder that danger lurked in that dark water, danger of all kinds.

I glanced across the street at the house kitty-corner from ours, and saw that the garage door was open and several parents from the neighborhood, young couples who were about my age now but had seemed so old to me when I was a child, were gathered there. Everyone had a drink in hand. Many were smoking.

One of the men was flipping burgers on a grill in the driveway while the others supervised earnestly. There was my dad, holding court as he always did, telling stories that had the other men in stitches. He looked so young and handsome, dapper in his short-sleeved, red-and-white-striped shirt. I watched as he turned his gaze to the group of women who were standing near the makeshift bar, and he caught my mother's eye and smiled. She lifted the drink she was holding, beaming back at him. He lifted his. A private toast amid a crowded party. So like them.

My mother. She was wearing a brightly colored sleeveless sundress printed with big psychedelic flowers. She was wearing flats—uncharacteristically, since she wore heels every day—her dark hair in curls around her face. She held a cigarette in one hand and a drink in the other, and she was laughing.

I often thought she had a Jackie Kennedy air about her—sophisticated, always dressed to the nines. She bought her first pair of jeans when she was in her eighties, and then went hog wild and got a jean jacket, too, embroidered with flowers like the ones on my white pants. But on this day, and for most of my childhood, she was Jackie O.

She looked across the street and saw me watching her. She smiled. "Mom," I whispered.

"You want to go back, but you can't."

I snapped my head around. There, sitting on the couch in front of the window, was my grandma. She had lived with us while I was growing up. She rarely went along when my parents socialized with the neighbors, preferring to stay home with my brothers and me instead.

She had died when she was ninety-one, after suffering a series of ministrokes. I went with her to the hospital when she had the first one, a TIA they called it. She had been sitting on the couch in our living room, in the same place she was sitting now in my dream, telling me a story, but then her words stopped in midair. Her amused expression dissolved into one of confusion and even fear. She held my gaze for a terrible moment in which time seemed to stop. It was like she was paralyzed.

"Gram?" I had said. "Are you okay?"

She just stared at me, unblinking, but I knew her eyes were pleading with me to do something.

"We need an ambulance," I called out to my brother, my mom, anyone who was within earshot. "Now."

She had come back to herself by the time we got to the hospital and was joking and laughing with the nurses. One of the nurses, clipboard in hand, asked her about the medications she was currently taking.

"I don't take any medications," my grandma had said.

The nurse had turned to me and, in a stage whisper, asked, "What meds is she on?"

My grandma winked at me, and I smiled back. "None," I said. "She hasn't been to the doctor since my mom was born. Sixty-five years ago."

The nurse looked at me, openmouthed, and then left the room. I could hear her talking to the other nurses. "I've got an eighty-eight-year-old woman who isn't on any medications!"

That was my grandma. A feisty, funny Finlander, a daughter of immigrants. She never took any sort of medication with the exceptions of a white chalky mint when she had an upset stomach and a hot drink of brandy and honey when she had a cold.

Many people in my culture don't get the experience of living with their grandparents, and that makes me feel sorry for them. She added so much laughter to my life. When my parents imposed rules on my headstrong teenager self, Gram was my confidante and sounding board and, oftentimes, my partner in crime. When I would come home as a broke college student, she was always the one who would slip a folded twenty-dollar bill into my palm, giving me a wink. "Have fun with it," she'd say.

And here she was, in my dream. I hadn't seen her in so long.

"Gram," I whispered. But when I got to the couch where she was sitting, she was gone.

And then the house crumbled around me. The scene across the street, the playtime at the creek, the parents and their laughter, all of it disappeared. I was standing in a pile of ash.

My eyes shot open, and I sat up in bed, my heart racing. My face was wet with tears. I hadn't even known I'd been crying.

I blew my nose and took a sip from the glass of water on my nightstand, glancing at the clock. Just fuzzy red symbols. I squinted. Two o'clock? Three? My glasses were on the nightstand, but whatever time it was, it didn't matter. It was dark, and I wanted to disappear into my dreams again, back into my past, a world that had long since disappeared, and yet had seemed so tangible and real when I was dreaming about it. I lay back down and drew the covers up to my neck, curling into a ball. I was cold deep inside.

CHAPTER FIVE

I must've fallen back asleep because I woke to a new day, the sun streaming in. I stretched, and then it came back to me. The voice in the hallway. The dream about my childhood. I shook my head, trying to rattle the thoughts out of it.

I looked around the room, but saw nothing unusual. There was the dresser, my minifridge, the television. The bathroom door was slightly ajar, just as I had left it. My glasses were on the nightstand. I slipped out of bed. It was the second day of my new life.

I swallowed my morning pills with a big gulp of water. The doctors said they would help. I wasn't so sure. But I was taking them dutifully anyway, just so nobody could say I was part of the problem. Or all of the problem.

The night still hung in the air around me, like fog. Coffee was definitely in order. I ran a brush through my hair, hopped into jeans and a T-shirt, and slid my glasses on, intending to head downstairs to the restaurant.

But as I was pulling my door shut behind me, I noticed Dominic sitting on the balcony at the end of the hallway, overlooking the lake, a full carafe of French press coffee on the end table next to him. He turned his head to look at me, as though sensing I was there.

"Good morning!" he called out. His expression was open and inviting, so I walked out on the balcony to join him, my heart pounding.

The lake shimmered. Down the street to the harbor I could see a handful of boats already moored to their slips. A sailboat floated lazily by, its colorful spinnaker unfurled, and the ferry that made its way to the islands every twenty minutes was chugging its way across the bay.

Wharton was the jumping-off point for travelers to explore the Redemption Islands, a chain of impossibly lovely wooded, mostly uninhabited (save a lighthouse or two) islands that attracted campers, hikers, and kayakers from around the world.

Only one of the islands, Ile de Colette, had a community of year-round residents and summer-cabin owners as well. I hadn't been there in a long time, but I was going to make it a point to hop on the ferry soon and take a look around.

"What a beautiful morning," I mused, still staring out over the water.

"Join me for some coffee?" Dominic asked, lifting up his French press. "There's too much for just me."

I smiled down at him. "I'll grab my mug," I said, and hurried back to my room, where I scooped it up and popped open my little fridge, grabbing my carton of half-and-half. Back on the balcony, Dominic poured coffee into my mug, and I watched as steam rose in the chilly air. It felt good, the cool nip on my face. I settled into the Adirondack chair next to him and, after splashing my coffee with half-and-half, took a sip.

"Thank you," I said, raising my mug. "Can't get the day started without coffee. Especially this morning."

"True that." Dominic smiled. "Long night?"

I leaned my head onto the back of the chair and sighed. "First night in a new place, I guess. I didn't sleep much."

"I get it. A new environment, new sounds at night. Unidentified creaks and groans. It can take a while to feel comfortable."

New sounds, indeed. I wasn't intending to bring it up, but I heard myself saying the words.

"Did you hear anything in the hallway last night?" I asked him.

He narrowed his eyes and grinned. "No," he said. "Should I have?"

I took another sip of my coffee. "Well, you did say the place was haunted."

Dominic laughed then, a deep chuckle that made me feel warm on the inside. "That's what LuAnn says. You should talk to her about it. Or Gary. He's got the stories. Did you hear something ghostly? Chains, maybe?"

"No, just the odd moan or two of the undead," I said, raising my eyebrows. We both smiled, but I cleared my throat. "I did hear someone, though. A woman."

He held my eyes in his gaze for a long moment. "What did she say?"

I winced. "She asked if anyone was there, and if I would let her in."

Dominic's eyes grew wide. "Let her in? What? Hell no!"

I dissolved into laughter at the horrified expression on his face. "That's exactly what I thought," I said.

"So, you didn't let her in?"

"A disembodied voice asks me to let them into my room in the middle of the night? I'm going to go with no every time. It's one of my rules to live by."

Dominic laughed and shook his head. "Sensible."

"Are there any other guests?" I asked him. "I was thinking it was just you and me, and Gil and Jason, but another of the rooms could be rented."

He shook his head. "I didn't hear of anyone checking in, but I went to bed pretty early last night."

"Same here," I said.

Both of us exhaled then. We stared out at the water for a while, and then Dominic broke our silence.

"Now that your day has started, what will it hold?"

I took a last sip. "I thought maybe I'd ramble around town this morning and get reacquainted with the place. It's been a while since I've been here."

He nodded. "What brought you back?"

The inevitable question. "I just needed a break," I said. "I'm a professor. I was on sabbatical last year, and I'm gearing up to go back to work in the fall. Not sure I want to, actually."

I winced at the thought of it. I hadn't admitted this out loud to anyone, but I wasn't sure I had it in me. The first student—or worse yet, his or her mother—who complained about a grade would do me in.

"A professor, huh? What do you profess?"

I smiled at that. "Modern American literature."

"Is that right?" he said. "Why literature?"

"Why?" I asked, furrowing my brow.

"Why do you spend your life focusing on that? What's important to you about it?"

His eyes were filled with curiosity, looking not so much at me, but into me. I couldn't remember if anybody had ever asked me that before.

"I've loved reading since I was a kid," I said. "But I noticed that, in college, I wasn't reading much. Not for pleasure. Just the books I was assigned to read for classes. I hadn't read anything current in years. So, when I decided I wanted to go into teaching—I loved the idea of spending my life on a college campus—it just made sense to me to follow my passion where it led. As it turns out, I really love the idea that I'm giving students the opportunity to read fun and interesting current works of fiction in contrast to all of their schoolwork. I like to think I'm giving them a respite from studying."

"Now that doesn't sound like a lady who doesn't want to go back to teaching."

I had said the words, and meant them, but I couldn't imagine getting back to the normalcy of my job. September would indeed arrive.

Students would file into my classroom. I'd get through it, one way or another. That was what the doctors said, at least.

He took another sip of his coffee, and I noticed his perfectly chiseled jawline.

"So, did you write the great American novel on your sabbatical?" he asked, eyeing me over the rim of his coffee mug. "Isn't that what literature professors do?"

I winced. "Not exactly," I said.

The image of my mother floated into my mind.

"This is going to be so hard for you," she had said, looking up at me with sunken eyes from the bed where she lay dying. They were the last words she ever said to me. But they were not the last words she spoke.

I had turned my parents' guest bedroom into a hospice, bringing in a hospital bed for her and hiring nurses to come in around the clock. They had wanted to move her to an actual hospice facility, but I wouldn't hear of it. I was the one making the decisions then; my dad was too strangled by his grief and terror to do anything but hold her hand and tell her how much he loved her. They had started their lives in that little house in the small town where they both grew up, and that was where my mother would end hers if I had anything to say about it, not in some sterile hospital room hooked up to God knew what kind of machines.

My parents had met just after my dad returned home from serving in World War II. He was making his way through the crowd on the main street of their little town to find a good place to watch the Fourth of July parade honoring the returning vets. The street was packed with townspeople, waving flags and wearing red, white, and blue.

"Wilder!" It was his best friend, George, standing with a handful of guys, the usual suspects with whom my dad had spent his youth. "Old man Stinson says we can watch from the roof of the White Cross."

They'd all shuffled into the White Cross Pharmacy and headed up the back stairs to the roof, just in time to see the high school marching band making its way down the street. They were playing "In the Mood." Leading the band was the drum majorette, throwing her baton high in the air and twirling around before catching it on the way down.

My dad nudged George. "Who's that?"

George gaped at him. "Who's that? It's Claudia Cummings, brainless! Every guy in town is after her. Get in line, pal."

He didn't get in line. He marched right to the front of it. On their first date, he took her to a supper club he couldn't afford that featured live music, and they danced the night away. They were engaged shortly thereafter, and he spent the next year trying to convince her father and grandfather he was worthy of this extraordinary girl.

They were married a year after that, and moved into a little story-and-a-half house they built, not unlike other postwar houses around town. Word had it, they bought the first television in town, and friends and neighbors would come over to watch this brand-new form of entertainment in my parents' living room.

My dad was transferred for his job—sales—several times during the intervening years, ending up in Minneapolis, where I was born, in the house by the creek where the snapping turtle lurked.

But as my parents neared retirement age, their thoughts drifted back toward their hometown. By chance, the little postwar-era-style bungalow they had built when they first got married went on the market, so my dad bought it as a surprise for my mom, and they settled into their last chapter in the house where they had begun their first.

My mom was delighted to find that, all of those years later, the art deco fixture she had picked out for their bedroom ceiling light when she was a young bride was still there.

It was the last thing she saw before we transferred her to the hospice room we had set up for her.

A framed picture of the two of them as a young married couple hung on the wall, and it always gave me an unsettling feeling about the passage of time. There they were in that photo, so young and beautiful, dressed up for a night on the town, my mom in a flowy green dress and my dad, dapper as ever, in a suit and bow tie. Nearly seventy years later, she lay dying in that same house.

She had often said that the years had passed so quickly, in an instant, an entire lifetime filled with home, children, love, loss, career success and then retirement, my parents' golden years spent kicking up their heels with friends and family until my mother couldn't kick anymore.

One minute, she was a young bride, the next a powerful career woman in corporate America—she used to tell me she was Wonder Woman in disguise, and I believed her, and still do—and the next, she was dying. Fragile as a baby bird. Emaciated by not just cancer but the treatment meant to hold it at bay.

"This is going to be so hard for you."

It had all happened so fast.

On her last day, they had arrived with the hospital bed in an effort to make her more comfortable, but then there was the matter of moving her into it. She was completely immobile at that point—all her muscle was gone; she couldn't even raise her own head. She claimed to be ninety pounds, but I didn't believe it. Seventy? Eighty? She was the definition of *skin and bone*. That was what the cancer had done.

To move her to the hospital bed in the guest bedroom, my brother and I just scooped her up and carried her there, holding each other's arms to create a sort of chair, her riding in the middle.

"I feel like Cleopatra!" she'd said, smiling from ear to ear.

Earlier, the minister had come and given her the last rites. He asked us all—my dad, my brother, and me—to hold hands around her bedside while he said some words I didn't hear or understand. I held one of her hands; my dad held the other. At one point I caught her eye, and she gave me a little smirk. Too much fuss for her.

Her longtime doctor had visited, too, earlier in the day. My dad noted several times at the funeral that the doctor was famous for not making house calls, and yet there he was. He came for my mother.

"You have taught me so much about how to live life to the fullest," the doctor had said to her, holding her hand. "It has been my honor to know you."

I watched from the doorway as he'd put a hand on her cheek. "You are an extraordinary woman," he said. "You have lived an extraordinary life. You have raised a wonderful family together with your husband of a million years. Such a marriage you've had. We're all envious of it. You have so much to be proud of. To look back on. You will live on in your son and daughter and their children if they ever get busy and get on with their lives. You will not be forgotten."

My mother managed a smile and a nod.

"Be at peace, wonderful lady," he said. "You will leave this earth better than you found it. That is all any of us can ask."

I had never seen this—a deathbed farewell. So that was how it was done. I hadn't done it. I couldn't. I hardly said anything to her that day.

My mom looked up at her doctor and smiled. "Take care of him," she said, and I knew she meant my dad. "He's going to need all hands on deck when I'm gone." Her voice was thin and papery.

A solemn look passed between them. "Like I would care for my own father," he said, and I watched him wipe a tear from her eye.

Later, after my mom had closed her eyes, the hospice nurse pulled me aside. "She's in a lot of pain," the nurse said. "We usually give them morphine at this stage to keep them comfortable."

I nodded, my own grief strangling my words into silence.

"Do I have your permission to—" She held my gaze. "You don't want her in any pain."

I looked into this woman's eyes, and I knew what she was saying to me. My mom weighed all of eighty pounds at this point, and she was in terrible pain. She'd had her last rites, and her family was gathered. This was the end.

My mom was already drifting into another world, her eyes fluttering open and closed. I wondered if Gram, who had passed a decade earlier, and my other brother, Randy, who had died of a heart attack shortly thereafter, were nearby.

"Please do what you can to keep her comfortable. We don't want her in any pain."

And I knew it was the end. A feeling of utter panic shot through me. One dose of morphine and the person who had loved me first and fiercest, my rock of steadfast support during every crazy and ill-advised decision I had ever made, my touchstone who made me laugh during good times and cried with me and shored me up during hard times, the woman whose wit and wisdom were razor sharp, would never open her eyes again and, soon, would not be alive on this earth any longer.

How could that possibly be? And then what would I do?

I had been with her through it all, from the day we sat in her oncologist's office and heard the diagnosis of stage four cancer, through three years of chemotherapy every other week that eventually took her hair and fifty pounds off her already-small frame.

She didn't care one bit about the hair. The day she got her wig, she texted me: "I look ten years younger! Why didn't I do this earlier?"

Texting. That was a new thing for her. I had bought her an iPad for Christmas that year to replace the dinosaur of a desktop computer she had been using for eons.

"Hey, look who is texting," she wrote in her first-ever message. She and my dad had zipped off for a weekend in Wharton after a round of chemo. As she always did, she contacted me to let me know they had arrived safely. "We are staying a couple of nights. Why not? The weather is gorgeous. We live our lives day by day. So far, so good! Love, M & D."

All of it came flooding back as I was sitting on the deck with Dominic that morning in Wharton.

"I didn't write the great American novel," I said to him, finally. "I was taking care of my mom. Cancer."

The words burned on my tongue. I was afraid to look him in the eye, to have him see the tears in mine.

"She passed." It wasn't a question. He knew.

I nodded. And those tears came.

He reached over and took my hand. "I'd say I'm sorry, but that just doesn't cover it. Not when you lose your mother, the kind of mother I believe you had." His face was unbearably kind.

"She was the best," I squeaked out.

"I hope you'll tell me about her sometime. When you can."

I knew her passing was coming, during the last year of her life. Even so, I was wholly unprepared for the vast emptiness she left behind.

Our eyes locked, and I couldn't look away. My grief had thrown me overboard yet again, and I was searching his eyes for a lifeboat.

"Feel like walking down to the lake?" he asked. And there it was.

"I would love to," I said, pushing myself out of my chair. "I'll meet you downstairs in five minutes."

I hurried to my room and closed the door behind me. I blew my nose and splashed water on my face before wetting a washcloth and holding it over my eyes. This simple act always comforted me when I was a little girl, and it did the trick now, holding back the flood of tears that lived so close to the surface. I looked at my image in the mirror. *Get it together.* I took a deep breath and held my own gaze. *You've got this.*

A few minutes later, Dominic and I were walking out the door into the chilly sunshine. It was early in the season, but even in the warmest months of the year, and the coldest, Wharton was oddly temperate.

We walked down the hill toward the water, passing by shops and restaurants that were opening their doors. Shopkeepers looked out at us and smiled, holding up hands in greeting. As we walked past the bookstore, Just Read It, Beth poked her head out the door.

"Hi!" she called out. "Brynn, right?"

"That's right," I said, smiling at her. "This is Dominic. He's one of the other summer lodgers."

Beth hurried out onto the sidewalk, hugged me, and gave his arm a quick squeeze. "I've seen you. Glad to finally meet."

"Me, too." He smiled and put a hand on her arm. "We're headed down to the lake to contemplate the day. Care to join us?"

"I'm opening the store, but thanks for the invitation. I'll take you up on it sometime." She gave my hand a squeeze. "Have a good day, loves."

We walked down the hill toward the lake, then settled on a bench in a small lakeside park near the city dock. The dozen or so slips were filled with boats, most big enough to brave the ocean-size waves this lake could kick up, if it was of a mind to. We sat for a while, just watching the water lapping at the rocky shore.

I didn't want to talk about my mother. I had that memory locked up tight, as I usually did. But there was something else I was curious about.

"LuAnn told me she shut up one room for the summer," I said. "Do you know what that's about? Remodeling, maybe?" I had visions of workers and banging and noise.

Dominic shook his head. "Not remodeling. She didn't feel right letting the room out to people this year. Out of respect. That's what she told me."

A feeling of dread washed over me as he said it, but I couldn't explain why. I shifted to look him in the face. "What happened?"

He cleared his throat. "I'm not sure it's my story to share, but since it's a police matter now, I guess it's public knowledge."

"A police matter?"

"Yeah," he said, rubbing his chin. "You know that LuAnn doesn't have the place open in the winter for a few months, right?"

I didn't know that. I had made my arrangements with her for the summer via email, and it just didn't occur to me she might be elsewhere.

"She goes to Hawaii," Dominic said, a smile curving his lips. "She told me she likes the *leis*."

I couldn't help laughing. "She's incorrigible!"

"One of a kind, for sure," he said, chuckling. "She's a great lady. Anyway, when she opened the place back up in March, she found a woman had been living there over the winter. And, I'm sorry to say this, but the lady died in one of the rooms. Room number five, I think she said. So now she's got it shut up for the season."

I took a quick breath in. "Oh no."

He nodded. "Yeah, it was pretty awful for LuAnn coming back and finding a body."

I couldn't imagine. My stomach tightened into knots. "Who was it?"

"Unknown. The police have no leads."

"Homeless, maybe? Or a squatter?"

"LuAnn has no idea who it was," he said. "The stranger thing is, nobody in town saw anyone coming or going during the winter. That's what LuAnn told me, anyway. No lights on. No footprints in the snow. Nothing to indicate that anyone was living there. But apparently, from the condition of the place, she had been there awhile."

A shiver ran through me. We sat in silence, each with our own thoughts. I was contemplating the circumstances that would lead a woman to break into an empty inn and live there with no lights to illuminate the darkness.

"No wonder she doesn't want to rent out that room," I said softly, making a mental note to talk to Kate's husband, Nick Stone, the police chief in Wharton. Maybe he knew something.

Dominic pushed himself up from the bench and stretched. His arms and chest were massive, and I couldn't help staring.

"Gotta start my day, for real this time," he said, looking down at me with a slight smile on his face. "Seems like you're okay to start yours, too."

A wave of warmth ran through me as I realized this had been deliberate. He had been giving me something else to think about other than the loss of my mother. I smiled back at him.

"Thank you," I said. "It was a nice morning."

He smiled at me. "The first of many, I hope."

As Dominic walked back up the hill toward LuAnn's, I stayed by the water. *Peace,* the water seemed to be saying to me. *Peace.*

On my way back to my room, I noticed Jason and Gil's door was open. A woman about thirty years old was sitting at the table just inside their suite. She was reading some papers, but looked up when I passed and gave me a smile.

"You must be Brynn," she said, gathering the papers into a neat pile and pushing her chair from the table. "I'm Rebecca. Jason's daughter."

"Oh!" I said. "Hi!"

"My dad told me you're living down the hall for the summer."

"Yes," I said. "I met your dad and Gil just after I arrived yesterday. They're great."

She held my gaze and gave me a sad smile.

"Since you're living so close, I wanted to make sure you know what's happening. I mean, the guests come and go, but you and one other person are going to be here all summer, too, right?"

I furrowed my brow and squinted at her. "Right," I said, drawing out the word. "What do you mean, 'happening'?"

She sighed. "Okay, so they haven't told you."

I shook my head. "Told me what?"

45

"Do you have a minute?" she asked, her eyes welling up with tears. "Maybe two?"

She was a stranger to me, but in that moment she looked so fragile and vulnerable, as though she might break into a million pieces, that I wanted to hug her. I walked toward her and took her hands into mine. "Of course. What's this about?"

The tears came, but she talked through them as though her face weren't wet and her shoulders weren't shaking.

"I took care of her for as long as I could," she said, the words flowing out quickly, in a long stream. "But I have three kids, all under the age of ten. I mean, at first it was fine. Wonderful, even, to have her there. But she has started to . . . well, she tends to wander. I'll turn my back for a second, and she's out the door, down the block."

Rebecca took a deep breath. "I love her, but I can't do it anymore," she said, grasping at my eyes with hers, seeking . . . what? Understanding? Forgiveness? But, why? Why seek forgiveness from a stranger?

We stood there for a moment, looking at each other. "Who are we talking about?" I asked finally.

"My mother," she said. "She was diagnosed with Alzheimer's five years ago."

I took a quick breath in. "I'm so sorry," I said to her, tears welling up in my own eyes. I knew all too well what it was to lose a mother. But mine was fully herself until she closed her eyes for the last time. I couldn't imagine how devastating and terrifying it would be to watch your mother slip away mentally, as though her very essence was draining, drop by drop. Maybe not even knowing you at the end.

"It was time to start thinking about nursing homes," Rebecca said, her words coming in one long stream. "So, we started looking at places, but Dad just couldn't . . ." She wiped away tears. "Dad just couldn't bear putting her in there. He wouldn't have it."

"Sure, I get that," I said, still wondering what, exactly, she was trying to say to me.

"So, she's moving in here," she said finally.

My reaction must've surprised her because she smiled. "Yeah, I know," she said. "But Dad wanted to do it. He wouldn't have it any other way, and Gil was right behind him."

My mind was going in all directions at once. "They're taking in your mom." It was a question and a statement at the same time. That's what Jason and Gil had been trying to tell me.

"She's already here," Rebecca said. "She spent the night last night."

The voice in the hallway, I thought back. Not a ghost after all. I peered beyond Rebecca into the suite. "Is she here now?"

Rebecca shook her head. "She didn't have a very good night," she said. "I spent the night here, too. She didn't know where she was. It unsettled her. So today they took her on the boat. The water always relaxes her."

She let out a heavy, world-weary sigh. I knew that sigh.

"I'm going to head out," she said. "I think it's best if I leave before they get back. She might think she's going home with me."

The look on her face tore my heart to pieces.

"You're a very good daughter," I said to her, my voice gentle and low. "You took her in and did all that you could, for as long as you could." I might have been speaking to myself.

She grasped my hands and looked into my eyes, and I saw my own pain of the past three years reflected back.

"I look forward to meeting her," I managed.

A few hours later, I did. I'll never forget the moment I met Alice. I was sitting downstairs at the bar talking to Gary before people started arriving for happy hour.

Jason walked through the front door with a woman on his arm, a beautiful woman in her sixties with blonde hair cut in a chic bob. She was slender, wearing khaki slacks and a floral sweater, a bright scarf wound around her neck. She looked for all the world like she had been plucked from a society magazine.

But behind that beauty, I saw something else. Fragility. Even fear. She seemed to be trembling, deep inside. Her enormous blue eyes searched the room, looking this way and that.

I took a quick breath in. Could it be? Was she the woman in my dream the night before? A chill seemed to wrap itself around me as I looked into her frightened, searching eyes.

CHAPTER SIX

She couldn't be the woman I had dreamed about. It had to be a coincidence. I had never seen her before. I tried to cast my mind back there, to the beginning of that dream, but the memory of it was already floating in a watery haze, disappearing into the ether. I couldn't say for sure if I had dreamed about Alice or not.

"Brynn!" Jason called out a little too cheerily, and waved. He turned his eyes to Alice. "Honey, come and meet Brynn."

Alice looked up at Jason and smiled. "Of course," she said.

I pushed myself up as Jason led her my way.

"Honey, this is Brynn," he said. "She's living down the hall this summer. In the Yellow Lady room. We're neighbors!"

She took her eyes off him for a moment to glance at me. "The Yellow Lady," she said.

"Brynn, this is Alice."

She looked me in the eyes then. "Brynn," she said. "I probably won't remember your name." She laughed and shook her head. "I have trouble remembering things lately. But I'll remember your face. I'm good with faces."

My heart swelled, and I chided myself for feeling uneasy when I met her. So many people were uncomfortable around those with this terrible disease, as if it were contagious. I made up my mind right then not to be one of them.

"It's okay if you don't remember my name," I said. "I'll remember yours."

She unwound her arm from Jason's and took my hands. "That's a deal," she said. "I have a feeling we're going to be friends."

"I think so, too," I said, squeezing her tiny hands, taking care not to squeeze too tightly.

"We've had a fun day," Jason said. "I showed Alice around town, and we took a quick boat ride."

"I like the lake," Alice said. "And there's a lot of good shopping in town, isn't there?"

"I've been meaning to check out more of the shops," I said.

"Let's do that together sometime soon," Alice said.

"Hon, it's time for your nap, remember?" Jason said to her, putting a hand on her arm.

She gave him a mock scowl and smiled at me. "He's such a mother bear," she said, her face glowing.

"I'll see you later, Alice," I said.

Jason steered her toward the door and looked over his shoulder at me. "I'll be right back," he mouthed.

I nodded and sank back down on my barstool. Gary appeared and set a glass of wine in front of me.

"Oh, the tangled webs people weave in their lives," he muttered before disappearing back into the kitchen.

A while later, Jason joined me. "Gil's upstairs paying some bills while Alice has a nap, so I'm off the clock for a minute." He took a glass of wine from Gary and smiled at me, rather sheepishly, I thought. "So. Life. It's complicated, huh?"

Simple words with profound meaning. "I met your daughter. She filled me in."

"We have two kids, actually, Bec and Jane," Jason said, taking a breath in and exhaling. "I know this might seem a little bit weird, and truthfully, it is."

I shook my head. "Life is weird," I said.

He smiled and went on. "I was married to Alice for thirty years. We were high school sweethearts. Went to the same college, got married even before we graduated. We had a wonderful life together, we really did, raising our kids, starting and growing our careers. It was awesome. She was awesome. But."

His eyes held mine, and I saw tears well up as he ran a hand through his thick white hair.

He shook his head. "When our kids were grown . . ." He sighed.

"You had to be who you were."

He nodded. "Back when we were growing up, gay wasn't . . . well, you know. It wasn't accepted. I didn't deceive Alice, not really. I loved her. More than you can imagine. I still do. I wanted a life with her. I wanted us to make a home together. Children. We were really happy. But I always knew. And when times changed . . ." He sighed. "I was fifty-five years old and thought, if I'm ever going to truly be who I am, I have to do it now."

"It must've been really hard."

"It killed me to tell her. It killed her, too. But she said part of her already knew."

The pain in his face broke my heart.

"We were cordial, if a bit distant, for a few years," he said. "We'd talk about the kids and the grandkids. We'd spend holidays together as a family. When I met Gil, though, it all changed. We didn't see each other as often."

He took a long sip of his wine. "She called me when she got the diagnosis. I was totally devastated."

He wiped his eyes with his napkin and heaved a long sob.

"It took me a while to get my head around it. That Alice wasn't going to be Alice anymore. That she would diminish, little by little, until she was gone. I couldn't quite grasp it. I thought of her, our kids. What we would all be losing."

I reached over and took his hand in mine.

"I felt so guilty. Like I'd caused it somehow."

"I can't imagine."

He shook his head. "I think I went through the five stages of grief in one afternoon." He managed a chuckle.

"I took her to our favorite vacation spot, St. Thomas—with Gil's blessing—and we spent a week laughing and crying and enjoying the beach and the water and the food. We talked about our kids and how great they turned out. We talked about our past. We talked about our grandkids' futures. We talked about us."

He stopped for a moment, taking a deep breath, as if the words themselves were heavy.

"I could see the signs of the disease creeping to the surface even then. My kids had been telling me something was wrong with her for a few years, but I was in denial. Total denial. I shrugged it off, telling them it was nothing, just the forgetfulness of age."

I knew that denial well. When my mom was diagnosed with stage four cancer, I had the firm belief that she'd beat it. I could not imagine the disease winning, not against the fortress that was my mother.

The utter terror of knowing that the person closest to you in the world had a death sentence hanging over their head was a powerful motivator for wrapping yourself in a comfortable blanket of denial.

"I totally get that," I said. "You have to see it for yourself. It has to be undeniable before you'll let yourself believe it."

He nodded, wiping tears from his eyes.

"How was she then, during that week? You said spending time with her like that convinced you the diagnosis was true."

"It wasn't anything much that she said or did, although there were some incidents," he said. "It was the look in her eyes. Fearful. Lost. As though she was slipping off a cliff and trying to hang on to something, but knowing she'd ultimately fall."

"She has that same look now," I said. "I've seen it."

He nodded. "She kept trying to pay for things with the room key. Once, it's not such a big deal, I mean, those key cards do look like credit cards. But over and over?"

"What's the old saying about dementia? If you forget where you put your keys, you're fine. If you forget what your keys are for . . ."

"Exactly right," he said. "Spending that week with her told me it was true. She had Alzheimer's. Oh my God, it's hard for me to even say the word. All I wanted, Brynn, was for her to have a happy life after we split up. Maybe find someone. Travel. Do the things we always wanted to do when we retired. And this death sentence—crueler than a death sentence—is what was waiting for her. Goddamn it. It's unfathomably cruel."

We let that statement sit for a moment. He was right. It was unfathomably cruel.

He took a deep breath. "She moved in with Bec when we got back and was with her for about five years. It just got too hard, with the kids. And now here we are."

"Your daughter said something about a nursing home?"

He winced. "I went looking with Bec and Jane," he said. "There are some nice facilities. Beautiful places. Caring nurses. But . . . everyone in there is so . . ."

"Old?"

He nodded. "Yeah. Old. Twenty years older than Alice. Some more than that. And all of them living in their own little worlds, if I'm speaking the truth. I couldn't stomach putting Alice in a place like that. She'd be scared to death."

My eyes filled with tears. "And Gil?"

"I love the man more than ever, if that's possible." He took a sip of his wine. "One night when I broke down after touring yet another nursing home, he suggested we take her in. I couldn't believe it."

"Breathtaking," I said, my voice barely a whisper.

"Gil's parents were immigrants from Japan. In his family, nobody ever went into a nursing home. He and his sister cared for their parents until they passed, just like his parents had taken care of their parents. It's just what they did in his family."

"So, this wasn't an out-there concept for him," I said.

"Not a bit," Jason said. "It's such a puzzle, how life works sometimes. I left Alice to be true to myself and found the love of my life. My leaving crushed her heart and spirit. My finding that love crushed her even more. Then she got the diagnosis nobody wants to hear. And it was that love—the love of my life—who took her in, saving her from living her last years in a nursing home."

It might not have been my place to say it, but I had to ask. "So, what does Alice think? Of the arrangement, I mean. Does she know you and Gil are married?"

"She's not quite sure who he is or what he's doing here. But he's so warm and funny that she can't help but like him. As for telling her we're married—she knows. Or knew. When we got married, she sent a lovely card and a gift, saying how happy she was for me." He smiled, his eyes filling with tears. "That's Alice," he said. "That's the kind of woman she was. Is."

He stared off into the past. "When our kids were little and I'd get home from work, we'd have a family dance party in the living room." He wiped away tears. "You'd think I could stop crying already."

I shook my head. "No. It sucks what's happening to her. I'd be crying every minute of the day."

He turned to look at me. "It does suck," he said, a fierce tone in his voice. "Gil and I are going to give her a beautiful summer. Boat rides, dinners out. Wine on the beach watching the sun go down. Dancing. She deserves every moment of happiness we can give her."

Gary appeared with a tray of snacks and set it down in front of Jason and me. "Bon appétit, kids."

I smiled at him and popped a slice of salami into my mouth, and only then did it dawn on me. It was well after three o'clock.

"Where is everybody?" I asked Gary. "Isn't it happy hour?"

He wiped the bar absently with a rag. "LuAnn thought it would be better if it was just residents tonight," he said, looking from me to Jason and back again. "To help the new lady get settled."

Jason nodded. "Alice doesn't do well with crowds," he said. "I wanted to ease her into her new surroundings without overwhelming her. LuAnn was gracious enough to cancel it for today. You could hear the crestfallen groans all the way up Main Street."

I chuckled at this. Then we got back to chatting. I asked about his daughters and grandchildren. He asked about my mom.

"And your dad?" Jason asked. "Is he still with us?"

I took a sip of my wine. I wasn't quite sure how to answer his question. My parents had been married for more than six decades when my mom passed. Theirs was the perfect pairing of two souls. They were so funny together, always laughing about something, each playing off the other like a vaudeville act. When she died, most of him did, too. His life force was dripping away every day he was on this earth without her. He was still living on his own, but I could see change in the wind. I didn't want to think about it.

"He's in England this summer," I said, finally. "Cornwall. My brother took him over to follow some ancestry leads. He's into that, tracing our heritage, and has found limbs of our family tree dating back to the fourteen hundreds there."

"Wow," Jason said. "That's really interesting! A nice distraction for your dad, too."

That's exactly what it was, and I was grateful to my brother for providing it. It let me have the summer to regroup and heal without worrying about my dad's grief, too.

Just then, Dominic appeared with Alice on his arm. He looked massive in contrast to Alice's delicateness.

"This lady was looking for you," he said to Jason, his velvety voice caressing my ear.

Alice was smiling, but I saw that she was also trembling, ever so slightly. "Jason! There you are."

"I'm right here, honey." Jason beamed at her. "We have happy hour here every day. It's just us today, but tomorrow the whole town joins in."

"The whole town?"

"Oh, it's just a few people," I said to her, waving my hand. "And everyone's so nice. I'm new to town, too, so we can be new together."

Alice turned to me, then. "Brynn." She smiled broadly. A triumph. "The Yellow Lady."

"You remembered!"

"I don't think I could forget you," Alice said, looking at me deeply. It was like she was looking into me.

"How about some wine, honey?" Jason said, holding out a glass of white wine.

Alice narrowed her eyes. "Am I supposed to have this? Rebecca never let me have wine."

Jason smiled. "Well, she's not here. Why the hell not?"

CHAPTER SEVEN

I tossed and turned that night. Even though my body and spirit were dead tired, sleep would not come. So many thoughts were racing through my mind. The tragedy of early-onset Alzheimer's for Alice and her entire family—the cruelty of that situation juxtaposed with the love it brought out in everyone involved—just wouldn't let me go. I wondered if I could love someone that much, or if anyone would ever love me that much.

Then, the mysterious man across the hallway floated into my thoughts. Dominic was a stranger to me and yet felt so familiar somehow. It was like I knew him deep in my bones.

I was mentally going through various times in my life—public school, college, my first jobs, even spring break trips with girlfriends—trying to find some connection between us, someplace we might have crossed paths. On the playground as a child? In a bar in Cancún? Did he sit next to me in physics class? Did he work nearby, and I'd seen him on the bus during my morning commute? Was he in the chemo room next door with someone as I sat with my mom during her treatments? It was useless. There was nothing.

I felt myself drifting off to sleep when I heard my name.

"Brynn." The voice was paper thin and whispery. "Brynnnnnn."

I held my breath. Where was it coming from? Inside my room? The moon shone in through my window, a shaft of light illuminating the darkness. My white curtains billowed in the breeze.

"Come out in the hallway," the whispery voice said. "I'm here."

I thought about it for a minute—should I answer?—but in the end, I slid out of bed. It had to be Alice, just like the night before. I pulled on my robe and listened at the door. Nothing. I unlocked the door and twisted the knob, wanting to get to her before she wandered onto the deck or downstairs. I pulled open the door and poked my head out into the hall.

"Alice?"

Alice was not in the hallway. It was empty. Moonlight was streaming in from the window on the door to the deck, shining down the full length of the hall. I noticed the dead bolt on the deck door was locked, but I stepped over to it and peeked outside anyway, just to make sure she wasn't out there somehow. She wasn't. The deck, and the street below, were deserted.

I turned my gaze back to the hallway. All was quiet and peaceful. The house was asleep.

I must've been dreaming, I told myself. Nobody was calling my name. I was stepping back into my room when a shaft of light shone down the hall. Not moonlight. Electric light.

What in the world? A feeling of dread took root deep down in the pit of my stomach and squeezed.

The light flickered into the hallway from the alcove by the shower rooms. Somebody was awake. An overnight guest? Maybe that's who I'd heard? But how could they have known my name? And why did they turn their lights on at the very moment I was in the hallway? It didn't make any sense.

I crept down the hall toward the light, stopping when I got to the alcove. I poked my head around the corner. Alice was standing there, in her nightgown.

"Alice?" I whispered. "What are you doing out of bed?"

"It's important," she said, her eyes clear, her voice strong. Nothing of the baby-bird fragility existed in her at that moment. "There's something in this room you need to see."

"Let's go back to your room, Alice," I said. "You should be in bed. Jason will be worried about you."

"Don't trouble yourself about that." Alice smiled at me. I noticed her face was lit up with a warm glow. "I'll be back in bed before you know it. You weren't hearing the calls, so I had to wake you up to see this. Go into the room, Brynn."

And with that, Alice flickered and faded from view. It was like she evaporated into the night.

The door to the room in the alcove was open. A light was on inside.

"Hello?" I said softly, not wanting to awaken any other guests who might be in earshot.

I walked slowly toward the open door. "Hello?" I said again.

I knew I shouldn't go toward that door. Why the guest had it open and the light on at that hour of the night was none of my business. I should've simply gone back to my room and crawled back into bed. But I couldn't stop myself. It was like something was compelling me to come closer. Calling me. Just as it had called my name.

My heart was beating harder with each step I took toward the door. When I reached it, I held on to the doorframe with one hand and poked my head inside.

Just as my room and Gil and Jason's suite seemed to be from different moments in time, the same was true with this room. It might have been taken from a Victorian-era mansion.

The bed took my breath away. Its enormous gleaming wooden headboard and footboard were carved with an intricate pattern of leaves. A rose-colored floral quilt and a cozy nest of throw pillows was the perfect complement.

On the carved wooden nightstand sat a lamp that looked to be a century old or more, its delicate light-green glass globes painted with purple and blue flowers. Soft light shone from both globes. It reminded me of the oil lamp my grandma had in her room in my childhood home.

Whenever I wanted to hear a story about the past, I'd light that lamp, and we'd sit curled up together on her bed, talking about her grandmother and great-grandmother, and what life was like for her when she was a child. Her job, growing up with her gaggle of brothers and sisters, was to make sure all the lamps and candles were snuffed and out before she went to bed each night. The most important job in the house, she often said.

But it wasn't the light from the lamp that had caught my attention as I stood in the hallway. A fire was blazing in the fireplace, its stone hearth extending a foot or so into the room, its face, of the same stone, arched over the opening. *Lake Superior stone,* I thought. The light from the fire was, undoubtedly, what had flickered into my field of vision, beckoning me.

I watched the flames dance and sway, and only then did I notice a rocking chair in front of the fire. Had it always been there? I wasn't sure. But now I noticed it was rocking back and forth slightly.

"Brynn."

I whirled around—was someone behind me?—but seeing no one, I turned back to the fireplace. An old woman was sitting in the rocking chair. She was smiling at me.

The woman was wearing a floral nightgown with a sweater over her shoulders. Her tortoiseshell glasses—a statement piece—framed clear brown eyes that were twinkling at me. Her face was lined with age but kind. She was familiar to me, somehow. The woman held a book in her lap, a small hardcover volume.

I couldn't move. I just stood there, staring at this woman. Why did everyone in this house look so familiar to me? She might have been an aunt or cousin.

"Did you call my name?" I asked her. "What do you want?"

She smiled and grasped the book in her lap. She held it out to me. I stepped close enough to her to reach the book, and took it from her. Its title caused me to drop it onto the floor, as though the book itself were on fire.

The Illustrated Man.

CHAPTER EIGHT

I awoke tangled in a snarl of damp sheets. My comforter was on the floor, pillows strewn everywhere. My bathroom light was on, and the fridge door was ajar.

What in the world? Had I been up and looking for something to eat in the middle of the night?

I slid my glasses on and looked at the clock. Almost nine thirty. I stretched as I listened to sounds of life, hustle and bustle out my window—Wharton was open for business, and tourists had descended.

I didn't usually sleep this late, but considering the restless night I'd had, it didn't surprise me too much. I slipped out of bed and pushed the door to the fridge closed on my way to the bathroom to splash water on my face. The coolness of the water was comforting and jarring at the same time.

My stomach growled. I quickly dressed and ran a brush through my hair. I couldn't remember how long Gary was serving breakfast, but I hoped I could still get some eggs. Within a few minutes, I was out the door and about to trot down the stairs to the kitchen when I veered off into the alcove. Last night had to have been a dream, but I wanted to take a look anyway.

The now-familiar sense of dread overcame me as I crept closer to the door and tried the knob. Nothing. It was locked.

When I saw the number on the room—five—my stomach seized up, and I hurried away and down the stairs. I very much wanted to be in the company of someone, anyone, else.

A few other diners were scattered at tables, so I took a seat at the bar. Gary appeared, pot of coffee in hand. He turned over the cup that was facedown on my place mat and poured. I added some cream that was sitting in a small silver pitcher nearby and took my first sip with shaking hands.

He furrowed his brow at me. "Rough night?"

"You could say that." I took another sip. "Either I had some weird dreams or . . ." I let my words trail off. It seemed too ridiculous to say out loud.

"Or?"

I set down my cup. "Gary, is this place really haunted like people say it is?"

He chuckled. "I could tell you stories."

I winced. "Bad stories?"

"Why?" he asked, leaning against the bar. "Did something happen?"

"I'm not sure," I said, wrapping my fingers around my coffee mug, enjoying the warmth radiating off it.

"Listen," he said, taking out his pad and a pen. "Let's get you ordered, and then I'll sit with you awhile, and we can have a talk."

I had lunch plans in a few hours, so I just ordered one scrambled egg and a piece of toast. Gary was horrified at this, which made me laugh, defusing some of the night's terror. He emerged from the kitchen with my plate, setting it down in front of me before wiping his hands on his apron. All the other diners had left, and we were alone in the restaurant. He took the stool next to mine and poured himself a cup of coffee.

"Okay, so let me just tell you, this place is one hundred and fifty years old," he said. "Maybe older than that."

I held his gaze. "Really?"

He nodded. "Listen, this house has been standing a long time. You know it used to be a boardinghouse back in the day, right?"

"Yes, LuAnn told me that."

"So, a lot of living and dying has happened here. Some of it, not so pleasant. Those were harsh days, back when this place was first built. The people who stayed in the house, largely Scandinavian immigrants trying to carve out a life by fishing and logging and mining, were often-times at odds—to put it mildly—with the Native Americans who had always been here."

I nodded.

"What I'm saying, doll, is, this place has a restless vibe. It always has. The tension, those traumatic, difficult times, they still hang in the air here. A hundred people, maybe more, have called this place home. Sometimes they come back. They pass through."

I held his gaze. "Pass through?"

He nodded, a solemn look on his face. "It can scare the living day-lights out of you. Is that what happened? You saw something?" he asked.

I told him about the knocking on the wall when I was taking a shower the first day I arrived, and that Dominic had heard it, too.

Gary nodded. "Yeah, that's pretty typical. Especially when somebody new arrives."

I wondered whether to tell him about what had happened the night before. I was staring down into my cup, remembering, when he put a hand on my shoulder.

"That's not all of it. Is it?"

I shook my head. "I've been having weird dreams. Or maybe they're not dreams. I don't know."

"Go on. No judgment here, Brynn."

"I heard someone calling my name from outside my room. So, I got up and went out into the hallway to check on her. I noticed a light on in another room. I saw—"

I couldn't even speak the words. And I certainly wasn't going to tell him about Alice.

"Which room, Brynn?" His expression serious, grave.

"Five. I heard about the . . . lady. The woman LuAnn found when she opened up for the season. I think I may have seen her."

Gary ran a hand through his hair. "Brynn, it had to be a dream. I'm not saying I don't believe you—of all people, I'm going to believe things like this—but five's locked up tight. Nobody is in there and won't be all summer. LuAnn is superstitious about that kind of thing. She's not going to open it up until they find out who the lady was and what she was doing here. It's a matter of respect for her."

I nodded, unconvinced. "Okay," I said, taking a last bite of my toast. I looked at the clock. It was just after ten. I was meeting Kate at the ferry dock at noon to go to the island for lunch. "Thanks, Gary. I appreciate the talk." I dropped my napkin on my plate and hopped off my stool.

"Anytime." He winked at me. "And for what it's worth, it's been your first few nights in a new place. You're going to have wild dreams. It's normal. Don't worry about it."

I wasn't so sure. I just hoped they'd stop.

Showered and changed, I headed off to the ferry dock a little early because I wanted to run a quick errand on the way.

As I opened the door to the bookstore, Just Read It, a bright-sounding bell tinkled, and Beth appeared from the back room.

"Morning!" she said to me. "It's another perfect Wharton day!"

"Hey," I said, warmed by her smile.

"No happy hour yesterday?" she said, chuckling. "The town nearly ground to a halt."

"I know! LuAnn wanted to give our newest summer resident some breathing space to get used to things," I said, not sure of how much to divulge. It wasn't my story to tell.

"Jase was in here yesterday afternoon with Alice," Beth said. "By now, everyone knows what's going on. He asked me to spread the word, actually. Didn't want anyone talking when he showed up here or there with her."

"She's a sweet lady," I said.

"It's a damn shame."

We shared a moment then, both of us filled with empathy. Grief. Sorrow.

"So!" Beth lightened the mood. "Did you just come in to say hi, or can I help you find something?"

"Do you have a copy of *The Illustrated Man*?"

"Ray Bradbury, huh? Let me check." Beth clicked on her computer and did a quick search. "We do!" she said, then led me into the science fiction section and pulled the slim paperback off the shelf. "This is one of my favorite books. I remember reading it in college, and it's always stuck with me."

I took it out of her hand, and mine started to tingle.

"Thanks," I said, staring at the cover, which depicted a shirtless man sitting down, facing away from us, his back completely covered in tattoos. "I've never read it. I'm ashamed to admit that because I teach literature—"

"Oh!" Beth broke in. "You're a teacher?"

"I am," I said. "I teach at the U down in Minneapolis. I've heard about this book, but, I don't know. I'm not really much into sci-fi, I guess, so it wasn't on my radar. Someone"—I stumbled on my words— "recommended it to me recently, and I thought it might be a fun read."

"It's a collection of short stories," she said, back at the register and ringing it up. "Do you know the premise?"

I shook my head. "No."

"It was written in, I believe, the late forties or early fifties, and it starts with a prologue in which a homeless man—they called them 'hobos' back in the day—is sitting in front of his campfire eating his dinner of pork and beans when another man comes by. Our narrator thinks it's sort of odd because it's a warm summer night and the guy has a long-sleeved wool shirt on, buttoned all the way up to his neck. But whatever, he thinks. The man asks if he can spend the night by the fire with our narrator, who welcomes him. Getting ready for bed, the man takes off his shirt and reveals that he's covered in tattoos. Beautiful, colorful, mysterious illustrations."

I took a quick breath in. No wonder Jason and Gil had given Dominic that nickname.

"The man tells our narrator that he got the illustrations, as he calls them, from a woman who turned out to be a time-traveling witch."

"Well, that's never good," I said, smirking.

"Nope. No good has ever come from a time-traveling witch. Right after getting the tats, the guy realizes they're not just simple illustrations. They're enchanted. They move and tell stories. Creepy, scary stories."

"The man tells our narrator not to look at him during the night, not to watch those illustrations tell their stories. And especially, he's not supposed to look at the one empty spot on the guy's back because his own story will materialize there. But, of course, he looks, right? Who wouldn't? He can't help himself. And the rest of the book consists of the stories told by the illustrations that come to life as the two men are lying by the fire."

"Wow," I said, gazing down at the book in my hands. "I can't wait to read it."

"One of the stories still blows me away," Beth said, leaning in toward me. "It's about this family who lives in what's basically a smart home. Bradbury calls it a Happylife Home. The kids' room is a virtual-reality chamber. Let's just say things end badly."

My mouth hung open. "You said it was written *when*?"

"I know! That's my point! All of the stories have a common theme about the conflict between technology and humanity. Just like we're dealing with today! It's totally amazing he came up with that more than seventy years ago. Hardly anyone had televisions for crying out loud, and he's writing about the dangers of virtual reality."

"Wow," I repeated. "Who's the time traveler? That witch or Ray Bradbury?"

"Exactly what I've always thought." Beth gave me a warm smile. "I knew I liked you for a reason. Come on back when you've read it, and we'll talk some more."

I slipped the book into my bag and headed off to meet Kate at the ferry dock. After the strangeness of the past few nights, a conversation about my favorite thing—books—brought me back to myself. I would make sure that conversation would continue over the course of the summer.

CHAPTER NINE

I was standing on the deck of the ferry, spray lightly sprinkling my face. Kate and I had just taken off from Wharton's dock, headed to Ile de Colette, a twenty-minute ride away, for lunch. I couldn't quite remember the last time I had been to Colette, but I knew it to be a laid-back community of a few hundred year-round locals that swelled tenfold during the summer tourist season.

Visitors could find high-end resorts, campgrounds, and everything in between. At the marina, you'd see multimillion-dollar yachts next to battered fishing dinghies. While Wharton was more Cape Cod, Colette had a hippie vibe.

One of the more popular bars on the island, Jimmy's, had partially burned down years before, and the owner had just put up a sort of quasi circus tent over the whole thing and never bothered to rebuild before reopening his doors. It wouldn't be unusual to see campers clad in swimming suits and shorts, no shoes, sitting at the bar or waiting for one of the two showers in the bathrooms.

Celebrities seeking an out-of-the-way vacation frequented Colette with no threat of paparazzi or prying eyes. Movie stars in baseball caps and jeans, trying to blend in, would be spotted bicycling around town; musicians who regularly sold out arenas would take the stage at Jimmy's on random nights, surprising patrons with an unplugged show; bestselling authors would rent houses on the water for inspiration.

Colette's streets housed a handful of small funky restaurants, one known for breakfast, one known for locally sourced dishes, another known for pizza, still another extremely high end, along with a coffee shop where most locals congregated in the morning.

And the beach. It was famous for being the only beach on all of Lake Superior with water so warm that anyone could comfortably swim. With its rocky bottom, it was shallow enough to walk out the length of a football field before feeling the familiar sting of the ice-cold lake. It was, in a way, surreal, walking into the Great Lake in what felt like bathwater until passing an invisible boundary where the temperature would plummet.

On the ferry, just a minute out of Wharton, my whole view changed. Standing on the deck, I could see tree-covered islands dotting the wide expanse of Lake Superior, its water undulating as though it were alive. Wharton got smaller and smaller as the ferry chugged along.

"I never get tired of this," Kate said, stringing an arm through mine as we gazed out over the vast expanse of the water, islands of pine and rock dotting the horizon.

"It's . . . I'm searching for the right word," I said. "*Majestic* comes to mind."

She nodded. "I thought it would do you good, getting out on the water." As we both took in the view, she pointed out a cormorant soaring past. It alighted on the water and floated, bobbing up and down on the waves.

"This is fun," I said, smiling at her. I couldn't remember the last time I'd said those words.

As we disembarked, walking down the dock toward town, we chatted, catching up on the past few years for both of us. Her new husband was the police chief in town, and I got to hear about her cousin Simon's current project, the newly opened ballroom at Harrison's House.

"And no word from Kevin?" I asked her, referring to her ex-husband, whose cheating had caused her to come to Wharton a couple of years earlier when their marriage fell apart. I had been at their wedding. Never liked the guy.

She shook her head. "It seems so long ago now that I was married to him," she mused. "Like it was another lifetime."

I knew that feeling. I was single myself after two decades of couple-hood. My old life had stopped when my mom got sick. I dropped everything and everyone—including him—to care for her. The long stretches of time apart while I tended to my parents took their toll on both of us, and when I was asked about our breakup, that was what I told people. But truthfully, he was angry at me for us being apart and resentful when I was home. After watching my mom fight the battle she would ultimately lose, I was left with the searing resolution that life was too short to be unhappy for even one moment, if you could possibly help it.

I did some soul-searching and realized I hadn't been happy in my relationship for a long time. Years. I loved the man, but I just didn't like him very much. So, after talking it over with my mother, I started looking for an apartment, something I hadn't done in twenty years. When I got the keys and opened the door for the first time, before my things arrived, the big empty room seemed to mirror what I felt inside.

Ultimately, I didn't find the happiness I sought. I was still unhappy, but now I was lonely, too. I didn't know whether I could get my old life back again. Or if I even wanted it. Suddenly, I had no tether. No moorings. I was floating, like that cormorant, going where the waves took me.

Kate and I were seated at a table in a dockside restaurant so we could watch the boats come and go while we had lunch.

Salads ordered and a bottle of wine opened, Kate raised her glass to me. "Here's to your summer in Wharton," she said. We clinked glasses, and each took a sip. "How do you like LuAnn's?"

I chose to sidestep the strangeness of the place. It was a bright, sunny day, and that odd occurrence in the still of the night seemed faraway and unreal.

"It's like a little soap opera already," I said. "I met Jason and Gil right away."

"Simon knows Gil from way back," she said. "They're a great couple."

"They are," I agreed. "Do you know what's going on with them?"

She furrowed her brow. "No," she said, a look of concern washing over her face.

Not believing I was betraying any confidences since Jason had been introducing Alice around town, I told Kate about their somewhat unusual living situation.

"Wow," she said, shaking her head. "I can't believe Simon didn't tell me. Maybe he doesn't know, either. And Gil's okay with it?"

"More than okay. He was the one who suggested it."

"Wow," Kate said again, sipping her wine and staring out over the water.

"I know. It's truly a beautiful thing they're doing."

It illustrated the point that love is love is love. It seemed rather lacking in my life just then.

"Have you heard from Robert?" Kate asked me, referring to my former partner of twenty years.

I shook my head. "Not lately. I've heard he's dating a twenty-five-year-old yoga instructor."

Kate bowed her head. "Namaste."

We both burst out laughing. "You've gotta laugh about it, or you'll cry," she said, refilling my wineglass. "I totally get it. You've had quite the year."

She wasn't kidding. Images from the past year of my life flashed through my mind then, like scenes from a movie.

Robert and I storming through the house, yelling at each other. Me sleeping in the guest bedroom when I was home to escape his simmering resentment about me being away so much, and my incredulity that he could possibly feel that way when I was taking care of my dying mother. Talking with my mom about my relationship, and finally, after years of just being happy-ish, making the decision to leave when she urged me to do so.

The utter devastation of my mom's death, followed two months later by the news that my beloved malamute—whom Robert had kept along with everything else—woke up one morning paralyzed because of what turned out to be a tumor on her spine. I held one paw and Robert held the other as the vet gave her the injection, with us both telling her how much we loved her as she slipped away. In a heartbreaking way, it melted the iceberg between us. Civility crept back into our relationship. I think the beloved dog we shared would've liked that.

And now, the icing on that cake was my own indecision about returning to a career I loved, but just might have run out of steam for. The lost look in my dad's eyes, and how childlike he was becoming.

"It felt like an assault. It really did. While it was all happening, I had an appointment with my doctor, who's known me for more than twenty years. She asked what was going on in my life, and I told her.

"She just stopped, put my chart on her desk, and said, 'You win.' I asked her what that meant, and she said, 'Patients tell me about the stressors in their lives every single day. I have never heard of anyone who has dealt with the breakup of a long-term relationship, moving, starting a new life, caregiving for a dying parent, the loss of that parent, career uncertainty, and the loss of a beloved pet at the same time.'"

Kate just stared at me. "Oh, Brynn. That's totally unreal. It's like the universe came after you, in all the places that you live. And love."

I nodded, the ever-present tears welling up yet again. I brushed them away.

"Did she suggest anything?" Kate asked.

"She asked me how I was coping, mentioned something about PTSD, and asked if I wanted antidepressants. I'm giving them a try."

Kate nodded and squeezed my hand. "How's your dad holding up?"

I shook my head and shrugged. "Better than I thought he would. I really wasn't sure if he was going to make it a day without her."

"A marriage like theirs . . ."

"I know. Once in a lifetime."

I could see my parents at their local watering hole, telling stories together, making everyone laugh. I'd never seen a love like theirs. Never had anything close to it. They were true soul mates, blessed to have found each other.

"My brother rented a house in Cornwall, England, for the summer," I said. "That's where my dad's ancestors are from. He's always wanted to go. They're going to spend a few months looking through cemeteries and chasing down living relatives, too."

"A distraction," she said.

"That's exactly what Jason said."

"And you came here."

I nodded. They had asked me to come along, but I really needed a break. My own distraction so I could focus on putting my life back together.

"This place can cure what ails you," she said. "I know. I came here broken and found the love of my life."

"Nothing like that on the horizon for me," I mused, picking at my salad. Anything to lighten the mood.

"I hear you're living down the hallway from the talk of the town," she said, grinning at me.

I could feel the heat rising to my face.

"You're blushing!" she laughed.

I couldn't help laughing, too. "He is ungodly handsome," I said. "But despite that, he's a really nice guy. Easy to talk to once you get over his . . ."

"His what?" Kate giggled.

I put my head in my hands. "Face. Chest. Shoulders," I admitted.

I looked up to see Kate wagging her finger at me. "Just be careful," she said. "Nick's got his eye on him."

"What?" I put down my fork. "Why?"

"It's not a big deal, or I would've said something earlier, but Nick is sort of quasi watching him because he matches the description of a man involved in"—she hesitated for a moment and took a long breath—"something down in the Twin Cities."

I felt a gnarling in the pit of my stomach. "What is it?"

Kate shook her head. "I can't talk about it. I shouldn't have even said anything."

"He's a person of interest in something? Kate, I'm living down the hall from this guy. We share a shower, for the love of God. Does LuAnn know?"

"She knows," she said. "When Nick saw him around town, he pulled her aside. It's not usually done, but, hey, we're all family here in Wharton, right?"

"What did she say?"

"She said it was ridiculous," Kate said, taking a bite of her salad. "You know LuAnn. And, for the record, Nick is not officially concerned about this guy. Don't worry."

"He's really nice, Kate." I said the words, and I meant them, but how much did I know about Dominic? Nothing at all, really. Just some pleasantries shared over coffee.

She squinted at me and gave me a mock scowl. "So was Ted Bundy."

I choked on a bite of salad. "What?"

Kate laughed. "I'm kidding."

"Seriously. What did he do? Or what might he be involved in?"

She winced. "I've said too much already."

"Kate, I need to know."

Kate took a deep breath and let it out. "It's just . . . there was a report of a guy who matched the description of your man—"

"He's not my man!" I broke in.

"*The* man," she said, "who was spotted with a woman who later turned up dead."

I put down my fork again. "Tell me you're not serious."

The one man I had even preliminary feelings for in years, and he was a murder suspect? This could not be happening.

"Well," she said, "yes and no. The thing is, the woman died of natural causes, so there's really nothing to it. But her children reported seeing a man who looked like Dominic—and you've got to admit, not too many men match his description—visiting her in the hospital a couple of times. They had no idea who he was. And her death was unexpected."

"Hospital. So, she was sick?"

"No, that's the thing. She was in the hospital for minor surgery, but there was a complication, so she had to stay a couple of nights while they monitored her."

"That's when the man visited?"

Kate nodded. "And then she died. Just died."

My stomach knotted. I didn't know what to think about what she was telling me. She probably saw, from the look on my face, that I wasn't sure how to process this information. Did it matter? Was it anything? She reached over and took my hand.

"If Nick were concerned about it, believe me, he'd be all over it. And he's not. I just wanted to tell you because you're living in close quarters with him. I figured you had a right to know."

"But," I began, not sure where I was going. "So, her kids reported a visitor who looked like Dominic. How did that alone lead police to him? There's a piece missing. I mean, police don't just get a random description and then magically have the person to question. Right?"

Kate nodded her head. "Nick had read the description and the report and then saw Dominic around town here in Wharton," she said. "Sometimes, it's that random."

"Speaking of Nick," I said. "Does he have any leads on the woman who died over the winter at LuAnn's?"

Now it was Kate's turn to be surprised. "Oh! You know about that?"

"Everyone's talking about it," I said. "LuAnn's got the room shut up for the season out of respect for the woman, until we find out who she was."

"I probably shouldn't be talking about this, either, but there's no leads whatsoever," Kate said. "Nick is getting pretty sick of women dying in Wharton and having no idea who they are or what happened to them."

"It's not the first time?"

Kate shook her head. "It's how we met, actually. I'll tell you that story some other time. The weird thing about this is, we live here. We were here all winter. We'd drive by LuAnn's regularly when she had the place closed for the season. And not just us. Everyone in town who stays for the winter looks after each other. Nobody noticed anything going on at LuAnn's. No lights. Nothing."

I let that sink in and took a sip of wine. All these mysteries swirling around me, and I had only been here a couple of days. What would the rest of the summer hold?

After lunch, we strolled around the island for a while, popping into this shop and that shop, talking about different things. But my thoughts kept drifting back to Dominic and the lady in room five.

CHAPTER TEN

Early the next morning, I found Alice wandering in the hallway. She was peering out the windows on the door to the deck, one hand above her eyes, blocking the morning sun.

"Hi, Alice," I said, a little too brightly. The images of Alice in my dreams swirled around me, and I felt a chill, wondering what that was about.

She whipped her head around, an alarmed look on her face.

"Oh! It's you! You're the one in the Yellow Lady room." She smiled then, the fear that had been on her face melting into happiness. "Don't tell me your name. Let me remember." She paused for a moment, squinting at me. "Rebecca?"

My heart broke hearing Alice call me her daughter's name.

"It's Brynn," I said, managing a smile.

"Brynn. Of course."

"Would you like to join me outside?"

Alice nodded, a little confused. I led her out to the deck, where we settled into the Adirondack chairs.

"It's a beautiful morning," Alice said, looking out over the water. "Look how it shimmers."

"Yes," I said, exhaling and taking it all in.

We sat in silence for a while.

"Where's Jason?" she asked me.

I smiled at her. "I'm not sure. But, don't worry. He'll turn up."

She smiled back. "He'll turn up," she echoed as she locked eyes with me. But then her smile slowly faded, and her expression turned dark. "I'm afraid of a lot of things now. I don't know why. It feels like bad things are lurking, waiting for me when Jason isn't around."

I leaned in toward her. "You know what, Alice?"

She tried to smile, her lips trembling. "What?"

"Don't be afraid. You're safe with me. I promise you that nothing bad is going to happen to you when I'm around. Even if bad things are lurking. They can't get past me."

Her eyes were wet with tears. She grabbed my hand. "I believe you. You are a warrior. You've had to be. You kept your mother safe. So I know you'll keep me safe, too."

I had no idea how to respond to that. She was right. I had indeed felt like a warrior during the last year of my mother's life—even said as much to friends—fighting to get her the care she needed and deserved. But how did Alice know that?

"Heads on stakes outside of the care center," she said, absently, staring out onto the water.

I took a quick breath in. "Alice, what did you say?" I asked her. "Would you mind repeating it? I don't think I heard you correctly."

She smiled broadly. "You put the heads of four nurses on stakes!"

I stared at her for a long minute. How could she possibly know that? She was referencing a joke (albeit a tasteless one) between my friend Mary and me about how I dealt with a situation at the rehab center where my mom had gone after being in the hospital.

A year before she passed, my mother had spent two months in the hospital fighting organ failure, and, when she had finally stabilized— which was a miracle—she was transferred to a rehab facility. The goal was to rebuild her muscle tone, which had all but evaporated, to allow her to be mobile again so she could resume her life at home. But it didn't work out that way. Every day, my dad and I would arrive at the rehab facility to find her sleeping. There was no rehab. They had her on a morphine drip all day, every day, and so she slept, floating in another world instead of getting back on her feet in this one.

I didn't question it at first, thinking maybe all of this sleep was a part of rehab somehow, getting her strength back before she began her therapy. No. That wasn't it. After two weeks, her care team called me in for a care conference. Only, it was anything but. Four nurses—all of whom I'd seen at one time or another when I visited my mom every day—and me, sitting around a table, my mom's chart in a file at the center of it.

The head nurse, Carla, cleared her throat. "There's no easy way to say this," she began, "but we need to talk about transferring your mother into our long-term-care wing."

I furrowed my brow. "I don't understand," I said. "She's supposed to be here for physical therapy to regain her muscle tone so she can walk again. Get around. Dress herself. So she can go home. That's the goal, right?"

The four nurses gave me the same pitying look. "I'm afraid we need to adjust our goals for her," Carla said. "She's not responding to therapy." She leaned in and said in a conspiratorial tone, "She's not even trying."

I recoiled, as though she had burned me. "What do you mean, not trying?" I asked, a little louder than I had intended, looking from one to the other.

"It's our policy," Carla went on. "It's actually dictated by insurance. Patients in the rehab wing need to actively participate in therapy. We need to be able to document progress, consistent upward progress, for insurance purposes. If there's no progress, we need to move them to the long-term-care wing, or insurance will stop paying the bills."

"Why? I'm sorry, but I just don't understand what you're saying."

"It's a matter of insurance, as I said, but it's also a matter of beds," Carla said. "If your mother isn't participating in therapy, we need to move her out of that bed to make room for someone who will."

"Okay," I said slowly, considering what they were telling me. "So, she's moving upstairs into the long-term-care wing. Will she receive the same therapy there? Will she get what she needs to regain her muscle tone so she can go home?"

Carla shuffled the papers in front of her. The others looked down or away from me.

"Well?" I prompted.

"They don't get the same kind of therapy in long-term care," she finally said. "Those adjusted goals I mentioned? The goal is not to get them home. It's to make them as comfortable as possible. It's just a matter of some paperwork, and we can get her transferred today."

Like hell they would. I thought of my constantly sleeping mother and the morphine drip they had her on, and rage bubbled up from deep within me, the kind of rage I'd never experienced.

"You have her on a morphine drip," I growled. "She is sedated! Get her off that morphine drip, and then we'll see about 'trying' and 'progress.'"

They were blinking at me, as if they had no idea what I was saying. "It's doctor's orders," one of them said. "We're just carrying them out. We can't just—"

I broke in. "When's the last time the doctor was here? I haven't seen him since the day my mom was transferred from the hospital."

Crickets. The four of them looked from one to the other, shaking their heads.

"My mom has been here, what, two weeks now? When is the last time the doctor saw her?"

"He makes his rounds once a week," Carla said. "It's his view—"

"You don't have eyes?" I pressed. "You're nurses! She's lying there sedated all day and night and you have the nerve to tell me she's not participating in therapy?"

They stared at me, eyes wide.

"I want her off that morphine drip immediately."

"We can't just change doctor's orders on the whim of a family member," Carla said, squaring her shoulders.

Oh, this is going to be a battle, then? I was prepared. I leaned forward, resting my arms on the table.

"Here's the way I see it." I smiled at them. "I understand that your facility makes a lot more money shifting people into long-term care and keeping them there for the rest of their lives rather than giving them rehab therapy for a few weeks to get them back on their feet and get out of here," I said, my teeth bared.

"You have no—"

I lifted my hand to shut down her words. My rage had settled into a quiet, simmering vengeance.

"Here's what's going to happen now."

They shifted in their chairs.

"Tomorrow morning, I am going to come back here at nine o'clock. I fully expect my mother to be off the morphine, up and around, sitting in her chair, and eating breakfast. When she's finished with her breakfast, I will accompany her to the therapy we're paying you to give her."

"We can't just take her off her medication."

"Yes, you can. She is not going to be sedated into a stupor for one more day. She is going to get the therapy we're paying you for. And if I walk into this facility tomorrow and find her in bed, unresponsive, as she is now, I'm calling my friend John Stanich. Do you know John? He's the district attorney."

They fidgeted some more and exchanged glances.

"What you're doing sounds like patient abuse to me. If I have to get John involved, he will start an investigation. And I will make sure the whole matter ends up on the front page of the newspaper, with photos of the four of you to go along with it."

My phone had been sitting on the table in front of me. I picked it up and hit the photo app.

"Smile, ladies." Click.

None of them said anything. I pushed my chair back and stood up. "I'll see you at nine o'clock tomorrow morning," I said over my shoulder as I walked away, tears of rage and fury stinging at my eyes.

I got in the car and headed for home but pulled over a few blocks before I got there. I shut off the car and let the flood of tears wash over me, crying until there weren't any tears left. My dad was back at the house, and I didn't want him to see me break down. He had asked me to handle all of the particulars of my mother's care—he was completely overwhelmed and not up to it—and I needed to come back from this meeting cheerful and upbeat. I blew my nose and put my glasses on, hoping he wouldn't notice my puffy red eyes.

That night, I sat outside on my back patio with my friend Mary. I told her what had gone down.

"Oh," she said, grinning. "That explains why I saw four heads on stakes outside of the rehab facility when I drove by this afternoon. I was wondering."

The devilish look on her face and the absurdity of what she had just said flipped some sort of switch in me, and I started laughing and then couldn't stop. It was one of those "inappropriate laughter during a solemn moment in church" moments where something—the intense need to release stress, maybe—overtakes you and won't let you go. Both Mary and I laughed until we cried.

A tasteless joke, yes, but sometimes you have to descend into the ridiculous during extremely stressful situations to prevent insanity from setting in. We talked about how tragic it was that not everyone in my mom's situation had an advocate willing to go into battle to make sure they got the care they deserved. How people just ended up alone and at the mercy of the system at the end of their lives.

But all of my threatening worked. The next day, lo and behold, I arrived to find my mother up and around, sitting in a chair and eating breakfast. I accompanied her to therapy that day and every day for weeks until she was strong enough to go home.

She lived another year after that. A good year, taking fun overnight trips with my dad, entertaining family, basking in the love we all had for her, never once complaining. And then it all became too much.

I hadn't thought about that day in a long time. I looked at Alice, who was staring at the lake, the morning sun shimmering on its surface, making the water dance with life. Her face was the picture of innocence. She turned to me and smiled.

How could she possibly have known?

CHAPTER ELEVEN

Jason poked his head out through the doorway. "Hey, honey! There you are! I told you I had a phone call. I didn't know where you got off to. You okay?" He stepped out onto the deck.

"I'm here with Brynn," Alice said to him. She looked at me for a long moment. "Brynn. I'll always be safe with Brynn." And then, in a stage whisper to me: "Repeating names helps me remember them."

"That's great!" Jason said, catching my eye. "But now it's time to go. Gil already left for the dock."

Just then, Dominic came through the door carrying his French press full of coffee and a mug.

"Morning, y'all," he said, setting the pot on the table. He turned his eyes to me. "I made a full pot. I thought you might like to join me again this morning."

"Oh!" I said, pushing myself out of my chair. "Great. I'll grab my mug. I was going to make my way downstairs, but Gary's coffee . . ." I made a face.

Jason snorted. "Tell me about it. Swill!" He raised his eyebrows at me and grinned before patting Dominic's shoulder. "Good morning, sir."

Dominic smiled at him. "And to you." He turned to Alice. "Lady Alice, I hope you slept well." He took her hand then and brought it to his lips.

She giggled.

"Brynn is my warrior, you know," she said.

"You're lucky." Dominic grinned. "I'd love to have a warrior like her in my corner."

"Come on, honey," Jason said as he helped her up from her chair. "The lake awaits!"

After they had gone and I had retrieved my mug and half-and-half, Dominic and I sat on the deck, drinking our coffee and staring out over the water.

"What was that about, do you think?" I asked him. "Alice, I mean. It's like she's afraid."

He took a deep breath in and let it out in a long sigh. "She feels herself slipping away. I've seen it before in people with Alzheimer's or dementia, in the early to middle stages. Whatever evil has ahold of them, they feel it. They know it before it overtakes them."

"I've never heard anyone call Alzheimer's evil," I said to him.

"Then you've never watched someone you love slip away because of it." He gave me a sad smile then. The pain behind it was tangible.

He went on, staring out over the water as he spoke. "In some cases, it's like they submerge into . . . I don't know what. The collective. The otherworld. The beyond. They're so close to death, they dip into it. And they're gone from us for a while. Still here, but in another world, too, at the same time. They don't know us. Don't remember our names or anything about the life we lived together. But then, without warning, they can pop up. Put their heads above the surface. They slip back into our world and know us. They can call us by name. They become themselves again for a brief moment. Just a brief moment. Then it's back down into the abyss."

He took a deep breath. "You wonder where they go, when they're in that abyss."

I reached over and put my hand on his. "I'm sorry. It sounds like you have personal experience with this."

He threaded his fingers through mine. Electricity shot through me, energizing and calming me at the same time. It was like I could feel my blood pressure dropping and my heart racing simultaneously. I couldn't remember the last time I had felt so much.

He looked at me and shook his head, and I could almost see his painful memories shake out of it. "Too much." He loosened his fingers, wrapped them around his coffee mug, and took a sip.

I toyed with telling him about what Alice had said to me, and about how she had appeared in my dreams, but decided against it. It sounded too out there, too strange to bring up to a man I barely knew. And I didn't relish telling the story that went along with it. Memories swirling through my mind were one thing. Making them palpable by saying them out loud was something I didn't want to deal with just then.

He broke the spell of my thoughts. "What are you up to today?"

"No plans. I thought about renting a kayak. But it sounds like a lot of work right now. The wet suit. The paddling."

"I feel you. There's something about this place that brings out the inner need to chill. I've got nothing going on today and was thinking about hitting the beach on the island. Sand, sun, water, a good book. Come along?"

Twenty minutes later, after a grueling battle trying to tug my bathing suit onto a body that hadn't seen it in a good three years, throwing on a cover-up, and packing a tote with a change of clothes, a hairbrush, a towel, and a paperback—not *The Illustrated Man*—we were driving down to the ferry dock in Dominic's fancy sedan. We pulled onto the ferry, Dominic turned off the car and hit the parking brake, and we climbed the rickety metal stairs to the upper deck. There, we stood at the railing and watched Wharton disappear from view.

After we got to the island, we pulled off the boat and cruised through town, past the stores and cafés where people were congregating for the day. We passed the small marina, where an older man was washing his boat, his dog supervising the effort, and headed onto the road toward the beach. Vacation homes—some grand houses, others small cabins—dotted the landscape here and there, and a wide expanse of grassland sat between the road where we were driving and the lake. The sky was deeply blue, not a cloud to be seen, and the sun shone down gently. I leaned my head back and exhaled.

Dominic pulled off the road and into the parking lot for the beach, and we headed down the long, winding wooden staircase to the lakeshore, choosing a spot adjacent to a stand of huge pines. It seemed an odd disconnect, pine trees next to a sandy beach, but then again, nothing was ordinary here in this enchanted place.

Settling onto our big beach towels in the warm sand, I cringed slightly at the idea of taking off my cover-up and revealing the reality of me in my bathing suit to this handsome man. But I forgot all about my modesty as Dominic peeled off his shirt.

I knew his shoulders and chest were broad, but somehow, without a shirt on, they seemed enormous. His arms and chest were heavily muscled. His stomach, rock hard. That would have been jaw-dropping enough, but the tattoos took my breath away.

Every inch of his arms and torso was covered. Strange, ancient symbols and hieroglyphs ran down one arm. On his other arm, a woman intertwined with a snake, along with a wolf and a lion, who reclined side by side. A hodgepodge of faces and animals—was that a turtle?— symbols and words and ancient-looking weapons decorated his chest and stomach. I stared, openmouthed. I couldn't help myself. I couldn't look away. It was just like the book.

Dominic turned to get something out of his tote, revealing his back. What I saw made me gasp aloud.

In the middle of his back was the image of some sort of beetle, its two enormous wings outstretched, reaching all the way up to his shoulder blades and meeting at the base of his neck, where they seemed to be holding up the sun. The wings were decorated with an intricate, colorful pattern of shapes—deep reds, blues, greens, and purples—that made them look like ancient Egyptian art, or a stained-glass window in a church.

Along the full length of his spine, symbols from world religions were superimposed over the beetle. A crucifix, a star of David, the star and crescent, the ahimsa hand, the nine-pointed star, the yin and yang, and other strange and exotic-looking symbols I didn't recognize.

He turned back around and caught me staring. The look on my face brought a smile to his.

"I thought it would be best just to get it over with," he said, his eyes twinkling. "It tends to be a little . . . jarring . . . to people seeing it for the first time."

It was then I realized my mouth was agape. I stammered out a couple of syllables. I couldn't find any words.

He smiled even broader than before and let out a chuckle. "I get that a lot."

Finally, I found my voice. "I have so many questions, but I don't even know where to start. Your back—oh, Dominic, it's like a work of art. It's breathtaking. Can I look at it again?"

Dominic rolled onto his stomach and rested his chin on his forearms. I crossed my legs and leaned over to gaze more deeply at the design. The level of detail, the artistry of that beetle alone. The wings! I could hardly fathom it. I wanted to touch him, to run my fingers along those delicate lines, to trace the wings. But I barely knew this man. It seemed like too much of a violation to touch him like that. I wanted to respect this artwork on his body, revere it, not objectify it.

"Why a beetle?" I asked, finally.

He looked up at me and smiled a slow smile. "A lot of people have seen it on my back and commented on it. Not a lot have asked why. Thank you for asking."

"Obviously it means a great deal to you, considering the real estate that illustration covers on your body."

He chuckled. "You could say that. It's a scarab. It was one of the most important religious and mystical symbols in ancient Egypt."

I was right about the Egyptian connection.

"It symbolized a lot of things, one of them being the sun, which people worshipped."

Hence the sun at the base of his neck.

"But more than that, the scarab was a symbol of transformation, resurrection, protection, and immortality. Reincarnation. Eternal life. People who wore scarab jewelry felt protected, knowing they were going to rise again."

I didn't know quite how to respond to that.

"They were also used in funerary art in ancient Egypt, so that the dead would be protected and transformed."

A shiver of cold ran through me, even though we were sitting directly in the warm sun.

"Are you of Egyptian heritage?" I asked him. "Or just interested in the mythology and lore?"

He rolled over and sat up. "Well, African heritage for sure, but probably not Egyptian." He grinned. "And yes to the interest in mythology and lore. But I'm most interested in the transformation part of it. That's what's important to me."

"People turning their lives around, you mean? That kind of transformation?"

"You could say that." He got to his feet. "I'm going to take a dip in this cold Lake Superior water. Join me?"

No more questions, then. I'd respect that. I knew all about deflecting prying questions.

He extended his hand, and when I took it, there it was again: the electricity shooting through me. He pulled me up to my feet and we walked down the beach together.

The warm, soft sand gave way to small stones at the water's edge. That was what lined the lake bed here and elsewhere around Superior's shores. The rocks were smooth, not uncomfortable to walk on in bare feet. Almost like cobblestone.

Dominic and I waded into the water, which was refreshingly chilly on this warm day, but not ice cold as it would be elsewhere around the lake. I scooped up a stone and held it out to him.

"We don't have scarabs here, but we have these," I said. "Some people believe it's a way to take the lake's spirit home with them. For protection and good luck. Not so different from your scarab."

I tossed it to him. He caught it and slid it into his pocket. "We can use all the good luck we can get." And then he kicked back and floated on the water's surface.

All at once, he wasn't there anymore. I looked this way and that. Where did he go? I was scanning the lake's surface when he popped up behind me and picked me up at the waist, flinging me into the air so I'd come splashing down into the water.

The moment I submerged, time seemed to stop. I opened my eyes in the crystal-clear water and saw the beautiful mosaic of stones on the lake bottom in grays, browns, blacks, whites, and ecrus. Some speckled, some solid colored.

Turning my head up, I saw Dominic's wavy, shimmering image above the surface. The sound of the lake whispered in my ears. It was so peaceful, so calming, I wished I could grow gills and breathe underwater to stay there, just like that, forever. It was like being a baby in the womb, nearing the moment of birth, the new world hazy and wavy and just a moment away.

I came up for air, laughing. "No one has done that to me since I was a kid," I said.

"I went under, so you had to go, too. That's how it works."

We stood there, waist deep, smiling at each other for a moment, that same electricity passing between us as forcefully as if we had been holding a power line. I could see by the look on his face that he was feeling it, too.

He moved closer to me and picked me up at the waist again, but instead of tossing me back into the water, he pulled me close, his enormous arms encircling me. I wrapped my arms around his neck and my legs around his waist as he walked farther out into the lake. It deepened with every step until he was up to his chest in water, and then he pushed off, sending us floating.

Our arms and legs intertwined in slow motion, the water giving us permission to touch each other in a way we—at least, I—felt unsure of doing on land. Somehow, it was okay out here to have my legs wrapped around this man, his arms around me, our bodies touching.

We floated out like that until we hit the famous barrier of icy-cold water just off this beach that separated the deep cold of the lake from the warm water of the shoreline. It was like a physical wall of chill well known to frequent swimmers there. We crossed it.

"Whoa! Damn!" Dominic cried out, dropping me into the water, our dreamlike floating spell broken.

I swam up to the surface and dissolved into sputtering, watery laughter as we both scrambled back to the warm side, him grumbling the whole time.

"What in the name of Poseidon was that?" he sputtered.

"Gitche Gumee, if you please," I laughed. "He's this lake's great spirit, not Poseidon. Have a little respect."

"Well, Gitche Gumee just opened up a can of whoop ass," he said, as we waded back to shore. "That was like the arctic, right there. And I'm not a damn seal." The look on his face, so affronted, so aghast as he scowled at the water, made me howl with laughter.

"It's sort of a famous feature of this beach," I said. "The invisible barrier."

"Invisible barrier? So that's how it is here? This is what you do? No warning? No signage: 'Beware of the invisible cold-ass barrier!'"

I laughed even more as he ranted on.

"No warning! You take a man out into the water. An unsuspecting, innocent man. From California, by way of Georgia. Do you know what we have in Cali? The ocean. It's cold, don't get me wrong. But there ain't no *invisible barriers* like that in the Pacific. Seals, yes. Walls of ice-cold water that just come out of nowhere, no."

I bent over at the waist, laughing harder than I had in a long time.

"You're swimming with an unsuspecting man who is going to freeze his nuts off after he hits an *invisible barrier*—and you know it's coming! You're just floating there, all serene and happy like a mermaid—la-la-la, isn't this nice—knowing the whole time we're bobbing toward an iceberg."

I was trying to catch my breath. "I'm sorry," I squeaked out, drying my eyes.

"Oh, I can see that, all right. I can see you're very sorry." By now he was laughing, too, his eyes dancing. "Sorry my ass. That's how sorry you are."

We waded out of the water and onto the sand, collapsing onto our towels. We lay on our sides, facing each other. I couldn't stop laughing.

"And don't get any ideas, either," he went on. "I might have kissed you. In fact, I was planning on it. Not now. No, ma'am. Shrinkage is real! I'll be lucky if my manhood ever comes back."

I shook with the force of the laughter that was coursing through my body. I wiped my eyes. "I think that just added a decade to my life," I said.

"My work is done, pretty woman," he said, running a hand through my wet hair. "It stands to reason, if stress and sadness take it away, laughter can give it back."

We fell silent as the air thickened between us. His body was so close to mine, close enough for me to feel the energy radiating off him. I wanted that kiss. I longed to slide closer and kiss his perfect mouth, feel what it was like to have his lips on mine. But I shook it off. I hadn't dated anyone since my relationship broke up, and I was definitely out of practice. We weren't in the water anymore, and a shyness overtook me.

I cleared my throat. "What do you want to do now?" I asked him.

"Not go back in the water, that's for damn sure," he said, squinting darkly out over the lake. "But I brought a book."

I sat up. "Me, too!"

"Great minds," he said, reaching into his tote.

Mine was a suspense thriller—I had felt weird about reading *The Illustrated Man* with the Illustrated Man, so I brought another. His was a true-crime novel. He leaned back on one elbow, crossed his ankles, and cracked his book as I struggled to get comfortable. He put an arm around me and pulled me into him.

"I make a pretty good backrest," he said.

I turned around to grin at him. "Are you sure?"

"Lean on in."

So I did. I stretched out and leaned my back into his chest. We sat there together, heads inches apart, each reading our own books, for the rest of the afternoon as the lake lap, lap, lapped into shore. Truth be told, I was enjoying being close to him more than the plot of the novel I was reading. The lake's "invisible barrier" had broken one down between us.

Just the act of leaning against his vast chest made me feel safe and protected and ready for my own transformation I'd hoped to find in Wharton, as though he himself were the scarab.

CHAPTER TWELVE

As the afternoon wound down, Dominic and I gathered up our things and climbed back up the long and winding staircase to the parking lot. In the changing area, I peeled off my wet and sandy swimsuit, splashed some fresh water onto myself, and dried off before changing into the sundress and sandals I had stuffed into my tote earlier. I gave my hair a quick brush. Reasonably de-sanded and clean, I looked in the mirror—it would have to do.

Both Dominic and I emerged around the same time, me in my sundress, him in his shorts and black V-neck T-shirt.

"Well, look at you," he said. "Just as quick as that, you're ready for action."

"What now?" I asked. "Back to LuAnn's?"

"Hell no." He smirked. "I've got one fine lady on my arm. It's not time to go home just yet."

I could feel the heat rising to my face. "I suppose the troops can carry on without us. But you realize we'll be the talk of happy hour if we're both not there."

He laughed. "Then let's give them something to talk about. How about heading over to Jimmy's for an adult beverage and maybe an early dinner?"

That sounded perfect to me.

We hopped into the car, and he drove us back into town, his hand resting on my thigh. Was that appropriate? I wasn't sure what to do with my own hands so I kept them folded in my lap until we pulled into Jimmy's, the bar with the circus tent for a ceiling.

The sun was still high in the sky—it was only about five o'clock—but inside, the whole place was lit up by fairy lights wound around the wooden poles holding up the tent. I saw countless signs with various messages: "Well-behaved women rarely make history," "Obey only the good laws," and many others adorning the wooden walls that remained standing after the fire.

Candles of different sizes and shapes flickered on the tables. Everything except the tent was rustic, as though an island castaway had crafted it from materials at hand—the bar itself was wood, the barstools hewn from tree stumps, and the wide-planked, rather haphazard floor seemed to have been laid in a hurry without much attention to detail. It reminded me of the Lost Boys' lair in Peter Pan. We might as well have been in the trunk of an enormous tree.

I looked around at the other patrons, some wearing swimsuits, others wearing hippie dresses, others wearing shorts and T-shirts. They could have been lost, too, looking for their Pan. Maybe I was one of them.

We found a table, and our server sidled up.

"What can I getcha to drink?" she said. "Just so you know, we've got a taco truck outside in the back parking lot right now, just about ready to open. So that's what's for dinner. The entertainment starts whenever they want to start. And we don't take plastic. It's all cash. But you two don't look like plastic people, so I think we'll be fine there."

Dominic and I grinned at each other.

"Got any local beers?" he asked.

"Spotted Cow is on tap," she said, jutting out her hip.

"That'll do," he said.

She turned to me. "Make it two," I said.

Dominic raised his eyebrows. "I didn't figure you for a beer drinker."

"Hey, when in Rome." I shrugged.

Our drinks arrived, and he held his glass aloft. "To a lovely day with a lovely lady," he said, flashing that movie-star smile.

I clinked my glass with his, my face reddening. "Thank you," I said. "I had a really good time. For the first time in a long time."

"That's what it's all about, girl," he said, his face growing serious for a moment. "Enjoying life. People get so caught up in themselves and their dramas, or they get ensnared in their own sorrows and tragedies, they forget to appreciate the beauty around them."

"Or forget there even is beauty around them," I said, remembering how gray the world had looked for the past few years. "I'm guilty of that myself."

"Aren't we all at one time or another?"

We gazed at each other, and I lost myself in the beauty of his face. The perfection of creation, right in front of me. His face was angelic and devilish all at once with his sly grin, dancing eyes, his strong nose and mouth, blindingly white perfect teeth, and chiseled jawline. He was staring at me just as intently.

"I'm appreciating the beauty around me right now," he said, echoing my thoughts.

I lifted my hand to my cheek, trying to stop the blush. I couldn't remember the last time a man had told me I was beautiful.

After we finished our first beer, he popped out back to get us some tacos with all the fixings and a decadent plate of nachos with guacamole and salsa.

"If I could eat only one thing for the rest of my life, it would be nachos," I said, peeling a cheese-laden chip off the mound.

"For me, it's my grandma's broccoli casserole," he said. "Gooey, cheesy comfort food."

We sat there for a long while, nibbling on our Tex-Mex, getting to know each other, talking about everything and nothing. Politics, town gossip, favorite movies, and fun trips we'd taken.

He asked me all about my life and childhood, which I freely told him—growing up by the creek in the suburbs, my grandma living with us, and everything else there was to tell about my background and then some.

"So, what's your story?" I asked him.

"There's not much to tell," he said, taking a bite of a chip. "Pretty ordinary stuff. You're more interesting than me."

"Oh, I doubt that." I grinned at him. "Where did you grow up?"

"Here and there," he said, looking down at his plate. "Lots of places."

I took a sip of my beer and eyed him over the rim. "Like where? You said California back on the beach, right?"

He fidgeted in his chair. "I don't love talking about my past," he said. "It's not what defines me."

I was going to say "Okay" and leave it at that. But it wasn't.

"I think a person's past, good or bad, idyllic or horrific, shapes who they are," I said. "But I don't believe it defines them."

He held my gaze for a long minute. "My first memory is of finding a gun in my living room and shooting my father in the chest when I was four years old. So that gives you a little taste of it."

I had no words to respond. I simply locked eyes with him and reached over to take his hand. How could I possibly relate to that? My childhood had been written in a storybook, decidedly not Grimm's. Nothing bad ever happened to anybody I knew—literally. No family members or neighbors died when I was a kid. Nobody went bankrupt. Nobody lost their home. Nobody even lost their job. No children went missing. No kids in school got seriously sick; no family members, either.

Everyone in my neighborhood liked and supported each other. No neighbor dramas. No bad apples on the block. We kids ran wild without any thought of danger, playing Star Light, Moon Light on summer nights, hiding in the dark until our friends found us, without any fear of strangers. My parents were blissfully happy and created a happy life for us, made even more so by my grandma. I came home from school every day to her running to the door with open arms, so happy to see me. There were always warm cookies, fresh out of the oven.

All in all, I had had a pretty good run up until the past few years. Gratitude seeped into my heart for the first time in a long time.

And here, this lovely man sitting across the table from me in this strange hippie bar had started his life with a nightmare. God only knew how it had gone for him after that. The look on his face shredded my heart. I could clearly see that four-year-old little boy in his eyes.

"Oh, Dominic."

He smiled sadly. "I know. It's kind of a conversation stopper. My story doesn't improve much after that, either. It's why I don't really talk about my past."

"Did he—"

Dominic shook his head. "It went through his shoulder and out. He survived. The cantankerous old bastard is still kicking."

"May I ask why a loaded gun was where a four-year-old could find it? Was your dad a cop?"

He sighed. "Hardly. Do you really want to know?"

"Of course I do. That doesn't mean you have to tell me."

He winced. "I was hoping to keep it all to myself until you knew me better," he said. "Or, you know, forever."

All at once, a sense of protectiveness washed over me. Clearly his past was a source of pain for him. I didn't need to know anything. Jason had told me Wharton was full of busybodies. I was determined to not be one of them.

"How about those Twins?" I grinned. "They're having one hell of a year so far. People are saying they just might make it all the way to the World Series."

His face softened in a way I hadn't seen before. "Thank you," he said. He gazed into his bubbling beer glass for a few moments, and then he looked up at me and said, "There was love and happiness in my childhood, though. A lot of it was a nightmare. But I lived with my grandmother for many of my growing-up years."

"She loved you."

His eyes were brimming with tears. "'To the moon and back' is what she always used to say."

"And she made broccoli casserole."

"The best in the world."

"Is she still with us?" I said, leaning in.

He shook his head. "She's with me all the time. But she crossed the bridge a few years ago."

Just then, the band took the stage with the clatter of setup for their guitars, a violin, banjo, bass fiddle, and drums. The singer's microphone looked like it could have been from the 1930s—a silver square on a stand—and the guitar he threaded over his shoulder seemed to match the era. When they started playing, a mixture of bluegrass and country, everyone quieted down to listen. Several people took to the dance floor, some in groups, others in pairs, one hippie dude swaying this way and that by himself.

Dominic pushed himself to his feet and took my hand, and before I knew it, we were two-stepping to the music, with him twirling me every so often and pulling me back in close. A sort of hazy reality set in.

The fairy lights and candles, the music from another era, the strangely familiar face of this man so close to mine. It was as though we were taken out of the river of time for a moment, like people in old folktales who stumble onto a fairy ring on a crisp autumn evening and dance the night away with them, not realizing they're dancing through years, decades, even centuries.

CHAPTER THIRTEEN

All was dark when we got back to LuAnn's. It was after ten o'clock, and the restaurant was closed and clean, ready for the breakfast crowd. Dominic led me through the dining room to the doorway, and we crept upstairs quietly, not wanting to wake anyone.

In the hallway, we saw light coming from under Jason and Gil's door. They were still up. The rest of the house was quiet. I glanced into the alcove. All dark. I hadn't told Dominic about what I had experienced two nights earlier. And didn't want to think about it myself.

We reached his door and passed it. "I'll walk you to yours." He smiled down at me.

At my door, just down the hallway, my heart was thumping in my chest. I was so out of practice with dating—was that what we were doing?—I wasn't sure what came next. Invite him in? Or was it too soon? Was it wise at all? Should I play hard to get? I had no idea what to do.

He took the key from my hand and opened the door before turning on the light and scanning the room. My curtains were billowing in the cool breeze. All was just as I had left it.

"Looks like you're set," he said.

We were standing close to each other, and although our arms and legs had been intertwined in the water, and we had danced together all night long at Jimmy's, this felt different. I wasn't sure whether to touch him or not, but every cell in my body wanted to.

"I had such a good time today," I said to him. "Thank you."

"Me, too," he said, his voice low.

He wrapped his arms around me and pulled me close, and I lifted my face toward his. He pressed his cheek to mine, and I could smell his scent—musky, spicy, comforting. I melted into him. And then, his lips were on mine, and I could feel the force of the kiss coursing throughout my entire body.

My heart was pounding in my chest as I navigated my first kiss with a new man in more than two decades. He pulled back, his arms still wrapped around me. I wanted nothing but for him to get closer.

"I've been wanting to do this all day," he said. "Longer than that, if you want to know the truth."

"Me, too," I whispered. My whole body was vibrating on the inside.

He slid a hand into my hair near the nape of my neck and took a handful of it, his eyes studying my face.

"Brynn, Brynn, Brynn," he said, his voice seeming to get an octave lower. "I'm going to leave it just like this. For now."

I nodded. "Okay."

"Coffee on the deck in the morning?"

"I'll be there."

He pulled me back into him and smiled slightly, his eyes holding mine, before kissing me again. And then he turned on that movie-star smile, and winked.

"See you tomorrow. Sleep tight, now." And he shut the door behind him.

As I locked it and turned back to my darkened room, it seemed so much emptier than it had just a moment before. It was as though his presence filled up not just my room, but me, too.

∽

The next morning, the first thing I was aware of, even before my eyes fluttered open, was the smell of the rain. I lay there for a moment, enjoying the fresh scent of water and grass and earth and lake. A chill wafted through the air in my room, making me want to curl down farther under my comforter and sleep the day away. A low growl of thunder rolled through the sky. I stretched and breathed it all in and out, in and out.

A knock at my door broke my meditation. I slipped out of bed, pulled my robe around me, and opened the door to find Dominic standing there with his French press and a mug.

"No coffee on the deck today. I thought I'd bring it to you instead."

"Wow, room service!" I smiled at him, running a hand through my hair, hoping it didn't look too much of a fright. I gave silent thanks that I was wearing my soft new pajamas, at least, rather than the old, ratty T-shirts I usually slept in. "What a nice way to start the day."

I opened the door wider and invited him in. I was about to close it behind him when he said, "We had better leave it open. We don't want to become the talk of Wharton too soon."

I had a feeling we already were, but I couldn't have cared less. I grabbed my mug and half-and-half, and we sat in the two chairs on either side of the small table by the window, the rain making hypnotic music as it fell.

As we listened to the storm outside, I wondered again about the storm he had undoubtedly endured growing up.

I didn't know much about him, not really. Still. There was something timeless about the feeling that hung in the air between us. In one sense, I didn't know him at all, and yet in another, I knew everything.

I smiled at him, a wholly unfamiliar feeling of contentment welling up inside of me. Even after just a short time, I was growing accustomed to starting my day with him.

"I had a good time yesterday," I said, taking a sip of coffee and catching his eye over the brim of my mug.

He smiled. "Yes, indeed. I think we're going to have more of those. I hope we do, anyway."

"We talked a lot about me," I said slowly. "And, I know you don't want to talk about your past, so I'm not going to ask. But what about the present? I don't even know what you do for a living."

He smiled that big smile. "A little of this. A little of that."

I raised my eyebrows at him. "Is that so? It sounds vaguely criminal. Tell me you're not a serial killer on the lam."

He chuckled. "No, no, no, no," he said. "Nothing like that. Let's just say I help people who are in transition."

More evasive answers. I was going to press on this time, though. I was falling for this man, too quickly—more like "tripped and falling"—and I needed to know more about what I was letting into my life, or it was going to be one awkward summer of running into him in the hallway. And with Kate's news that her husband had looked at him after a suspicious death . . .

"Like, a grief counselor? Or a hospice worker? Rehab sponsor?"

"Well, definitely not a rehab sponsor." He chuckled. "But, yeah, sometimes it's grief, sometimes it's hospice, but sometimes it's people who need to put their lives back on track after they've paid the price of falling. I have resources when they find they're completely out of them."

"People who are getting out of prison, you mean?"

He nodded. "Yeah. It's all that rolled into one. I have all different types of clients that I help. My overarching belief is that life is too short. Way too short, Brynn. You have no idea." He stopped for a moment. "That was insensitive. Yes, you do. You know it better, and fresher, than most right now."

I nodded, willing the tears to stay where they were.

"When people come to me, they're at their lowest point. If I can help them get back on the path toward a happy life, I do that. If I can't, I help with that, too."

It still wasn't clear to me—how did people find him? Was he a coun-selor affiliated with some group? Did he have his own foundation?—but I sensed this was a man who wasn't going to easily share anything. I could almost see his shield going up.

"So, what are you doing in Wharton for the whole summer?" I asked. "I know, I know, everyone asks it. But—are you on a sabbatical, like me?"

"I'm here to meet you, Brynn."

His smile was broad and warm, but a chill shot through me. We sat, staring at each other for a moment.

"What—"

He laughed then, breaking the spell. "Okay, that was the worst pickup line in history."

I put down my coffee cup and saw my hands were shaking. He saw it, too. "You don't know what was running through my mind!" I said finally. "What you're describing, what you do for people. I'm in that exact kind of transition right now. I was thinking someone called you. Or hired you. Or—"

He put his hand up to stop me. "I keep putting my foot in it this morning," he said. "Wow, I am one insensitive bastard."

I shook my head. "I don't understand."

"Okay. I was just trying to be romantic and seductive with that stupid line, not thinking of everything you've told me about your recent life."

I managed a smile. "Don't worry about it. It just hit a little close to home. I'm not your client, am I?"

He grinned. "Hey, I don't go around kissing my clients, lady. Or swimming across invisible barriers with them."

That brought a genuine smile to my face, and I chuckled.

"The truth is, I'm here for much the same reason you are," he said, pouring the last of the coffee into our two mugs. "When you do what I do, it takes it out of you. I get sort of, I guess you'd say depleted. I don't have a wife or family to restore me, obviously, and sometimes I need to detach and exhale for a while. Smell the fresh air. Recognize the beauty around me. Immerse myself in the garden of earthly delights where we live. Eat some pasta. I need to rejuvenate so I can give back to others."

"I totally get that," I said.

Just then, a loud boom of thunder pierced the quiet between us, and a sizzle of lightning crackled through the sky. Rain poured in sheets, the wind taking it sideways down the street.

"I love a good storm," Dominic said.

"Me, too. Sort of puts a damper on another beach day, though."

"True, that. Kayaking would be a similar bummer."

He smiled at me, and, as the rain poured down and thunder shook the house, a memory of another rainy night bubbled along the edges of my mind. At least, it felt like a memory. But it couldn't have been.

I was with a man I knew was Dominic. The two of us burst out of the door of a brick building into an alleyway. He was holding my hand, and we were running, both of us laughing and looking back over our shoulders. He pushed me into a doorway to get out of the rain—we were soaked to the skin—and he kissed me as the rain pounded down around us and lightning sizzled through the sky.

"The death of a good speakeasy," he said, his voice low in my ear. "It's always so sad."

"They nearly caught us all," I said. "How did you know they were coming?"

"A gentleman's intuition," he said, an impish grin on his face.

Dominic's voice—in the here and now—brought me out of my imagination. "Brynn?"

I took a sip of coffee. My hands were shaking.

"Where did you go?" Dominic asked. "You zoned out for a minute."

I ran a hand through my hair. "I'm really not sure," I said.

He grinned at me then. The same impish grin.

CHAPTER FOURTEEN

Just then, Jason poked his head into my room. "Hi, kids!" he said, looking from me to Dominic and back again.

I held my cup aloft. "We were just having coffee."

"I'll bet you were," Jason said. "You missed happy hour yesterday. Everyone was wondering what became of you."

Dominic laughed. "And there it is."

I laughed, too, but felt the blush rising in my cheeks. "We went over to the island for the day," I said.

"Oh!" Jason said, elongating the word so it contained many syllables. "Did you, now? I see, I see, I see. I can't wait to tell Gil."

Both Dominic and I dissolved into embarrassed laughter at the look of sheer delight on Jason's face.

"Hey," Jason said. "Speaking of the island, I have a huge favor to ask of you."

"Sure," I said. "What is it?"

His look of delight morphed into a chagrined cringe.

"After this storm passes, Gil and I need to go over to Colette to look at a property we're toying with buying," Jason said. "We're supposed to be meeting with the Realtor. I thought maybe we could have lunch there afterward, just the two of us."

I nodded, not quite understanding what he was getting at.

"I know it's a lot to ask," he went on, "but is there any chance you could sit with Alice while we're gone?"

"Oh!" I said, raising my eyebrows. "Absolutely."

"Are you sure?" Jason asked.

I shrugged. "I'm happy to do it. No problem at all."

Jason took my hands. "Thank you so much. I hired a woman here in town to be our sort of . . . I don't want to say *respite care person*, but . . ." His words trailed off, and he shook his head.

"Alice didn't like her when we did a trial run yesterday. She kept wandering off, looking for me."

I winced. "That's not good."

"No," Jason said. "We're going to try again with her. Jocelyn is her name. She's completely lovely, so I don't know why Alice didn't take a shine to her. But I just don't feel right about leaving for that length of time when she's not comfortable with her caregiver."

"Of course," I said.

"She likes you, though," he said, looking from me to Dominic and back again. "Both of you. She feels safe with you. I don't know. Maybe because you're staying down the hall from us, you feel like family to her. I'm thinking that her need to find me, to go looking for me, will be lessened if she's with you. I just feel so . . ."

He sighed and looked up at me, his eyes searching. I tried to give him what he needed to hang on to right then.

"No need to explain. You and Gil absolutely need some time to yourselves. You have to take it."

"Caregiving can suck the life out of you, man," Dominic broke in. "Brynn is right. A lunch here, a dinner there. It's not so much to ask of us, but it's vital for you. For your spirit. It's what you need to recharge along the way so you can help Alice in the long term. Brynn and I were just talking about a similar thing."

He caught my eye and smiled, shyly, I thought.

Jason exhaled loudly. "Oh, you're a godsend. Both of you."

He went on. "So, I was thinking you might want to watch a couple of movies in our suite with her while we're gone? Would that be okay? Alice is at home there. We've got that big flat-screen TV above the fireplace. We'll light a fire since the weather is so crummy. We'll get some lunch and snacks and wine for you."

"That's not necessa—" I started.

"Oh, it's necessa, missy." Jason smiled. "It's the least we can do."

"I'll join you, if you'd like," Dominic said to me. "We'll make it a party."

All at once, my room, which had been bathed in gloom because of the darkness of the storm outside, felt like it was filled with light.

"So, ten thirty? Our place?" Jason confirmed.

"I'll be there," I said.

When Jason had gone, Dominic turned to me. "I have a few things to take care of this morning. Knock on my door when you're on your way down to Jason and Gil's suite, and we'll make an afternoon of it."

I nodded at him, and he grinned as he shut the door behind him.

So, ten thirty it was. I had a little more than two hours. Enough time for a long bath with a good book. I grabbed the copy of *The Illustrated Man* that I had bought at Beth's a couple of days prior and headed down to the tub room, hoping the lady from number five would leave me in peace this time.

CHAPTER FIFTEEN

At ten thirty, fresh from my bath, in a pair of skinny jeans, a white T-shirt, and a necklace with blue, white, and green glass beads dangling around my neck, I stepped out of my door to find Dominic leaning against the wall next to his.

He was wearing a black V-neck T-shirt and gray sweatpants, comfy slippers on his feet. He hadn't shaved, and his usual neat goatee was morphing into a full beard. He shrugged, smiling. "Too casual? I've been attending to some things this morning and didn't have it in me to, you know, give it the full treatment."

I grinned at him. "The full treatment?"

He raised his eyebrows. "Oh, I give it the treatment, lady, when I'm going out. A man's gotta bring it. But, I figured, we're staying in, so . . ."

"I think you look great," I said.

"You clean up pretty nicely yourself," he said, fingering my necklace and letting his hand stray to my cheek.

At the end of the hallway, Jason opened his door. "Hi, you two. Alice, look who's here." His words were a little too enthusiastic. But I understood.

We hurried down to their suite, all smiles. Alice was curled up in an armchair by the blazing fire, an afghan thrown over her legs.

"Hi, Alice!" I said to her.

"Brynn, in the Yellow Lady," she said to me, then turned her eyes to Dominic. "And the big man. My knight."

Dominic laughed at this. "I guess you could call me that." He crossed the room and bowed, holding out his hand. She slipped hers into it, and he brought it to his lips. "Lady Alice. How are you this fine day?" Alice giggled, and a blush rose to her cheeks.

Jason and I shared a smile behind Dominic's back, and Jason made a heart sign with his thumbs and forefingers over his own heart, beaming at me.

Gil emerged from the bedroom. He took in the scene of Dominic and Alice and exhaled.

"Let's make sure to take our rain shells, hon," he said to Jason. "I have a feeling this isn't going to let up anytime soon."

Alice trembled. "Are you going somewhere?"

Jason crossed the room and sat on the ottoman across from Alice's chair. "Remember, honey? Gil and I have to go across to the island to take care of some business. We thought the weather was too bad to bring you along."

She blinked at him.

"Remember? You're staying here. We'll be back in a couple of hours."

"I'm staying here?"

"Yes!" Jason said, a little too brightly. "That's why Dominic and Brynn are here. They're going to spend the afternoon with you, until we get back. We didn't want you to be all by yourself."

"Dominic and Brynn," Alice repeated.

"That's right, honey. You three will have a little lunch. Watch a movie together. Maybe you'll want to take a nap after that. You'll be safe with them."

Alice smiled at me. "I know that."

"Okay!" Jason said and kissed Alice on the cheek. "We're off."

Jason and Gil grabbed their jackets off the hooks by the door.

"This is for you," Jason said, pointing to a big plate of hors d'oeuvres—cheeses, meats, veggies, dips, crackers—on the kitchen counter. Two bottles of wine sat in an ice bucket, with three glasses nearby. I hadn't noticed it when we came in.

"Jason, you didn't have to do this," I said.

"Of course, silly," he said. "If you feel you want some lunch downstairs, just put it on my tab. Alice likes the tuna melt."

"Oh!" Alice piped up. "It's wonderful. They put avocado on it."

Interesting, I thought, what her mind remembered and what it didn't. I wondered if there was a science to it, or if it was just random, different for each person, depending on which brain cells were going to sleep.

After they had gone, Dominic poured both of us a glass of wine and cocked his head in Alice's direction, a questioning look on his face. I shrugged. Jason had given her a glass or two at happy hour, so I guessed it wouldn't hurt. I joined him in the kitchen and brought the tray of hors d'oeuvres and some napkins into the living room where Alice was sitting, and set it on the ottoman that stood between the couch and the love seats.

Dominic handed Alice her glass, and we all clinked together. "To a lovely afternoon," he said, his voice smooth. And comforting, I thought.

Jason had suggested we watch movies, but I just felt like talking. I thought Alice did, too, by the way she leaned toward me, her eyes expectant.

"Alice," I began. "Tell me about your daughters. Their names are Jane and Rebecca, right?"

She beamed. "That's right. Jane and Rebecca. Jason says they're both mothers now themselves, although I can't quite believe that because I'm too young to have grandchildren." She smiled at this. "Rebecca has a few kids. Four? Jane has just one, I think." She was staring off then, as if trying to get a look at her family in her mind's eye.

She didn't have to search her memory for their faces. I spied a photo on the coffee table. It looked like Jason, Alice, their daughters, sons-in-law, and a whole gaggle of kids. I pushed myself to my feet and stepped over to it, picking up the frame. I held it out to her.

"This is your family, right?"

She took the frame and studied the photo within it. Her brow furrowed. "Well, that's me. And that's Jason. But I don't know who these women are. Or the men. Or the children. Are you sure they're my family?"

I knelt next to her. "This is your daughter Rebecca," I said, pointing to the woman I had met a few days prior. "And this is your daughter Jane."

She scowled at the photo. "They're so old! They're adults! My kids are small. But it looks like a beautiful family, doesn't it?"

"That's right, Alice. You've raised a beautiful family. Your girls have husbands and children of their own now."

Alice held my gaze for a moment and then looked back to the photo. She pointed to one of her grandsons.

"He will die young," she said. "Cancer. Jane won't be able to handle it. I won't be here to help her."

I took a breath in and shot a look at Dominic, who shook his head quickly.

"Lady Alice," he said, slowly taking the photograph from her hands and putting it facedown on the table. "Tell us about how you and Jason met."

Alice beamed. "We were high school sweethearts. It's always been Jason and Alice, for as long as I can remember. He asked me to a dance when we were juniors in high school. I wore a pink chiffon dress. He wore a pink tie with his suit, matching. And that was it. There was nobody else for me. He was so handsome."

"I'll bet you were a beauty back in the day," I said to her. "You still are."

She put a hand to her cheek. "I don't know about that." She smiled then, her eyes focusing on that night in the past.

"Jason wasn't a very good dancer at first." She giggled. "You should have seen him! Maybe you did. Maybe you were there. I'm not sure. He was so gangly! All legs and arms. But then he became quite good at it."

Dominic smiled at this. "Do you like to dance, Lady Alice?"

"I love it. When our girls were young and Jason came home from work, we'd put on records and we would have a dance party, right in our living room," she said. "Every night. We'd play everything, from big band oldies to Elvis to sixties rock. Even into the seventies!"

"Who was in charge of choosing the music, you or Jason?" Dominic led her.

"Usually I chose. I liked to have something on the stereo when he came home. I'd be in the kitchen finishing dinner, and I'd go out into the living room, and he'd be dancing with the girls, everyone singing along with the songs. In the summertime, we'd go outside, and the neighbors would join in."

"It sounds wonderful," I said.

"It was," Alice said.

"Who were some of your favorite singers back then?" Dominic smiled at me, and my eyes shone back.

"Jason loved Aretha Franklin—we both did—so, we'd play her a lot. We'd dance with those kids. Everybody laughing. We wore them out!"

"I love me some Queen of Soul, too," Dominic said. "I never danced at home with my mother to her music, though. That's something special you gave your kids."

Alice was in another world then, another time. She was gazing back to those nights in their living room, humming a familiar tune. Dominic fiddled with his phone for a moment, and soon an Aretha Franklin song began to play. He stood up and held out his hand to her.

He twirled her around, and they swayed to the music that was in Alice's memory and playing in the room, and both of their faces truly lit up with joy.

My heart melted at the sweetness of it and ached at the sadness. What kind of breathtaking man was this?

She collapsed back into her chair in laughter. "Those girls would dance all night if we let them."

"And did you, sometimes?" Dominic asked, grinning.

"Oh, heavens no. That was just a short, fun time to welcome Daddy home before dinner." She smiled, looking at both of us, her eyes brimming with tears. She brushed them away with her hand. "Where's Jason? Isn't he supposed to be home by now?"

"He'll be back in about an hour, Alice," I said. "He's on the way home."

She smiled and settled into her chair. "He's on the way home. So, he's not far." She looked at Dominic, then me. "Jason is the love of my life, you know."

"Did you ever date anyone else?" I asked her. "You're so beautiful, Alice, I'm sure you had lots of men buzzing around, wanting to take you out."

She shook her head. "No, I didn't see the point," she said, more lucid than she'd been all afternoon. "You're lucky if you get one great love in this life. I had mine for thirty-plus years. After it was over, there was no other man who could possibly compare. I have my kids. That was enough. They still need their mom."

"And your grandkids, too, right?"

She furrowed her brow at me and pushed herself out of her chair. "I really need to get home," she said. "How long have we been talking? My kids are going to be home soon, and I need to meet the bus."

Dominic and I exchanged a glance. I wasn't sure how to respond to this. But he jumped in.

"Jason's going to meet the girls at the bus today, Alice," he said, his voice low.

She looked at him, a vacancy in her eyes I hadn't seen before. "That's silly. Jason's at work."

Dominic shook his head. "Not today. Today he's coming home early, and he said he'd meet the girls at the bus because you came here to visit with us."

She slumped back down into her chair. Her eyes were darting this way and that.

"And who are you?"

"We're your friends," Dominic said, handing her a piece of cheese on a cracker. "I'm Dominic. And this is Brynn."

She popped the cheese and cracker into her mouth and chewed thoughtfully.

"Brynn," Alice said, searching my face to find something familiar. I could see her working for it, straining to reach back into her mind. "My protector."

"That's right." I smiled at her. "And I'm always just down the hall in—" I was going to say "the Yellow Lady," but didn't get a chance. Alice turned toward the door, her eyes becoming glassy and unfocused.

Then she snapped her head around to look at me. Her pupils had all but disappeared. Only a cloudy blue remained. "You're in number five."

CHAPTER SIXTEEN

Neither of us pressed Alice to explain that remark. Frankly, I didn't want to know what was behind it. Instead, we turned on a movie, and Alice dozed, leaning on Dominic's chest.

"Time for a nap?" he said to me in a whisper.

I nodded. "Seems like a good idea."

He gently roused her. She smiled sleepily at him and let him lead her up the stairs.

"This is where I stay," I heard her say as he opened the door and helped her inside. "Jason doesn't sleep with me anymore. We have separate bedrooms."

I picked up my wineglass with shaking hands and took a sip. And then another. A few moments passed, and Dominic emerged from Alice's room, quietly closing the door behind him.

"That was weird," I said to him as he slid down next to me on the couch.

"What was weird?"

"All of it, I guess," I said, not quite knowing what more to say.

"You haven't spent a lot of time around people with Alzheimer's," he said. "It's actually quite typical, all of that back and forth in time. It's like they're living it all at once—past and present. Even future sometimes. That linear time construct? It dissolves for them."

That sent a shiver through me, but I wasn't sure why. "What do you mean, exactly?"

"When she was talking about having to go home to meet her kids at the bus, I'm not sure that she wasn't really back there. Part of her. Her spirit, maybe, was actually back there living that moment again."

I just looked at him. I had no idea how to respond to that.

He chuckled. "Okay, I guess that was a little woo-woo for a rainy afternoon. I've often wondered about it, though. It's like, who's the one with an impaired mind? Us, or them? Maybe they're the ones seeing clearly. Not us."

"Speaking of that . . ." I wasn't sure how to continue.

I wasn't so much concerned with Alice reliving, or living, her past. I hadn't told him, or anyone, about my somewhat strange encounters with her.

"You're going to think I'm crazy," I said to him finally.

He smirked. "I just told you I believe Alice was back there, thirty years ago, actually living that moment while at the same time she was right here with us, and *I'm* going to think *you're* crazy?"

I couldn't help smiling back at his devilish grin.

"You've got something on your mind, woman," he said. "Out with it."

I fidgeted, wondering just how much to say. "It's like she knows things she shouldn't."

He frowned at me and leaned forward. "What do you mean? I don't follow you."

I told him about the "heads on stakes" joke, and the battle at the care center that precipitated it.

He chuckled. "I think I'd like that Mary friend of yours," he said. "And I pity the fool who messes with anyone you love."

"Well, obviously." I grinned at him. "But the point is, how did Alice know about it?"

He shook his head. "You've got me on that one."

"And that's not all. Did you notice what she said about one of her grandchildren? That he'd die young? Of cancer."

He put an arm on the back of the couch between us. "I did notice that," he said. "How I took it: the boy does have a childhood cancer of some kind right now. She was just being a worried grandma."

I nodded my head, but something inside told me that wasn't the case. And there was no chance I was going to ask Jason about it. That'd be all he'd need.

"Maybe," I conceded. "But then she said I was staying in number five."

He shrugged. "I didn't follow that. She was just mistaken. Five's shut up tight."

I took a deep breath in and let it out again. "I was in there, Dominic. In number five."

"How?" he asked. "Did you get the key from LuAnn? I'm surprised she gave it to you. She's superstitious about—"

I shook my head, and it stopped his words. "No," I said. "The other night, I was awakened by someone calling my name. I went into the hallway, and Alice was there, saying she wanted to show me something. And then she was gone. Disappeared. I saw a light coming from the alcove by the shower rooms. I went down there and . . ." I couldn't say the words.

He leaned in toward me. "And what?"

"And the door to number five was open. That's where the light was coming from. I went in there and saw . . ." I took a deep breath. "Dominic, I think I saw the lady who died over the winter."

His eyes grew wide. "You saw her dead?"

"No," I said, slowly. "She was sitting in a chair by the fire. I think she's the one who was calling my name."

"Was anybody else there with her?"

"No. Just her."

I omitted the part about her giving me the book titled with his nickname. He didn't have to know everything.

"Brynn, it had to be a dream," he said, his voice gentle and low. "I'm not calling you crazy, but LuAnn has five locked up."

I shook my head at him but held his gaze.

"Listen," he went on. "What if you were sleepwalking? Okay? In a dream state, but not, at the same time. And say you made your way down the hall to number five. There is no possible way you could open the door."

"I didn't open it," I pressed on. "It was already open. Like she wanted me to come in."

But then, all at once, I backpedaled. What he was saying was absolutely true.

"Say I did dream the whole thing. It was like Alice knew about it, because she was there. She said I was in number five. I was! That was my dream. Or whatever it was. It's been bothering me ever since."

"And you're thinking you saw the spirit of the lady who died in number five?" he asked me. "Did she—I don't know—say anything to you?"

I shook my head. "No."

"Well, a whole lot of good that dream was, then." He gave me a mischievous look. I tossed a throw pillow at him.

"Next time you dream about the dead, ask them questions! Who was behind JFK's assassination? What's in Area 51? Does God hear NFL players praying before games? If so, does he have a favorite, because it seems to me the Patriots have some sort of upper hand."

I dissolved into laughter. "That's what you'd ask the dead?"

"Damn straight," he laughed, his eyes lighting up and his face beaming like a little boy's. "What would you ask them?"

"I'd say: Describe the afterlife. In detail."

"Oh, that's what you want to know?"

"Doesn't everybody?"

I didn't mention that I'd really like to know how my mom, brother, and grandma were doing. I didn't want to bring down the mood. It was too light for that. The laughter, too easy. That was how it was with this man.

It occurred to me then that he was bringing the laughter back into my world, and that revelation stopped me for a minute. The joie de vivre he radiated somehow found its way into the crevices and fissures in my wall built of grief and sadness and loss. It had been a long time since I had laughed as easily and completely as I did when I was with him.

Dominic pushed himself up from the couch. "I'm going to check on Lady Alice," he said, making his way up the stairs to her door and carefully, soundlessly cracking it open just a sliver. He peered inside and closed it just as quietly. As though he were checking on a fussy toddler who had finally fallen asleep.

He nodded at me. "Out like a light," he said, trotting down the stairs and sliding back down next to me on the couch. "She looks like Sleeping Beauty."

"I wonder what she's dreaming about," I said.

Dominic looked at his watch. "We've got a couple of hours or so before the guys get back," he said. "Movie?"

He put his feet up on the ottoman and laid his arm against the back of the couch between us.

"Curl in," he said.

And so, with the rain still pounding away outside, an occasional rumble of thunder growling through the sky, I leaned into him and exhaled. None of these strange mysteries—Alice, the lady in room five, even Dominic's secretive past—seemed to matter so much then.

The movie had just finished when Jason and Gil came through the door, wet rain shells, sodden umbrellas and all.

"Not the best day for a trip to the island," Gil said. "But it was nice to get away for a minute." They hung their rain shells on the hooks by the door.

"How was the house?" I asked.

Gil and Jason gave each other a look. Jason grimaced. "Not great. We won't be pursuing it. But that's not important. How did it go here?" Jason asked, wincing. "Do I want to know?"

Dominic and I both pushed ourselves to our feet.

"It went great!" I said. "We talked for a bit, had some snacks, and then she said she was tired, so she went to lie down."

"She didn't want to run away?" Jason asked. "She tends to wander and fret when I'm not around. Or so I've been told."

Dominic shook his head. "It was all just fine. She was wondering about where you were, but our answers satisfied her. We had a nice talk. She's a lovely lady."

Jason pulled out one of the kitchen chairs and sank into it, exhaling. Gil slid over and began rubbing his shoulders. "See?" Gil said. "I told you it was going to be okay."

"Completely!" I said. "Really, Jason, it was no problem at all. We both enjoyed it."

Jason ran a hand through his hair, and I could see the tears brimming in his eyes. "What a relief. I don't know how to thank you."

"No thanks necessary," Dominic said. "We had a nice time." He put a hand on the small of my back. "Now, we'll leave you to it. I'm sure you're ready to relax and put your feet up in front of the fire. A rainy crossing on the ferry is no fun."

Just then, Alice poked her head out of her room. "You're back!" she said to Jason.

Jason pushed himself to his feet. "See? I said it wouldn't take long. And here we are."

Alice turned to us. "We had a nice time," she said, parroting Dominic's words.

"Yes, Alice, we did." He smiled back at her.

She looked from Dominic to me and back again. "Can you see it?" she asked.

He and I exchanged a glance. "What?" I said.

"The light between you," she said. "It's beautiful. I saw it as soon as you came in. It's your souls rejoicing."

But then her smile faded, and a darkness descended over her face as her pupils receded. "I'd ask the dead if they have a place prepared for me," she said, her voice monotone. "I'm going to be joining them soon."

CHAPTER SEVENTEEN

Dominic and I took our leave, shutting the door behind us. We made our way down the hall, which was dark and gloomy in the constant rain. At his door, he turned and wagged a finger at me.

"Don't say it," he said. "I know you're dying to say it. But do not say it."

"Say what?"

"I told you so."

I held his gaze for a moment. "I'd never say that," I said, finally. "Okay, yes, I would. I'm that petty, as a rule. But I'm just glad I'm not the only one who noticed."

"Yeah, no denying it," he said. "I checked on her, and she was out like a light when we were having that conversation."

"You have more experience with people who have Alzheimer's than I do," I said. "Have you ever seen anything like this before? It's like she's . . . I don't want to say *clairvoyant*, because it sounds so dramatic, but I don't really know what else to call it."

He shook his head. "No, I have not," he said, overenunciating every word for emphasis. "I'm still trying to get my head around it. Do you know if she had psychic abilities before? I mean, a lot of people sense things, right?"

He was absolutely right. My mind hadn't gone there, but maybe Alice did have psychic abilities before. It wasn't unheard of. People did. Maybe that was what this was.

He glanced down at his watch. "I need to make a couple of calls," he said. "Are you going down for happy hour?"

"Yeah, I thought I would."

He winked at me. "Okay. I'll probably see you there."

I stood in the hall, watching him disappear into his room. But not even a moment later he came out again and walked over to me. He took me in his arms and pulled me close, putting his mouth on mine. He backed me into the wall and kissed me with a force, an urgency, a passion that took my breath away. This wasn't just a flirty kiss. It was serious business.

He pulled back, just a bit, smiling slightly. "I couldn't leave you without doing that," he said, his voice soft and low. "I'll see you later."

And then he was gone, leaving me standing against the wall, breathless.

Back in my room, I retrieved my book off the nightstand and settled into my comfortable nest of pillows. I groaned when I noticed the appointed hour, three o'clock, had come. People would be filing in downstairs. I was comfy reading in my bed and might have stayed there all evening, but Kate had mentioned she was going to try to stop by with her husband, so I rousted myself and padded into my bathroom to freshen up.

I splashed some water on my face, and as I reached for my towel, I caught a glimpse of something—someone?—in the mirror. There had been movement, a dark shape, behind me. I was sure of it. I whirled around and grabbed my glasses.

"Hello?" No response. I took a few steps out of the bathroom and looked around, my heart pounding. I was still clutching my towel. "Is anyone there?"

I took a deep breath and let it out. Nobody, then. Maybe I had imagined it. I stepped back into the bathroom, dabbed on some makeup, and brushed my teeth. My eyes kept glancing into the mirror, which reflected the interior of the bedroom. I felt cold, deep inside. All at once, the bustle of happy hour didn't seem so bad.

A few minutes later I was descending the stairs—no sign of Dominic—and emerged into a chattering throng of locals. I made my way toward the bar and caught Gary's eye.

"There she is!" he rasped, coughing the words out. "Missed you yesterday! Wine?" He didn't wait for an answer and handed me a glass.

"Thanks." I smiled at him and took a sip.

I surveyed the room. LuAnn was circulating, in full denim from head to toe, bedazzled jacket and shoes and all. I saw Beth deep in conversation with a woman I didn't know. I made a note to talk to her when I could. Plus lots of people I didn't recognize. No Jason, Gil, or Alice. No Dominic. I'd stick it out for a while, I told myself, before retreating back up to my room.

The door clattered open, and Kate with, presumably, her husband, Nick, and another man entered the room.

The other man looked familiar. I'd met him before, I was sure of it. Kate caught my eye and smiled, and the trio snaked through the crowd. The two men headed to the bar, and Kate made her way to me. She wrapped her arms around my waist and squeezed.

"You know you're the talk of the town," she said, giggling in my ear. "I hear you and the Illustrated Man went to the island yesterday."

I laughed. "Well, that didn't take long."

"Are you kidding? LuAnn saw you drive off toward the ferry dock in his car with totes and beach towels. That's as good as sending up a flare."

Kate waved to her husband and the other man, and they came to join us.

"Nick, this is Brynn Wilder," Kate said, squeezing her husband's arm. "Brynn, my husband, Nick." She looked up at him. "It's still weird to say that."

"Get used to it, baby." He smiled down at her. "You'll be saying it for the rest of your life."

He turned to me and held out his hand. "Welcome to Wharton," he said. "Any friend of Kate's, as they say. She's told me all about you."

"Thanks!" I said. "I've heard a lot about you, too, so it's nice to finally meet."

The third in their trio was smiling at me over Nick's shoulder.

My eyes grew wide. "Oh!" I said, the flash of recognition setting in. "You're Simon!"

He muscled past Nick. "I was wondering if you'd remember me," he said, kissing me on both cheeks. "It's been a lifetime since Kate's starter wedding. That was the last time we've seen each other, I think. You look exactly the same, and, I must say, I resent it. Unless you'll share your secrets to eternal youth. Then I won't resent it as much."

I laughed at this. *So much laughter here in Wharton,* I thought.

"You're welcome up at the inn anytime," Simon said as LuAnn sidled by and pinched his arm. "If you want to get out of her clutches, I've got a room for you," he said, in a loud stage whisper.

"The poaching of paying guests is frowned upon in some circles." LuAnn sniffed at him.

And the evening began. We talked of island gossip, the incessant rain that day, and the bridezilla Simon and Kate were dealing with at the moment.

"The mother is worse," Simon confided. "The mothers are always worse."

Nick didn't add too much to the conversation, but I got the impression that was normal for him. A lot of listening, not a lot of talking.

I kept an eye on the door to our upstairs realm, but Dominic didn't walk through it. I wondered where he was. Soon, though, Jason and Gil appeared with Alice. I saw that her eyes were darting back and forth, scanning the packed room. I sensed an undercurrent of panic radiating off her, and noticed her squeeze Jason's arm tighter.

"It's about time!" Simon called out as they made their way toward us. He went directly to Alice and took her hands.

"You must be Alice. I'm so glad you'll be here in Wharton with us for the summer. I love the pearls, darling! So classic. They make your outfit."

Alice beamed at him, and so did Jason.

"Honey, this is our friend Simon," Jason said to her. "You'll be seeing a lot of him."

"Simon," she said. "Good. I think I like you."

"I knew you were a woman of good taste the moment I laid eyes on you," he cooed. I could see Alice visibly exhaling.

We all chatted for a bit, nibbling on the snacks LuAnn was circling around on trays. Before long, though, I noticed Alice becoming more and more distracted. Simon, Jason, and Gil were deep in conversation, and Kate and Nick were talking with some other people in the crowd. Only I noticed Alice's unsettled eyes, her trembling hands, her frightened expression.

I moved over to her side and took one of her shaking hands. "Is everything okay, Alice? Can I help?"

She looked into my eyes. "She's going to die," she whispered to me. "I don't think I'm supposed to say anything, but she is."

My stomach tightened. "Who, Alice?"

She clutched my arm. "It's happening right now."

I tried to catch Jason's eye—clearly it was time to take Alice back upstairs. But I didn't have a chance to do it because, just then, I saw Simon and Nick fish their cell phones out of their pockets at the same time and put them up to their ears.

Simon was standing nearest to me, so I heard what he said clearly. "Hi, Jon—" And then nothing. Silence, as he listened to whatever the caller was saying. His eyes grew wider and wider. "Oh my God," he said, his voice low. "I'll be right there."

Nick was looking at Simon over the tops of several heads in the crowd. "You might want to stay here with Kate for the time being," Nick said to him.

Simon was still holding his phone to his ear. "And you might be insane."

"What?" Kate asked, looking back and forth between the two of them.

"Come on," Nick said. "I have the squad car parked outside."

"Something's happened at the inn," Simon said to us quickly, grabbing Kate's hand and following Nick out of the room. And then the three of them were gone.

Sirens roared down the street, and I saw an EMT vehicle and a fire truck speeding by, its lights illuminating the rain-soaked cobblestone. The sirens pierced the room, making everyone fall silent until the sound faded as the vehicles headed up the hill toward the inn.

"What in the Sam Hell . . . ?" LuAnn let her words evaporate. We all wanted to know the answer to that.

The party broke up shortly thereafter, with people, unsettled and worried, leaving for the comfort of their own homes or businesses. Soon it was just Jason, Gil, Alice, and me, along with LuAnn and Gary, and the guys in the back kitchen.

"Where's Dominic?" Jason said.

CHAPTER EIGHTEEN

My stomach knotted up. I didn't know where Dominic was. Should I? Did it matter?

Part of me wanted to hurry up the stairs and knock on the man's door. Maybe he had fallen asleep? He had said he was going to meet me for happy hour, hadn't he? Or had he? When I thought about it, I wasn't sure. But that kiss had said it. Hadn't it?

Another part of me didn't want to do anything of the kind. Did I want to knock on his door and find nobody there? Why should I knock on his door at all? A coolness washed through me as I realized I didn't want to know.

Jason turned to take Alice upstairs. I was going to follow, but Gil touched my arm.

"Do you feel like staying for one more?" Gil asked me, his eyes expectant, almost pleading. I didn't, but I could sense that he wanted, perhaps needed, to talk.

"Sure," I said and settled onto a barstool next to him.

"Jase, I'll be up in a minute," Gil said.

We sat there in silence at the bar for a moment until Gary brought our drinks and the last of the happy-hour snacks. Cheese, crackers, salami, and a couple of dips with a veggie tray. That would more than do for dinner for me.

"I don't suppose we're going to hear what happened at the inn for a while," I said. "If ever."

"Simon will tell me when he can," Gil said. "I'm thinking maybe somebody had a heart attack or something like that."

It sounded right to me, despite the fact that my stomach had knotted up. I wanted to change the subject.

"How's it going with Alice?" I asked him, popping some cheese into my mouth.

Gil shrugged. "This is what you do for family, right?" he said, his eyes betraying the sadness he didn't want to let on. "It's hard. I'm not going to lie."

I covered his hand with mine. "I know."

"She doesn't really know who I am or what I'm doing there," he said. "And Jason doesn't tell her. I understand why. But sometimes I feel like a third wheel." He took another long sip. Gary sidled by to refill Gil's glass and was gone again just as quickly, ever discreet. "A third wheel with my own husband."

"I was going to say, 'I know' again, but I really don't," I said. "This is brand-new territory you're in."

And then the tears came. He couldn't hold them back. "Jason was the love of her life," Gil said, his words choked by his own sobs. "But he's mine, too."

My own eyes filled with tears. So many thoughts were running through my mind at once. I hoped I could coalesce them into something Gil would understand.

"What you are doing is allowing Alice to live the end of her life, while she still has some of herself left, with her great love. You are, in a sense, stepping aside—even though you're still very much there—but allowing her to live out her dream at the end of her life."

Gil snorted, bringing a napkin to his face.

"You're also allowing Jason to find some . . . I don't quite know what to call it. Solace? Closure? He has confided in me that he feels a great weight of guilt for leaving Alice."

Gil nodded. "He broke her heart to find his own happiness in life," he said. "For other people, that might not be a problem. But for Jason . . . he's such a kind and decent person. A genuinely good human being. He does feel the weight of his decision. You're right."

"It's beautiful, what you're doing for her," I went on. "And for him. I've never seen a more selfless act of love."

He sighed and caught my eye. "There was no other choice. My upbringing . . . it's what you do. You care for your own. You owe them honor and respect."

"It doesn't mean it's easy," I said.

"Sure, it's hard for me," Gil said. "But I love Jason more than I've ever loved anyone. This is the right thing to do. For him. For Alice. For their kids and grandkids. And, ultimately, for me."

I put my arm around his shoulder, and Gil rested his head against mine.

"If I ever need to get away, can I come talk to you?"

"Of course," I said. "I'm living here, so the way I see it, we're in this together."

He took my hand and buried his face in my sleeve.

"Dominic, too," I went on. Just saying his name made my stomach do a flip. "He has a lot of experience with people with Alzheimer's. He was great with her today."

"We really appreciated it," Gil said. "Jason has found someone who is going to be sort of like a caregiver."

"He told me Alice doesn't like her."

"Yeah," he said. "We're not going to put a burden on you, but Alice feels safe around you. Would you be willing to be with her, every once in a while, so we can get away?"

"Of course," I said. "Gil, can I ask you something?"

"Of course, Brynn. Anything."

"This is going to sound weird," I said, wincing.

"Honey, nothing is going to sound weird to a man who is living with his husband and the husband's ex-wife, who thinks they're still married," Gil said, laughing as he wiped away tears.

"Okay," I began. "Do you know . . . has Jason ever said if Alice has ever had any"—I winced again—"psychic abilities?"

Gil looked at me for a long moment. "Oh my God. You, too?"

I exhaled, the relief palpable. "Yes! She has said a few really strange things to me," I said, my words coming out in a stream. "It's like she knows things, private things that she shouldn't know."

"I hear you," Gil said. "She's doing the same thing to us. That's not all of it, though."

I held my breath.

"It's like she's invading my dreams," Gil said, his voice a whisper. "It sounds crazy when I say it out loud."

"No, it doesn't," I said, holding his gaze.

The air thickened between us.

"Are you dreaming about her, too?" he whispered.

I nodded. "But, it's like . . ." My words trailed off. I didn't quite know how to describe what I was trying to say.

Gil finished my thought. "It's like, in the dreams, she doesn't have Alzheimer's. She is totally lucid. Completely herself."

"In charge, almost," I said. "Like she is directing things."

Gil exhaled loudly. "I am so glad I asked you to stay and talk. I thought it was just me."

"Me, too!" I said. "It was starting to feel like I was losing it."

He shook his head and laughed. "Tell me about it."

"Have you mentioned any of this to Jason?"

Gil took a sip of his wine. "Jason shuts it down every time I bring it up. He won't acknowledge it, even though he's right there when she starts talking about something that happened to the two of us that she couldn't possibly have known about. It's like he's in denial. He got angry when I asked him if she had psychic abilities before. Even like a sense of, I don't know, women's intuition. That sounds so dated and stereotypical, doesn't it? But I'm trying to find anything to explain it."

"Is he dreaming about her, too?"

Gil shook his head. "I have no idea. If he is, he hasn't told me. And he totally shut me down the other day when I told him about the fact that I was."

I turned to him. "What do you think this is?"

He shook his head. "It's like . . ."

"What?"

"Okay," he said, exhaling. "I'm just going to say it. To me, it seems like the veil between this world and the next is so thin where she is right now." Gil looked down into his wine. "It's like that veil is in tatters, and she can see through the holes."

I felt goose bumps on my arms.

"Dominic thinks much the same," I told him. "He thinks, when she's sort of . . . I don't know. Delusional? Saying things like she has to pick her kids up from school. He thinks she's not delusional at all. That somehow, she is really back there. Not just remembering a moment in time. Really living that moment, in the past, and also the moment with us in the present at the same time. It's like time as we know it is different for her."

I considered what I was about to say next. "You know how sometimes she just zones out and doesn't seem to be really . . . present?"

Gil nodded. "That's common among Alzheimer's patients, I guess."

"It's almost like she's submerging into . . . something. Someplace else. Maybe that's where she's going, back to the past."

Gil let out a strangled laugh. "Do you know how crazy that sounds? And yet here we are, seriously talking about the fact that she really, actually, goes back to being the young wife making cookies to have them ready for the kids when they get off the bus."

I nodded. "That's what Dominic thinks."

"I'm not saying he's wrong. Who knows what really happens when we're nearing the end? What sort of doors open."

We stared at each other for a long moment.

"For all we know, Alice could live another twenty-five, thirty years," he said. "I hope she doesn't. And not just because of me. I know it's terrible to say. I'm not trying to be ugly, but . . ." He frowned.

"I get it."

"Her body is strong. Her heart is strong. There's nothing wrong with her physically that isn't happening in her brain right now. But it's out there. Waiting for her. When she loses all recognition of her family—I cannot imagine how much it's going to hurt Jason and the girls. And the grandkids. And, somewhere deep inside of the shell of herself that she'll become, Alice, too."

"I'd never want to be in that place. Be a burden to my family." I let out a harsh laugh. "If I had one."

"Oh, honey," Gil said. "You'll have one if you want one. Don't even."

I shrugged.

Gil pushed himself to his feet. "I guess I'd better get back up to the suite," he said, sighing.

"Hang in there," I said to him. "Remember, if you ever want to talk, I'm just down the hall."

He gave my shoulders a quick squeeze and made his way toward the upstairs door.

I looked at the clock. It seemed so late, considering everything that had happened that day, but it was only a bit after four. I had plenty of time for the errand I was dying to do.

CHAPTER NINETEEN

After dashing upstairs to get my purse, I was on my way down the street. The rain had stopped, but the cobblestones were still glistening, a fresh scent of flowers and the lake and the rain wafting through the air. The sun was poking through the gray clouds and shining down in rays.

I pushed open the door of Just Read It and was greeted with the now-familiar tinkle of chimes. Beth poked her head out of the back room.

"Hey, you!" she said. "How are you liking *The Illustrated Man*?"

It took me a moment to realize she wasn't talking about Dominic.

"I loved it!" I said. "I read the whole thing in one sitting. Or one soaking, you might say."

She laughed. "You're a bathtub reader, too!"

"Yes, indeed," I chuckled. "I really loved the book. I may add it to my curriculum this year."

I actually hadn't thought anything of the kind until I said it, but the very thought of it sizzled through me. I couldn't wait to hear what my students would have to say about those short stories. And all at once, it occurred to me: a reason to be excited about going back to work.

I sighed. "You know, this is the first time in a while I've found myself looking forward to the coming year," I told her. "I haven't been able to conjure any sense of happiness about the prospect of being back on campus and had seriously doubted I was up to the job. And now here I am, excited about talking to my students about *The Illustrated Man*."

"The power of books," Beth said.

"The power of a bookseller," I said.

She smiled. "I was just pouring myself a cup of tea. Care to join me?"

I nodded, and she disappeared into the back and reemerged carrying two steaming mugs. I took a sip of the savory, spicy drink.

"Turmeric and ginger," she said. "It's good for what ails you."

I leaned on the counter. "Have you heard anything about what went on at the inn?"

Beth shook her head. "I'm sure word of what happened will make its way through town soon—nothing is ever a secret here in Wharton—but as of now, no."

"I haven't heard, either," I said. "I was planning to call Kate later, but I don't want to be a pest. I hope everything, and everyone, is okay up there."

"Me, too. But that's not the reason you came in here," she said, raising her eyebrows. "Browsing for your next good read? I've got some recommendations, if so. I'm getting into genre fiction this summer."

"I'm always looking for a good mystery," I said, "but actually, I came in to find some books about Alzheimer's."

She furrowed her brow at me, but then the expression melted into recognition. "Oh," she said. "Alice."

"I'm going to be spending time with her this summer," I said. "She's very jittery and afraid with most people, but she feels safe with me for some reason. Gil and Jason wanted an afternoon away today and asked if I'd sit with her."

"And that was okay?"

"More than okay," I said. "She's lovely. It's no trouble at all, spending time with her. I told them I'd be happy to do it again. They'll need a break every so often."

Beth crossed her arms and leaned against the shelf. "You seem like a really nice person," she said. "I just don't want to see you get too caught up with what is, after all, Jason and Gil's situation. Alice is their responsibility, not yours."

"I know," I said, thinking of how I just came out of one caregiving situation and had somehow fallen headlong into another.

"So, you want to learn more about Alzheimer's so you'll know what to expect?"

"Not just that. It's . . ." I took a breath. "Do you have any books that explain a link between Alzheimer's and psychic abilities? I did a quick search online but didn't come up with anything."

At this, she raised her eyebrows. "Care to expound on that at all?"

"I know, it sounds weird, but Gil and I both have had some odd experiences with Alice," I started, not quite knowing how to finish the thought. "I was just hoping there was a real-world explanation."

Beth stepped over to her computer, sliding her glasses on. "I can't think of any right off the top of my head, but let me check." She tapped at the keys, searching her inventory. She looked at me over the top of her glasses. "Nothing's coming up."

"It was worth a shot," I said, shrugging.

Thanking her, I pushed open the door and made my way back up the street. I had suspected my search wouldn't lead to much, even though I had secretly hoped to find a volume or two outlining several scholarly studies on cases like hers.

I told myself I'd do a more careful search online, but something inside me made me realize there would be no rational, real-world explanation for the strangeness swirling through the halls of LuAnn's. It occurred to me it wasn't the first time that could be said of the place.

∼

I arrived back at the house to find Gary in the side yard stoking a wood fire under a giant cast-iron cauldron. Around it stood several picnic tables and assorted Adirondack chairs. A keg of beer sat on ice, along with several bottles of wine and glasses.

"Hey!" he called out to me.

"What's all this?" I asked him.

"Fish boil. We do it every Friday. Tonight's the first one of the season."

I grimaced at him, causing him to burst into laughter.

"Come on now, it's not that bad," he coughed out.

"What in the name of Julia Child is a fish boil?" I asked him, eyeing the cauldron darkly.

"It's a lake tradition," he said. "C'mon in the kitchen with me, and I'll tell you all about it. We're full up for the six-thirty seating, and Gus and Aaron are both out today, so I could use an extra hand or two for the prep. LuAnn said she'd help, but, really, the last thing anyone wants is that woman in the kitchen."

Not quite understanding exactly what he was talking about, I followed him through the back door to the kitchen, chuckling at him.

Gary was tossing an apron to me when we heard a voice calling to him from inside the restaurant. Dominic.

"Hey, man, do you know—" he began as Gary popped his head out of the swinging door separating the kitchen from the back of the bar. "Oh! I was just wondering if you've seen Brynn."

"She's in here with me," Gary informed him, wiping his hands on his apron. "Come on back. Make yourself useful."

Dominic did what he was told and followed Gary into the kitchen, where I was tying a clean white apron around me. Gary picked another off a pile of linens and tossed it at Dominic.

"We're washing dishes?" Dominic asked. "I'll pay my bill, I promise."

"Very funny, smart guy," Gary snorted. "We've got a full house for the fish boil, and Gus called in sick. Called in hungover is more like it."

I smiled at Dominic, knife in hand. His eyes twinkled at me.

"Just tell me what to do," Dominic said.

"I made the slaw before happy hour, so that's done. I'll handle the fish." Gary directed us to a giant bowl of red potatoes. "You two take these."

"What, cut them in half?" Dominic asked. "Or in slices?"

Gary's face was aghast. "No, no, no, no," he chided. "Cut just the top off each one. Just a little bit!" He took the knife out of my hand and sliced the top off one of the potatoes. "Like that," he said, tossing it into a bowl.

"Got it," I said. "But why just the top?"

Gary squinted at me. "You've really never heard of a fish boil before, have you?"

Dominic and I exchanged a glance. Both of us shook our heads.

As we sliced the potatoes and Gary worked with the fish, he told us the history of the fish boil.

"It started back when this place was new," he began. "We've got a little rivalry going with Door County on Lake Michigan over which area actually did it first. We did, obviously."

He snorted and went on. "It started as an easy, fast, and cheap way to feed a crowd of people, like the loggers and fishermen who worked these shores. Now people think of it as a regional delicacy, which is sort of funny. It's turned into something of an event at resorts in this area of the lake and in Michigan, too."

"What kind of fish are we talking about here?" Dominic asked as he sliced.

"It's whitefish—Lake Superior whitefish caught today and delivered half an hour ago. We boil 'em up with potatoes and corn on the cob in a pot. We serve it all with coleslaw and bread. And voilà, fish boil!

We do it here every Friday during the high season. The timing of the boiling really is an art, which I have perfected, if I may say so myself."

LuAnn popped into the kitchen. "Is he bragging on how he's the master of the fish boil again?"

Dominic and I chuckled at this. "Sounds like he has rights on this one," he said.

"I don't mean to sound disrespectful of a tradition or anything," I began, "but it sounds kind of . . . well, *disgusting* is an ugly word . . ."

LuAnn cackled. "Oh, you've stepped in it now," she said, wiping her eyes.

"Disgusting?" Gary repeated. "Oh, my dear girl. My dear delusional girl."

"But it's all boiled together? Doesn't everything taste like fish?"

"Aha!" Gary pointed at me. "You have hit on the magic of the fish boil. No, for your information, Julia Child, everything does not taste like fish. And when we're ready to do the boiling, you'll see why."

LuAnn stepped back outside to check on the gathering crowd as Dominic and I finished with the potatoes and shucked a few dozen ears of corn, cutting each one in half as directed by our taskmaster. Gary was clattering around in the cupboard, retrieving a massive well-used silver basket shaped like the cauldron.

"Okay," he said. "It's showtime!"

He handed Dominic the basket and picked up the huge bowl of potatoes, tucking a box of salt under his arm just as LuAnn reappeared in the kitchen.

"People are starting to arrive," LuAnn said to Gary. "How are we doing?"

"We are doing just fine," Gary said. "Did you get everyone's drink orders?"

"They're beered and wined," LuAnn reported.

"Great. Can you melt the butter without burning the whole place down?" Gary asked her.

"Doubtful," she said, pulling a saucepan out of the cupboard. "But I've got insurance, so we're good."

Dominic and I followed Gary out the back door and saw that the picnic tables were filled with people.

"Hey, folks," Gary called to them. "Let's get this party started!"

He instructed Dominic to place the basket into the cauldron of boiling water and poured the potatoes into it, generously salting the water.

"Why we cut off just the top of the potato," Gary said to me, loud enough for the crowd to hear, "is for the salt to get in there and flavor the inside of the spud. It cooks up nice and creamy in its own skin."

I nodded. Made sense.

"We do this thing in stages. When the spuds are half-done, we add the corn," he explained to everyone. This was a theatrical production, and he was at center stage, enjoying every minute of it. "When the corn's half-done, we add the fish. When that's done, we have the boil over."

"What's the boil over?" Dominic asked.

"The main event!" Gary smiled broadly. "It's what everybody waits for, buddy. You'll see."

While the potatoes were boiling, we helped Gary set out plates, silverware, and napkins. LuAnn came from the kitchen with wide platters and serving utensils. On Gary's word, Dominic dropped the corn into the boiling cauldron. I helped LuAnn carry out big bowls of coleslaw, one for each table, platters of sliced lemons, the melted butter, and baskets of bread.

I took a moment to appreciate the scene around me. I'd always loved entertaining big groups of friends, and hadn't done much of it in the previous few years, and none at all after my mom's illness progressed. Now here I was, with this group of relative strangers—Gary, LuAnn, and Dominic—who were somehow already beginning to feel like family, putting on this spread for the crowd. Gratitude coursed through me.

"Fish!" Gary called, and in a minute, Dominic came through the back door carrying the platter of whitefish.

"Drop 'em in!" Gary directed, and Dominic slipped the fish into the roiling, bubbling cauldron, which smoked and sizzled.

"Okay," Gary addressed the crowd. "We've got some fish-boil newbies here." He cocked his head in our direction. "Anybody else a first-timer?"

A couple of hands went up. Gary talked about the origin of the fish boil before asking, "Who can tell me why we salt the water?"

"For flavor?" someone called out.

"Yep, but there's something else, and it's important," Gary said. "Anyone?"

"The salt makes it so the fish oil rises to the top," an elderly woman said, her voice thin. I guessed she had been to a few fish boils in her time.

"Exactly right!" Gary said. "It's a chemistry lesson, kids. The salt raises the gravity of the water, whatever the hell that means. But what it does is, it sends the fish oil right to the top. See those foamy suds on the surface? Come on up if you want to get a look."

Several people—me included—gingerly approached the cauldron. Sure enough, I saw foam bubbling on the surface of the water.

"That's the fish oil. We don't want that oil, so we do the boil over. That's why the whole thing doesn't taste fishy. No fish oil." He looked pointedly at me.

"And now's the time for the main event, people!" Gary went on. A couple of kids in the crowd cheered as Gary looked around here and there. "Where's my kerosene can?"

Dominic and I exchanged a worried glance. "Kerosene?" he mouthed.

"This is the dramatic part, and I want everyone to stay back." Gary scanned the crowd. "You'll all get to see it, but nobody come up here too close. Got it?"

"Got it!" somebody in the crowd called out.

"That means you, too," Gary said to us, brandishing a can of kerosene.

"You are seriously not going to put kerosene on that fire," Dominic said, eliciting chuckles from the crowd.

"Newbie," Gary said, eliciting more laughter. "Stay back, everybody!"

He carefully splashed some kerosene on the fire logs. Whoosh, a tall eruption of orange flame engulfed the pot, sending the foamy suds boiling over and down the sides, which further ignited the flames. I jumped back, clutching Dominic's arm.

In a flash, it was over, and the flames died down.

I exhaled the breath I didn't even know I was holding. The look of horror on Dominic's face caused me to burst out laughing.

"They do not mess around here on Lake Superior," he said, his eyes wide. "That was some serious business right there."

"Come on, big man," Gary said to him. "Help me get this basket out of the water."

"Now?" Dominic said. "Are you sure that thing isn't going to erupt with the fires of hell again?"

Gary chuckled, as did many in the crowd, and he threaded a long pole through the basket's handle. "Here," he said to Dominic. "You take the other end."

Together, they lifted the basket out of the cauldron, pausing for a moment to let the excess water drain out before carrying it over to the buffet table. They worked to carefully scoop the potatoes, corn, and fish out of the basket onto waiting platters. A line of diners was already forming.

"Come and get it, people!" Gary called out as he filled two plates, one for Dominic and one for me. "Thanks for all of your help, kids. Make sure you get some slaw, too."

All of the tables were full, so Dominic and I settled into a couple of Adirondack chairs under the big oak tree in the backyard. LuAnn came over and set some drinks on the armrests for us. She kissed me on the forehead and leaned over and did the same to Dominic.

"You two are the best," she said to us. "Thank you for all the help."

"No trouble at all," I said to her. "It was fun."

"Agreed," Dominic said.

"You're welcome to be our extra hands again any time you feel like it."

And then she circled off through the crowd, taking drink orders, making sure everyone had what they needed.

I took my first bite of fish. To my astonishment, it was flaky and delicate and didn't have any hint of a fishy taste.

"This is delicious," I said. "I thought it was going to be mushy or gelatinous or otherwise gross because it was boiled."

"I know!" he said. "Have you tried the potatoes? They don't taste like fish at all."

Just then, I glanced up to the second floor and saw the curtains moving in one of the rooms. Someone had been watching us. I did a quick mental rundown. My room was on the other end of the building. Dominic's and two guest rooms were facing the other way. Jason and Gil's suite was at the end, its deck and windows overlooking the street. That left only number five.

CHAPTER TWENTY

We offered to help LuAnn and Gary with the cleanup, but they wouldn't hear of it.

"That's why we use compostable plates and silverware for the fish boils, kids," Gary said. "Cleanup's a breeze. We're just going to stuff these platters, bowls, and serving utensils into the dishwasher, and boom. We're good to go."

Satisfied that we weren't needed, Dominic pushed himself out of his Adirondack and held out a hand to me. I grasped it, and he pulled me up. "Care to go for a walk?" he asked me.

And so, a short while later, we were strolling through the streets of Wharton. As the evening wore on, I noticed lines at the ferry dock dwindling and the ferry running less frequently. I guessed going over to the island was more of a day trip, thinking back on our magical day there. I could still feel Dominic's arms and legs intertwined with mine as we floated in the water.

As if sensing what I was thinking, Dominic offered his arm to me, and I threaded mine through it. We walked in companionable silence for a while, watching the shopkeepers shut their doors, turn their "Open" signs to "Closed," and button their places up tight as the restaurants came to life with activity.

I toyed with mentioning seeing the curtains sway in number five, and the apparition in my bathroom mirror earlier, but in the end decided not to bring up those things. It felt like strange happenings were piling on, engulfing me since I got here. First the knock in the shower, then Gary's warnings about ghosts everywhere, the dream or whatever it was with the lady in number five, even the otherworldliness swirling around Alice. Now this. It was getting to be too much already. I wanted to talk about something real.

"I started thinking about going back to work today," I told him, finally.

"Oh? You said you were sort of dreading it."

"I was," I admitted. "I didn't know if I actually would go back. But today was the first day in a very long time that I found myself looking forward to it."

He looked over at me and smiled. "That's great, Brynn. I'm really glad to hear it."

I knew what was unspoken, there, in his comment. It was progress. Me seeing light at the end of the tunnel of my grief. Life was out there. And right where we were. I couldn't remember the last time I had thought of anything except simply slogging through another day, yet this day, the past few days, in fact, had been filled with joy and mystery and hope and fun, too.

We found ourselves by the water's edge and sat down on one of the benches. The lake was shimmering with life. I took a deep breath and drank it in.

"I was looking for you at happy hour today," I said, remembering Alice's comments. It seemed a lifetime ago already.

"I know," he said. "I came down a bit late, and everyone was gone. Gary said something happened up at Harrison's House, and it broke up the party."

I nodded. "My friend Kate was here with her husband, the police chief, and her cousin Simon, who owns the inn. Both men got phone calls at the same time as sirens roared up the street. A fire truck and an EMT, I think. So, yeah, something happened up there."

Dominic shook his head. "That can't be good. And you haven't heard anything more?"

"No," I said. "I went to the bookstore after happy hour broke up, but Beth said there was no word yet."

He grinned. "Odd, for this town. Word travels fast."

"So I'm learning."

He eyed me. "We could always walk up there. To Harrison's House, I mean. I hear they have a bar. We could just be going for an innocent drink."

"You're terrible," I chuckled. "But I don't want to intrude. What if somebody had an emergency? I mean, obviously there was an emergency, but we don't know what it was."

"You are the one person alive in Wharton who wants to mind her own business."

I knew it was a joke, but something about the way he said it sent a shiver through me. He was wrong. I intensely wanted to know about the emergency at Harrison's House, and why Dominic was late.

I cast an eye toward the skies and saw gray clouds moving in.

"It looks like we've got some more rainy weather coming," I said. "It rolls in quickly here. People say the lake makes its own weather systems. How that works, I have no idea."

He chuckled at this. "If that's the case, Lake Superior is telling us to go back to LuAnn's and stop thinking about pestering them at Harrison's House." Dominic smiled, getting to his feet. "What did you call it? Gitche Gumee?"

"Far be it from us to disobey the lake," I said, pushing myself up.

As we walked back to LuAnn's, scattered gentle raindrops began to fall, and I thought about how this man made his living helping people in transition. We hadn't known each other too long, but he was certainly there for me, always with an encouraging word as I made my way through this brave new world.

He said I wasn't a client—thank goodness—but I wondered if he was tired of working during his off hours. I knew doctors who hated going to cocktail parties because people would set upon them with stories of their various ailments. Did he feel the same? I made a mental note to keep thoughts of my "transition" to myself and to focus on the here, the now, and the future when we talked of things happening in my life.

The closer we got to LuAnn's, the more I was beginning to lament the fact that our evening together was nearly over. But then Dominic surprised me.

"How about watching a movie?" he said.

"I'd love that," I said.

The restaurant was closed, so Dominic used his key to let us inside the main door. We found the dining room dark, neat, and tidy, ready for the morning rush. No sign of LuAnn or Gary. All was quiet. A sizzle of electricity coursed through me as Dominic led me through the empty dining room and up the stairs.

When we got to his door, he opened it, but then turned to me.

"I'm going to get out of my fish-cooking clothes." He smiled shyly.

"Oh!" I said. "Good idea. I'll do the same and meet you back here in five minutes." That would give me time to freshen up and brush my teeth. Perfect. In my room, I went through my dresser, considering outfits and tossing them aside. What to choose? Pajamas seemed . . . forward. Finally, I settled on black leggings and a soft pink T-shirt and headed into my bathroom.

I peeled off my clothes and did a quick spot-shower with warm water from the sink and a washcloth to rinse the day off my skin. I washed and moisturized my face, and brushed my teeth and hair. I pulled on my leggings and big shirt and surveyed my image in the mirror. It would have to do. I slid my feet into my slippers and padded back across the hall.

I gave his door a soft rap and he opened it, inviting me in. He was wearing a white T-shirt and gray sweatpants.

I hadn't seen his room before, but I shouldn't have been surprised to find that it was wholly different than the others. Heavy masculine furniture dominated the room. The bed was an enormous four-poster made of cherrywood, covered with an eggplant-colored down comforter and pillows in eggplants and greens and whites lining the headboard. The dresser had a deep-purple marble top and an antique round mirror that was worn, warped, and weathered with age. A mission-style armchair and ottoman sat in the corner by the window.

Dark wood paneling covered the walls, which were adorned with paintings of tall ships. An old nautical map of Lake Superior hung in a rough-hewn frame that looked to be made of weathered barn wood. A flat-screen television was poised above a gas fireplace, which Dominic switched on. It sparked to life, bathing the room with a flickering soft glow. Outside, thunder rumbled.

All at once, I found myself grasping for something to say. When in doubt, talk about the weather. "This rain won't let up today," I said, peeking out of the window.

"I love a good thunderstorm," he said. "Bring it on."

I wasn't sure what to do next. I stood by the window, my hands feeling suddenly awkward. Should I clasp them in front? Put them on my hips? It was as though I had forgotten what people did with their hands when in a room with a ridiculously handsome man.

Dominic saved me from my descent into angst by settling onto the bed, propping the pillows against the headboard. He patted the spot next to him. "I won't bite." He flashed the smile that always took my breath away. "Hard." He laughed then, a deep, throaty laugh that warmed me from the inside out.

I slid down next to him, and I could feel my heart beating so hard in my chest I was sure he could hear it. He slung his arm along the back of the pillows, and I snuggled into him, curling up. He looked over at me and smiled.

We reclined there for a moment, gazing at each other. We were supposed to be watching a movie, but I couldn't find the words to bring it up. Being this close to him, I couldn't find any words. All I could do was look at his mouth, longing to feel it on mine again.

Without quite realizing what I was doing, I reached up and ran a finger along his lips, tracing their perfection. And then I pulled him into me, kissing him with the same sort of intensity with which he'd kissed me. Had it been today? The day before? Time seemed to melt into itself here in this house, especially when I was with him.

He pulled back, leaning on his elbow and running a hand through my hair. "Brynn, Brynn, Brynn," he said. "What am I going to do with you?"

I cleared my throat. "You said something about a movie?"

He reached over and grabbed the remote. We settled on a romantic comedy and snuggled in together, his arm around me. I curled into him, my hand on his chest.

About halfway through the movie, I noticed he wasn't watching it anymore. He was looking at me.

"Not feeling the love for the plot?" I said, my face heating up.

"Oh, I'm feeling something," he said, his voice an octave lower than it usually was, deep and rich and seemingly coming from somewhere other than himself. "Just not for the movie."

We slipped down onto the pillows, and all at once, he was above me, leaning on one elbow, his face inches away from mine. He stroked my hair with his other hand and looked into my eyes with an expression I hadn't seen on his face before. Intensity burned behind his eyes. I knew what this moment was. And I wasn't going anywhere.

I hadn't been with a man other than my longtime partner for more than twenty years. And he had lost all interest in bedroom activities long before I finally left. I couldn't remember the last time I had danced this dance. And here I was, lying inches away from the most beautiful man I had ever seen, as nervous as if it were the first time. In some ways, it was.

Dominic peeled off his shirt, and I couldn't help gasping. I had seen his tattoos during our day at the beach, of course, but his illustrations took my breath away at that moment even so. I ran my hands across his shoulders, down his arms, and across his chest, rapt by the intrigue of the stories those illustrations might tell.

He leaned down and kissed my neck, lightly at first but then with an intense power, as though his passion was possessing him. He kissed my lips then with that same power and urgency, taking my breath away.

I lost myself in his intensity, unleashing my own that had been buried for far too long.

Later, we were lying in a tangle of sheets as the fire crackled. Now was not the time for pillow talk. We were both breathless. My entire body was shaking from the inside out.

Dominic dozed, but I was lost in his illustrations, lit up by the firelight. They were intricate and detailed, and, there in the flickering light, they seemed to dance and sway along with the flames. I was mesmerized, completely drawn in, as I curled in next to him, my eyes running along his arms to his chest and his stomach and back again.

But then something didn't seem quite right. Didn't I see a lion on his arm before, when we were at the beach? I couldn't find it now. All of the illustrations seemed strange and new. A new face here, a symbol there. A house. A fireplace.

But it had to have been my imagination. He was completely covered with illustrations, every square inch of skin on his torso, arms, back, and legs. I had been trying not to look too closely at him when we were at the beach—I hadn't wanted to stare, and I was shy and nervous—so I must have missed the tattoo of this couple, legs and arms intertwined, right? Was the woman a mermaid?

My eyes traveled to an older lady, who was smiling in a rocking chair, a pile of knitting materials in her lap. She looked kind, welcoming. Next to her, two children were running into a field of sunflowers. The image looked idyllic at first, but then a darkness descended over it. Were they running to something, or away from something?

I didn't know how long I stared at Dominic's illustrations, trying to find deeper meaning in them. But at some point, my eyes grew tired, and I laid my head on his chest. I was reading too much into it, I thought. I had been so caught up in the book, *The Illustrated Man*, and knowing that Jason and Gil had given Dominic that nickname, he became a reflection of it, and it, of him. The lines were blurring between the two in my imagination. I knew I needed to crawl out of that rabbit hole. It was just my mind, making connections that really weren't there beyond the fact that Dominic was covered with beautiful illustrations, just like the book's namesake. I didn't really expect those illustrations to come to life and tell me a story as they had in the book. But I didn't look away for a long while, either.

I shook those silly thoughts out of my head. Dominic was just a man. A mysterious, wonderful, passionate, surprising man. A man who may have come from a sketchy, even dangerous upbringing, a man who had shot his own father at the age of four. A man who was probably guarded and closed and, yes, even afraid because of all he had seen and, perhaps, done. A man who chose to spend his life helping others transform, the way he himself had transformed when he left that little boy who had shot his father behind, along with the life he might have had as a result of that trauma. He was not some character from a sci-fi classic. He was a flesh-and-blood man to be respected and admired for all that he had achieved despite incredible odds.

My eyes fluttered closed. But then they shot open again. Why did it feel so comfortable to be lying next to him in the firelight, as though we had been doing so our entire lives? Why did I feel as though I had always known him, that we had always been here, lying together this way?

"Because we always have been," Dominic murmured in his sleep, as though he had heard my thoughts.

My breathing slowed as I wrapped my arms around him. Soon I drifted off to sleep and began to dream.

CHAPTER TWENTY-ONE

A jumble of images drifted through my mind. They seemed like photographs, but all of them were moving and vibrating with life, being set down on a table, one on top of the other.

A scene appeared, hazy and blurry at first, and then coming into clearer view. I was in the kitchen of a small, modest cottage. Low ceilings, whitewashed walls, scrubbed wooden floors, a fireplace with a stone hearth where a cast-iron pot hung on a rod over the fire. A heavy table stood in the middle of the room. I could see a couple of doors. One, I knew somehow, was the bedroom. I suspected the other was also a bedroom, but I couldn't be sure.

I was peeling potatoes in the kitchen for dinner when a man, tall, broad, dark-eyed, and bearded, wearing woolen pants and a dark-wool jacket came through the heavy wooden front door, ushering in a waft of cold, salty air with him. He closed the door behind him and smiled at me, and all at once, I knew he was Dominic. A different face, a different body, a different race. But Dominic all the same.

"Your man has come home," he said. But his voice wasn't his own. He had a sort of low-country English accent that, at once, I could barely understand and at the same time knew deep in my bones. He enveloped me in his arms and pulled me in close. My heart did a flip, even though

I knew this man to the very depths of my soul. I buried my face in his neck and drank in the scent of him.

"It's about time you came on home, mister," I teased him. My voice, like Dominic's, was my own, but not my own. "Your woman's been waiting here for you, casting an eye out to the sea."

He wrapped his arms around me tighter and kissed me, tasting of salt water. "No sea is going to keep me from you, wife," he purred into my ear. "Not when I have such a fine woman to come home to."

Then, the scene shifted. We were in our bed, a red floral quilt pulled snugly around us, our arms and legs intertwined underneath it. He was telling me a story about his day, of someone he encountered in town. His eyes were dancing as he told the tale, a devilish look on his face, his voice animated with amusement. I was laughing so hard my stomach ached. I rested my head on his chest and wiped away tears. He was laughing, too. The utter and complete joy between us was real and tangible and living.

This is what it is, I said to myself in my dream. *This is what life is for. This is why we are here. To find the person who can bring our souls to life.*

The scene shifted again. We were older now. I noticed lines on my man's face, crow's-feet around his eyes, testifying to a life lived in laughter. His hair was graying. Salt dotted his black beard. He was still devastatingly handsome; his eyes still danced when they looked at me.

He was outside, on the cliff, with our young son and daughter, showing them how to tie nautical knots. I stood in the doorway of our home, watching as he laughed and teased with them, underscoring the serious business of tying proper knots with fun and love and humor, ensuring they wouldn't forget. My heart swelled.

"Come on in for dinner," I called to them. "The stew is ready!"

The children ran to me. "Now, wash up," I said to them. "Make sure your hands are clean."

My husband took me into his arms and quickly kissed my neck. "Yes, milady."

I slapped him on the arm, giggling.

That scene dissolved, and another took its place. I was standing alone, outside the cottage, which I now saw was a one-story dark-stone affair, two mullioned windows facing out toward the water. It was situated on a cliff overlooking an angry, dark sea. Waves crashed into the rocky shoreline below as rain pelted down sideways. I shielded my eyes from the stinging rain.

The door to the cottage opened a crack, and an older woman with a kind face poked her head outside. "You'll catch your death, dear," she called out to me. "I've got the kettle on."

I shook my head. "I cannot leave him. He's out there."

"The children," she said.

"Please get them their supper," I said. "I'm staying here. For now."

"If the good Lord chooses to spare him," she said, "he'll make his way home to you. He always does."

"I want to be with him, out here, in this storm."

I pulled my coat around me, wound the scarf tighter around my head. I walked closer to the cliff, watching the angry sea churn and roil and rage.

At that moment, I didn't care how cold it was, how the stinging rain was slicing at my cheeks. I didn't care if I died right there on the cliff. Nothing in my body or in my soul would let me leave that spot, not while my love was still out there in that raging sea.

I fell to my knees, knowing in the depths of my heart what I did not want to know.

Then I was dressed in black, sitting in an old stone church alongside the older woman. She was clasping my hand. My children were seated next to us, stricken looks on their ashen faces. I could see his face in theirs, and my heart bled with the intensity of the grief that was engulfing me.

The pews were filled with people, stoic, serious. I stared straight ahead, feeling dead in my heart. Somehow, I knew my body was empty, my spirit in tatters. My soul ached for the man I'd never hold again.

And then it all went black. The dream was over. My eyes opened with a start, my face wet with tears. I sat up, panting.

Dominic was snoring lightly next to me, and the sight of him hit me like a punch in the stomach. He was right here. Flesh and blood.

I had just lived a lifetime with this man. I had loved him. Laughed with him. Had his children. Had been his widow. But it was just a dream. Nothing but that.

Yet, my heart swelled with joy at the sight of him. He wasn't gone. He wasn't swallowed up by that angry sea. He was right here, lying in the firelight, very much alive. I put my hand on his chest, letting it rise and fall with his breathing, and the rhythm of it brought me a sense of peace. All was well.

It wasn't real, it wasn't reasonable, but urgent, powerful gratitude washed over me—he was alive. I could touch him, hold him, cherish him.

I tried to shake those thoughts away. It was silly. We were just getting to know each other. We'd only spent a few days together.

I slipped back down next to his warm body, pulling the quilt over both of us, and I couldn't help but give thanks.

It was like he had come back from the dead. As though I had been given another chance to continue our beautiful life together. But, no. *It's just a dream, Brynn. Just a dream.*

I was about to close my eyes when I was jostled awake. Alice was kneeling beside me, on the side of the bed.

"Wake up," she whispered to me. "This is important."

She faded from view, and I noticed three straight-backed wooden chairs standing against the wall on the other side of the room near the window. I hadn't seen those before, had I? Maybe I had missed them. There was a lot going on between us when I had first entered Dominic's room, and afterward, we had fallen asleep. Perfectly reasonable to think I just hadn't seen the chairs.

I sat up. No, the chairs had not been there before. I was sure of it. I had been standing in that very spot by the window, awkward and unsure of what to do with my hands, when I first came into the room. There had been no chairs there.

Then I saw the chairs were bathed in a different sort of light than the rest of the room. The light was coming from above, shining down in a delicate shaft. As though they were in a spotlight.

I glanced down at the sleeping man next to me. I considered waking him up, but for what? To ask about three chairs? It was silly.

When I looked back, two elderly women were sitting in two of the chairs. One of the women had white hair, styled in neat curls against her head. She was wearing a cotton housedress with an apron tied around her waist. The other lady was wearing an ankle-length dark dress with a cameo at the neck and sensible shoes. Her dark hair was pulled back into a tight bun.

I didn't know either of these women, but they were familiar somehow. Strange as it was, their presence was comforting and calming after that unsettling dream. Both of them were smiling at me. I smiled back.

All at once, they grew serious and turned their gaze to the third empty chair.

The air in the room thickened around me. I didn't like this. I reached down to jostle Dominic.

"Dominic," I whispered, harshly. "Wake up."

He was in a deep sleep and didn't move, despite me shaking his arm. When I looked back to the chairs, the two women were gone. My mother sat in the third chair.

My throat seized up, and tears were stinging behind my eyes. "Mom?" I said, my voice torn to shreds.

She didn't speak. She turned her eyes toward Dominic's sleeping form, and then back to me. She smiled and nodded her head.

"Mom?" I squeaked out.

And then she, along with all three chairs, faded away, the shaft of light last of all.

I closed my eyes for a moment and exhaled a breath I hadn't known I was holding. I wiped the tears away yet again, reaching over to the nightstand to grab a tissue.

Nightstand? Dominic's bedroom didn't have a nightstand. Did it? All at once, I realized I was alone in the bed. Dominic was gone. The fire was out. The room was inky black and deathly cold. I shot out of bed and flipped the light switch.

And then I realized I was in room five.

I tried the door. Locked. But I saw the dead bolt was open. The door was locked from the outside? I turned the knob frantically, back and forth, back and forth. Nothing. I started pounding on the door with all of my strength. My hand was aching, but I couldn't, wouldn't stop.

"Dominic! Jason! Alice! Anyone! Help me! I'm trapped!"

"There's no escape, dear," a thin, wispy voice said.

And then everything went dark.

CHAPTER TWENTY-TWO

I awoke to my own screaming.

"Shhhhh." It was Dominic's voice, calming and reassuring me. "It's okay. You were having a nightmare."

I looked up at him, blinking. My heart pounded hard and fast in my chest, and I was soaking wet with sweat. I was panting and tears streamed down my face, like a child, as though I couldn't get enough air into my body. I felt like I had just run a marathon.

"Just a dream," he said, stroking my hair, his voice gentle and low. "Brynn, honey, it was just a dream."

"It was so real," I murmured. I looked around, wiping the tears from my eyes. We were in Dominic's room. Just as we had been. Not room five.

"The good ones always are." He smiled down at me. "Do you want to tell me about it?"

I nodded. "In a minute," I sputtered out, the tears taking hold of my voice.

I slipped out of bed and headed over to the bathroom. I shut the door behind me and splashed water onto my face, then dried it on a towel that smelled like Dominic. Just this simple act brought me back to myself. I gazed at my own reflection in the mirror. My breathing slowed. It was okay. I was not trapped in number five.

I opened the bathroom door half expecting him to be gone, but there he was, leaning against the headboard, holding two glasses of wine.

"I thought you could use this," he said.

I curled in next to him, taking the glass. My hands were still shaking. I glanced at the clock. It read 12:12 a.m. Something about the symmetry of the numbers sent a cold chill through me.

"So, what happened in this dream of yours?" Dominic asked.

I told him about seeing my mother and the two elderly ladies.

"It was the oddest thing," I said. "I dreamed that I woke up. So, I thought in the dream that I was awake and really experiencing what was happening."

I also told him about being trapped in number five with a creepy old woman. I didn't say anything about Alice.

"That's the second time you've dreamed about that room," he said, frowning. "I think we need to ask LuAnn to open it up tomorrow, so you can see for yourself that nothing is lurking in there, waiting for you."

I chuckled, a little half-heartedly, but when I looked into his face, I could see he wasn't joking.

"You really think we should?"

"Absolutely," he said. "The fact that an old woman died there over the winter has you spooked. I always find that the truth, reality, has a way of calming crazy thoughts." He stopped for a moment and smiled that movie-star smile. His face was illuminated by starlight. "Okay, I just called you crazy. I didn't mean that."

This brought a real smile to my lips. "No offense taken," I said. "It is pretty crazy, isn't it?"

"I'm serious, though," he said. "We're getting in there tomorrow."

We. I liked the sound of that. "Okay," I said.

"Let's get some sleep," he said.

Taking our glasses, he crossed the room and set them on the dresser and slipped back into bed next to me. I turned onto my side, and he spooned me, draping an arm across my waist and taking my hand in his.

I closed my eyes and wondered why I hadn't told him about the first part of my dream. The life together. It had felt too personal, too raw to share. Was that it? No, that wasn't it. I was shy about admitting to him that I had fantasized a life together as man and wife. *Way to scare a man off.* I smiled to myself.

As I lay there, replaying the scenes of that dream life with Dominic in my mind, I thought about why I would conjure that particular life in my dreams. It wasn't a fantasy. It wasn't pleasant, not all of it, anyway. Indeed, it seemed like a harsh life, there in a stone cottage on a wind-swept cliff by an angry sea. Me standing in the blinding rain, waiting for a man, the father of my children, who would never come home. He was obviously a fisherman or some kind of mariner, and had been lost out there. Why would I conjure that up?

It had been so real. I could picture him in that angry, dark, roiling water, taking his last breath before going under, perhaps thinking of me at the end. Tears stung the backs of my eyes as I felt the love, the great, enormous love we had shared. The magnitude of the loss of it was unbearable.

And yet, it was just a dream. I didn't really live it. Dominic and I were in the first stages of falling in love—at least I was. I had to admit that to myself. I was falling for this man. I wasn't sure how he felt, but it seemed to me he was falling for me, too.

But in the dream, it was like we were soul mates. I had never had that kind of love with anyone. I knew it existed because my parents had found it with each other. But as for me, that kind of deep love had been elusive. It was one of the reasons I had left my longtime relationship. I felt that maybe my great love was out there somewhere, waiting for me to find him.

Had I found him? Was that what my dream was trying to tell me?

CHAPTER TWENTY-THREE

Sunlight shining in from the window awakened me. I stretched and reached out. Dominic was gone. The bed was empty.

My stomach seized up for a moment, but then I remembered. He had said he had a busy day ahead . . . hadn't he? In any case, I could be assured Lake Superior hadn't swallowed him up. He was fine, off doing whatever he had to do.

I yawned and saw Dominic had set his electric kettle, the French press, and a bag of coffee on the dresser. I slipped out of bed, filled the kettle with water, and intended on plugging it in, and then thought, no. I'd shower and start my own day. Maybe get out of the house entirely and grab some breakfast someplace in town.

I opened the door and stepped out into the hallway, my head foggy from all the dreams the night before.

"Oh! What do we have here?" It was Jason, eyebrows raised, smiling from ear to ear.

I let out an audible groan. I had hoped to make it across the hall without anyone seeing me come out of Dominic's room.

"I'm just going back to my room to get some half-and-half for my coffee?" I tried, my voice cracking.

"Right," Jason laughed. "Honey, you're so busted. I saw the man leave half an hour ago."

I dissolved into laughter, too. "Of course I couldn't do this walk of shame without anyone seeing me."

"Shame? I'd be shouting it from the rooftops. If I were single, I'd have been after him, too," Jason said as he headed to the stairs. "Well played, Brynn. Well played."

I shrugged into my room. Was this what dating was going to be like in midlife? If so, I would be permanently mortified.

I showered, changed into fresh clothes, and decided to go out for breakfast. I wasn't sure how discreet Jason was, and I had no wish to field questions from the likes of Gary and LuAnn. Thinking about it, maybe that was why Dominic had left so early. Cover?

I avoided everyone by slipping out the back door and made my way down the street. The air smelled fresh after yesterday's rain.

I pushed open the door to the coffee shop and found Kate and Simon standing at the counter. They both turned to me and smiled.

"Hey!" Kate said. "Join us for coffee?"

In a few minutes, the three of us were settled at a table by the window, sipping our coffee and chatting lightly about the weather. But both Kate and Simon didn't seem like themselves. An undercurrent of apprehension was simmering. Simon kept glancing out the window, up toward Harrison's House.

"Is everything okay at the inn?" I asked, looking from one to the other. "I don't mean to pry, but you left happy hour in a hurry. And the police sirens . . ."

Simon and Kate exchanged a glance.

"We're here avoiding the media," Simon said, elongating the last word. He took a sip of his coffee and winced. "We abandoned Jonathan like the cowardly cousins we are. Normally, I'd love for the media to be swarming around me. Not this time."

"Media?" I asked, raising my eyebrows. "What happened?"

Kate sighed. "You'll find out anyway, so we might as well tell you," she said, shaking her head. "A guest died. It's going to spread around town like wildfire today, what with every news station in the vicinity on our doorstep."

A tendril of dread crept its way up my spine as a dark thought seeped in. "The media would not be dispatched to a small-town inn because a guest died of natural causes. Would they?"

Simon ran a hand through his hair. "Jonathan found her in the ballroom. He is completely traumatized. It's like he went into the sewer and saw Pennywise. I think he's milking it a little, to tell you the truth. The man has always had a flair for the dramatic. Every time he gets sick, he's Camille lying on a fainting couch. And now, finding a body? He is in a faux catatonic state."

I couldn't help smiling. "It's not Bridezilla or her mother?"

"That's a lovely thought," Simon said, "but no. It was an elderly lady. She was staying alone for the weekend. First-time guest. Lovely woman."

"So, how did she . . . you know. Die?" I gulped.

"Nick's investigating," Kate said.

"Why? It wasn't natural causes?"

"The coroner hasn't determined the cause of death yet. Like Simon said, she was in the ballroom. But . . ."

"But, what?"

Simon and Kate exchanged a glance.

"She was lying in the middle of the floor with her hands folded across her chest," Kate said.

"Like she was in *repose*," Simon added, raising his eyebrow.

I shuddered. "Well, that's creepy."

"Nick thinks she was posed," Kate said, her voice low.

"She had to be," Simon said, leaning in. "It's not like you're having the odd heart attack or stroke, and then, at that moment, you think, 'Wait, let me just lie down here and fold my hands neatly!' You're just falling down any which way."

"Very true," I said. "But I'm not crazy about the implications. I mean, who would do that?"

"Exactly," Simon said. "I want to kick everyone out of the inn. All the guests. Can we do that? On the off chance somebody's a killer."

"No," Kate said. "We can't do that. But I know what you mean. Someone in the house, either a guest or an intruder, posed her like that."

"The police"—Simon looked pointedly at Kate and narrowed his eyes, and I knew he was talking about Nick—"questioned all of our guests. It's like we're in an Agatha Christie novel." His tale was cut short by Jason, Gil, and Alice coming through the door.

"Hi, kids!" Jason sang out, steering Alice over to our table. "Honey, you sit here with Brynn for a minute while we pick up our lunch." Then, turning to us, he said, "We're headed out on the boat. I thought a picnic on one of the islands would be fun."

As he and Gil made their way up to the counter, Alice sank into the chair next to me. I took her hand. "Good morning," I said to her. "A boat ride sounds like fun."

She held my gaze for a moment. "You're tired today," she said.

I smiled. "Do I look it? I thought I did a good job covering it with makeup."

"Don't be silly, darling," Simon piped up. "You look beautiful."

But Alice shook her head. "You're exhausted. Time traveling will do that to you. You did a lot of it last night. I can see it, time, hovering in the air all around you. It won't be the last time."

Both Simon and Kate were staring openmouthed, Simon holding his coffee in midair, halfway to his mouth. I didn't know quite what to say.

"I had a night filled with vivid dreams," I finally said to them, glancing at Alice. "She's right, I'm really tired today."

"Oh, dear Lord, please, not another one who has vivid dreams here in Wharton," Simon said, causing Kate to choke on her coffee. "I've had enough of that to last a lifetime. There is something about this town that brings it out."

"Dreams can do that," Alice piped up. "They're not just your imagination." She was quiet for a minute, studying my face. "You love him. I can see that hovering around you, too. He's not who you think he is. He's more dangerous than you think he is. But he is your true love. For better or for worse."

I stared at her, my stomach seizing up. What did she mean by that?

Jason and Gil snaked their way from the counter through the tables to us, carrying a couple of bags and three big bottles of water. "Okay, honey, it's time to go!" Jason said.

"It's time to go," Alice parroted, pushing herself up from her chair. She turned to Simon. "You don't have to worry about any of your other guests. There was no crime. Death came for her. Your lady. It was her time to go, that's all. There was nothing you could have done."

Simon stared at her.

"She didn't suffer. It was quite pleasant, actually. Death is coming for me, too," Alice said. "Technically, death is coming for all of us. But for me, it will be soon. I'm not afraid."

Gil caught my eye, and we exchanged a charged glance as Jason led Alice away from our table. The bell on the door chimed as they left the coffee shop and it closed behind them.

Simon, Kate, and I sat there in silence for a bit.

"Well, that was unusual," Simon said, raising his eyebrows and taking a sip of his coffee.

I took a deep breath and told them the whole story of how Alice had been saying rather odd, prophetic things to me. Gil, too.

"What does Jason think?" Simon asked.

I shook my head. "According to Gil, he won't acknowledge it," I said. "They got into a fight about it, actually."

"Not surprised." Simon sniffed. "Jason is a very 'everything's fine!' type of person. Plus, he's grieving. As we all know, grief can mess with you."

He wasn't kidding.

"What do you think?" Kate asked.

"I don't have any idea," I admitted. "All I know is, she's onto something. Dominic thinks it's because she's near the end. The veil between this world and the next is thin, and she's sort of living in both."

"It wouldn't be the first time something otherworldly happened in Wharton," Simon said, winking at Kate. "But I don't doubt that she's . . ." He was searching for the right word.

"Seeing?" Kate offered.

He nodded. "Exactly." He rested his elbows on the table and leaned into me. "But enough about that. Who are you in love with? Do tell. You mentioned a *Dominic* just now."

"The Illustrated Man!" Kate said. "That's Dominic, right?"

Simon narrowed his eyes at me. "Wait, stop. Everyone stop what they're doing right now. Earth, please stop spinning. Are you talking about that ungodly handsome man with the chest and shoulders that would make Mr. Dwayne 'The Rock' Johnson weep with shame? The one with all the tattoos who has been walking around town leaving a trail of women—and men—swooning on the street in his wake? Not that I've noticed him."

I could feel my face heating up.

"She's blushing," Simon said to Kate.

"Is Alice right? Are you in love with him?" Kate asked, squinting at me. "Already? You just met the guy."

Simon chortled. "Said Kate 'Love at First Sight' Granger."

I raised my eyebrows. "Was it love at first sight with you and Nick?"

Kate smiled. "Not quite. But you might say it was love at first touch. Something weird happened the first time I held his hand. I saw our whole future laid out in front of me."

"A future with the living embodiment of Eeyore, revealed to her in one horrific instant," Simon added. "And she went for it."

Kate burst into laughter. "He is not!"

"Okaaay," Simon said, rolling his eyes at me. "You're laughing because you know it's true."

"Simon thinks he's too serious," Kate said, wiping her eyes. "He's a police chief! Of course he's serious."

"Brooding," Simon said. "The man broods more than a hen."

"But you fell for him right away," I said, holding Kate's gaze. "It's not so crazy, then," I said.

"It wasn't crazy for me." Kate smiled. "It felt completely right."

"Oh, this Nick-Kate affair is old news," Simon said, waving his hand. "I want to hear about you and the sexiest man alive. How, what, when, where, why."

I had told Kate a bit about Dominic during our lunch on the island the other day, but I filled Simon in about meeting him at the showers and having coffee in the mornings. Our day at the beach. The fish boil. I told them about his passion for helping people better their lives, leaving out the more personal details. And I certainly didn't mention the night before.

"It's weird," I said finally. "I just met him. But it feels like I've known him forever. The dreams Alice mentioned? She was right. They were about him. And traveling in time. I dreamed of Dominic and me, living as man and wife in a different place and time."

All at once, Kate wasn't laughing. "What place and time?"

I cast my mind back to the dream. "I'm not quite sure," I said. "But judging by what we were wearing, I'm going to say about one hundred-ish years ago. Give or take. And in terms of the place, it seems like it was in England, on the ocean. Very windswept and rocky."

"Tell me more," Kate pressed.

Tears stung at the backs of my eyes. "It was like scenes of a life," I began. "Snippets of happiness. Us laughing together. Loving each other. Being together. He came home to me. We lay in bed laughing. I watched him teaching our children how to tie nautical knots."

"Then what happened?" Kate asked, leaning in.

My throat seized up. I looked from one of them to the other. "He died." My voice was thin, not wanting to say the words out loud. "He drowned in the raging, angry sea."

All of me wanted to burst into tears, right there at the table. The grief was so palpable. But I held it together.

"It was only a dream," I said weakly. "But I've never felt anything like the love I felt between us in that dream. Nothing close to it."

Kate reached over and took my hand. "I know. I really do. The same thing happened to me. Well, similar. I wasn't dreaming of myself. I was dreaming of a love between two people I didn't know. But I had never felt anything like it, either."

I brushed away a tear. "I woke up feeling sort of . . ." I searched for the right word. "Cheated, I'd guess you'd say. I've been living on this earth all this time and have never found the kind of love the people in my dream had. Or even my parents had."

"I felt the same way," Kate said. "But then I met Nick."

I held her gaze for a moment. I had just met Dominic but . . . could it be?

Kate finished her coffee and set the cup on the table. "I hate to break this up, but . . ."

Simon nodded. "I know. We really should get back. We can't hide all day." He turned to me. "I know this goes without saying—"

I put my hand up. "Don't worry. I won't tell anyone about the woman's death. The posing. I know nothing."

"Thank you," he said.

The two of them gathered their cups and placed them in the tub on the counter.

"C'mon up for dinner after the dust settles in a couple of days," Simon said. "And bring that man of yours."

I smiled at him. "I will."

"You can tell him shirts are not required," he said as they walked out the door.

I fished my phone out of my purse as I was finishing my coffee and noticed an email from my brother. I clicked on it, and several photos popped up. The Cornish countryside, the town of St. Ives, a photo of him and my dad drinking beer in a pub. But then I clicked on one that took my breath away.

"Here's the place we're renting for the summer!" my brother's caption said. "Isn't it cute! All of the houses over here have names. This is the Widow's Cottage."

It was the cottage from my dream.

CHAPTER TWENTY-FOUR

The Widow's Cottage. Was I the widow? It felt insane to even think about it. But I had to know. It was nearly ten o'clock in the morning. I wanted to call my brother, but I wasn't sure about the time difference between where I was and Cornwall, England. Six hours earlier? Six hours later? In the end, I just dropped my phone back into my purse. What would I have said to him, anyway? *I dreamed about living in the cottage where you're staying?* He'd think I was an idiot.

I stared out the window for a moment, my stomach knotting up. *Screw it,* I thought. I retrieved my phone from my purse and dialed.

"Hey!" my brother said. "Pop and I are enjoying a beer at the local pub."

Six hours later, then.

"Hey, Jeff. Everything going okay?" I asked.

"Here! Talk to Pop!"

I heard Jeff say, "It's Brynn," as scuffling sounds came through the line.

"Brynn," my dad said, his voice bringing tears to my eyes. "How are you, sweetie?"

"Great, Dad," I said, trying to keep my voice steady. "Are you having a good time?"

"Wonderful! I wish you were with us!"

"So do I," I said. "You'll have to tell me all about it when you get back. I won't keep you long, Dad. I'm just calling with a quick question for Jeff."

"Oh, Jeff?" my dad asked. "Your sister has a question for you." More scuffling.

"What's up, sis?"

"This is going to sound weird, but I'm just wondering if you know anything about the history of the cottage you're renting. The Widow's Cottage."

"Not really," he said. "But I can ask the owner. Why?"

"The picture looked familiar," I said. "Like I'd seen it before. I'm curious."

"Sure, not a problem. I'm here digging up history anyway. I'll see what I can find out for you."

I thanked him, but truthfully, I wasn't fully sure I wanted to know.

Back on the main street, I watched the hustle and bustle near the ferry dock, people lined up on foot or in their cars, waiting to hop on the boat for a trip over to Colette. Everyone was happy, anticipating a wonderful day. The aura of it, the energy they all gave off, hummed and swirled in the air, touching everyone with droplets of joy. Maybe that was part of the mystique of Wharton, the magic that seemed to permeate everything here. Tangible happiness.

It was just what I needed to melt the ice that had frozen in my veins when I saw that photograph.

I stopped for a moment as an enormous bald eagle flew overhead, so close that I could see his talons and the fierce expression on his face. Eagles were common sights in Wharton, but seeing them never got old, never became mundane, even for residents. Everyone on the street stopped what they were doing to watch in reverence. The magnificent bird soared in slow circles, round and round without once flapping his wings, above the unusually calm surface of the lake.

All at once, he dove down like a bomber, stretching out his muscled legs and talons when he reached the water to snatch a fish, who was undoubtedly surprised by this unwelcome turn of events. Applause broke out along with oohs and aahs as the raptor flew away with his breakfast.

I made my way up the street to LuAnn's and found Dominic talking to the lady herself on the front lawn of the house. She was wearing hot-pink leggings, a long, black shirt tied at her hip, and a jangle of silver beaded chains around her neck. Her glasses were cat-eyed and studded with silver balls. I couldn't help but smile.

"There she is!" Dominic said, grinning at me. "How's your morning?"

"I just saw an eagle take a fish out of the lake," I reported.

"Did you?" LuAnn opened her eyes wide. "That's a sign of good luck, you know."

I wasn't sure about that, but I could use all the luck I could get.

"We were just talking about you," she went on.

"Uh-oh," I said, wincing. "All good, I hope."

"Oh, honey, don't be silly," LuAnn said. "You know my motto: if you don't have anything nice to say, come sit by me. But we weren't gossiping. This hunk of man was telling me you want to see number five."

I exchanged a glance with Dominic and scowled. Here in the bright light of day, it seemed foolish. Unnecessary. But he just shrugged at me. "I told you. We're getting in there today."

"So, what's it all about? He said you're having nightmares?" LuAnn wanted to know, crossing her arms. I noticed her fingernails were the same neon color as her leggings. "Why didn't you tell me?"

"Well, I—"

"'Well, I' my ass," LuAnn broke in. "Brynn, this place is as haunted as a graveyard on Halloween. Hell, all of Wharton is. If you're upset by anything strange that happens in my place, I want to know about it," she said. "Dreams qualify. Nobody's going to think you're crazy or making things up."

"Okay," I said.

"And I'm not snooping into your business, if that's what you're thinking," she went on. "I want to keep a handle on what's going on around here. You know? If there are spirits causing trouble in my house, I'm going to do something about it."

I smiled at her. A month ago, I would have thought this a totally ridiculous conversation. Now I was comforted by it. I liked the idea of any spirit bedeviling me having hell to pay, courtesy of this lady in the hot-pink leggings and cat-eyed glasses.

"I'm serious," she said. "I have a business to run. I can't have the odd spirit or two scaring people off. So, tell me about these dreams. Or whatever you've been having."

I glanced at Dominic.

He nodded. "It's okay," he said.

"I don't know quite how to describe it. A couple of times, I've found myself in number five with an older lady. Last night it was a dream for sure because I woke up screaming. The other night, though, I could have sworn it really happened. I was wide awake. Or, I think I was. I heard somebody call my name in the hallway. Then I saw a light on in number five." I didn't tell her about Alice.

LuAnn exhaled. "Okay. So, something about that room is calling out to you. That's pretty clear."

Dominic nodded. "That's why I want you to open it up. Let's get her in there. Let her see what it is. Maybe the mystery is playing with her imagination."

"Imagination? Oh, honey, you've got it all wrong. Brynn is not imagining this. If I have learned anything in all my years living in this haunted house, it's to believe people when they tell you something."

"Do we have any leads on who this woman was?" I asked. "Maybe knowing that would make this stop."

"Not a one," LuAnn said. "And, truthfully, I don't expect to find out. Nick can police this thing all he wants, but we all know there is more in this world than can be CSI'd at a crime scene."

"You're saying you think this was something paranormal?" Dominic asked her.

"No idea. But, honey, it happened here, and it ain't got no reasonable explanation. I'm not surprised."

I squinted at her. "LuAnn, what is this place? I mean, really."

She threw her head back and laughed. "If I knew that, I'd be selling tickets."

"Can we get into the room?" Dominic pressed.

LuAnn scowled at him. "You know I wanted it shut up for the season. Out of respect for whoever that woman was."

"Yep," Dominic said. "I know that. But now it's affecting Brynn. You know it, and I know it. I'm not saying open it up to guests. Just to us."

"Oh, all right," LuAnn huffed, stalking off toward the inn. "Let's go." We followed her inside.

She grabbed a key from behind the counter, and we went upstairs. When we started down the hallway and got closer to number five, my stomach seized up. All at once, I felt like I needed to get to a bathroom.

Without a word, I ran down the hall to my room, unlocked my door, and rushed into my bathroom just in time to vomit into the toilet. And then again. And again. Dominic was right behind me, mortifyingly enough.

He grabbed a washcloth off the towel bar and ran cool water over it, squeezing it out before handing it to me. I rubbed it over my face. The coolness was soothing, calming.

"I haven't thrown up since college," I said, my voice shredded from the violence of the act. "It's been two decades."

"Streak, broken," he said. He led me out of the bathroom into my room. "Do you want to lie down?"

I saw LuAnn hovering in the doorway, a look of concern on her face.

"No," I said. "I want to see what's in number five."

CHAPTER TWENTY-FIVE

LuAnn slid the key into the lock on number five, turned the knob, and pushed the door open. I stood in the hallway, my back to the wall, holding my breath and nearly closing my eyes. My sense of fight or flight was flashing code red, my heart beating so hard in my chest that I was sure the others could hear it. Everything inside of me was screaming *Run!*

But there was Dominic, holding his hand out to me. And LuAnn, already inside the room.

"C'mon, honey," LuAnn called to me. "Nothing in here's going to bite you."

I exhaled and took another deep breath. Maybe Dominic was right. Maybe seeing this room in the light of day would break whatever hold it had on me.

Dread wrapped itself around me like a shroud, but I shrugged it off. *It's just a room like any other,* I told myself. *Not a horror chamber.* I took Dominic's hand, and we stepped over the threshold together.

And there it was. The wooden headboard and footboard, carved with an intricate pattern of leaves, just like I had seen in my dream. The rose-colored floral quilt and a cozy nest of throw pillows. The lamp with the delicate light-green globes painted with purple and blue flowers. The stone fireplace with the rocking chair in front of it. Everything was just as I had dreamed it.

But unlike my dream, the room felt devoid of any life. It was as cold as the grave. The fireplace was dark. The rocking chair, empty.

Or was it? I squinted and thought I saw the faintest outline of a form. A human form. Was she there?

All at once, darkness fell, and the fire crackled and sprang to life. The globe lamp on the nightstand flickered and came on, shining with its soft light. The room, which had felt so cold and dead and empty a moment ago, shifted and changed into a warm, inviting place.

And there she was again. The old woman in the rocking chair.

She was wearing the same floral nightgown with the sweater over her shoulders that I had seen before. The same tortoiseshell glasses. But this time, she had a book in her lap and was writing in it. A journal? I looked over her shoulder and saw that her spidery scrawl filled the page. She didn't seem to know I was there and kept scribbling away, only stopping to dab a tear from her eye.

"Do you see what I'm seeing?" I whispered. No response. The room was dead silent but for the crackling of the fire. I turned around, but both Dominic and LuAnn had disappeared. Unadulterated terror wound around me and squeezed when I saw I was alone in the room with this lady.

I couldn't move. It was like I was glued to the spot. Or paralyzed.

I watched her, rocking slightly back and forth in her chair, calmly writing in her journal. She had a cup of tea—I hadn't noticed it before—and she took a sip every now and then. She was humming softly as she wrote.

All at once, I got the feeling I was intruding.

This lady had no idea I was there. I slowly realized, to my horror . . . maybe I wasn't.

I had been thinking she was the one haunting room number five. But right now, it was me. Maybe I was the ghost.

"Brynn!"

I opened my eyes with a start. I was lying in a heap on the floor. My head ached. Dominic was kneeling over me, holding my hand, a worried look on his face.

I coughed and sat up. "What happened?"

"You fainted," he said gently. "Or collapsed. Or something. You let out a scream and, boom. You were down. Are you all right? Your head hit the floor pretty hard."

I rubbed the back of my head and winced as I felt a bump beginning to form.

Gary appeared at the door with a lowball glass. An amber liquid sloshed around with two ice cubes.

"Thanks, babe," LuAnn said to him as she took the glass. "Will you go whip up some breakfast for her? LuAnn's special. With the works."

"You got it," Gary said, eyeing me. "She's okay, though, right?"

I smiled at this. "She's okay," I said to him.

"Don't go scaring us like that," Gary said, his voice gentle and low. "I'm going to make you something to eat. I'll see you downstairs in a minute."

As he left the room, LuAnn turned to me and handed me the glass.

I sniffed it. Whiskey? "It's ten o'clock in the morning," I said to her.

"Ten thirty, if you please," she said, putting her hands on her hips. "Anybody who faints in my presence gets a Scotch to settle their nerves, no matter what time it is. It's my policy, and I'm sticking to it."

I managed a smile and took a sip. I could feel the sizzle going down my throat and warming me from the inside out. She was right, I had to admit. I did feel a sense of calm, whether it was from the Scotch or the fact that she and Dominic were both by my side.

Dominic held out his hand and pulled me up. "I think it's time we get out of here," he said.

"Agreed," LuAnn said, ushering us out of the room. She closed the door and locked it behind her. "Honey, I don't want you coming into this room again. I should never have brought you in there, not after you lost your breakfast at the very thought of it. I should have known better. And now this. Whatever's going on, it's obvious it's affecting you in a decidedly negative way. We don't want that."

I nodded, finishing the whiskey. I wasn't eager to go back into number five. Not after what I had just experienced.

"C'mon down to the restaurant," she continued. "I want to get some food into you and hear about what happened in there. Don't even think about objecting."

Dominic and I exchanged a glance before following her down the stairs. My stomach was empty, and although the thought of food wasn't at all appealing, the thought of opposing LuAnn seemed futile. Plus, I thought she was right. I needed to eat something whether I wanted it or not.

The breakfast crowd had cleared out, and it wasn't yet time for lunch, so the restaurant was deserted. We took a table by the window. The sun shone happily through the glass, but I sort of wished for gloomy rain. I was shaking from the inside out.

Gary appeared with a plate that held eggs scrambled with sausage, onions, tomatoes, and broccoli in a nest of crispy hash browns, all covered with cheddar cheese. Salsa and sour cream were on the side, along with several pieces of toast.

"So, this is on the heart-healthy menu, right?" I said. Gary snorted.

"Low carb." LuAnn sniffed.

I took a bite. "Heaven," I said to Gary.

He beamed. "Thanks, doll," he said before disappearing back into the kitchen.

I handed a fork to Dominic, who had already confiscated a piece of my toast. "There's no way I can finish this on my own," I said. He dove in.

"Okay," LuAnn said. "Let's talk about what happened in there. I know you were shaky going in. But did anything . . . set you off, so to speak?"

I took a couple more bites and considered this. I wasn't sure what to tell them.

"I'm not sure," I said finally. "I've never fainted before."

I saw Dominic and LuAnn exchange a charged glance.

"I think I was wrong, pushing you to go into that room," Dominic said.

I shook my head. "No, you weren't," I said. I looked from him to LuAnn and back again. "Something did happen in there, but I'm not really sure what it was."

"Positive? Negative? A little of both?" LuAnn asked.

"I can't really say," I said. "In a way, it was almost as if I was dreaming. It was the strangest thing. What did I do?"

"You were staring at something," Dominic said. "Your eyes got wider and wider. I said your name, touched your arm, but you didn't respond."

LuAnn held my gaze for a long moment. "She was there, wasn't she? The woman who died in the room."

"I get the distinct feeling it was her, but I'm not sure," I said. "Who else would it be?" I looked from one of them to the other. "Did either of you see her?"

"No," LuAnn said, squinting at me. "I saw nothing. Don't get me wrong. I've seen ghosts in this house. Just not today."

Dominic shook his head. "I didn't see anything, either."

I took a deep breath, unsure about telling them any more. It was too strange to say aloud. But LuAnn immediately saw that I was holding something back.

"Out with it," she said. "Tell us what you saw."

"This is going to sound really weird," I said.

"Honey, I live here," LuAnn said. "We've got weird going on every day. Hell, look who I have in the kitchen. Believe me, you are not going to tell me anything I haven't heard."

So, I told them how the fire crackled to life, warming the room. How the lamp turned on. And how I saw the old woman sitting in the rocking chair, writing in her journal.

"You didn't see any of that?" I asked them. "The fire, the lamp? None of it?"

Dominic and LuAnn both shook their heads.

"The woman. What was she wearing?" LuAnn wanted to know.

"A nightgown," I said.

"With a sweater thrown over her shoulders?"

I nodded.

"It was the lady who passed in that room," LuAnn said. "No doubt. That's what she was wearing when I found her. I wonder what she's doing back here."

Tears stung at my eyes, and I wasn't sure why. I took a deep breath to try to keep them at bay. But Dominic noticed and placed his hand on mine.

"It's okay, Brynn," he said. "Seeing a ghost . . . it's not something that happens to most people. It's upsetting."

I shook my head. "That's not it," I said. "It wasn't upsetting or frightening. She was just sitting calmly by the fire. She had no idea I was there. I was the one in the room who was invisible, watching her, not the other way around."

LuAnn squinted at me. "I don't follow that. What do you mean, honey?"

"She wasn't haunting the room. I was."

CHAPTER TWENTY-SIX

After I finished eating, I felt like taking a walk alone to clear my head. The incident in room five, whatever it had been, was unsettling me, deep into my bones.

I wandered through town, window-shopping and people watching, letting my mind drift.

My mother floated into my thoughts. How I ached to pick up the phone and call her. I wondered if the white-hot pain of the loss of her would ever go away. She'd make sense of all of this. The image of her in my dream the night before tugged at my heart. It seemed so real, real enough to touch, as if she had actually been there. Had she? Was it just a dream, or did she come to me to say she approved of Dominic? Or was it something else? As I thought of it, I remembered that dream had dissolved into me being alone in room five. It was what had led Dominic to insist we get in there, for real.

It all seemed to circle back, to overlap, as though everything that had happened to me recently was connected somehow. My mother's death, me coming to Wharton and specifically to LuAnn's, meeting Dominic, the house in Cornwall, the mysterious woman in number five, Alice, even the odd death of the woman at Harrison's House. A thread was running through it all, I just knew it, but I couldn't see it clearly enough to pull it.

I found myself passing by the police station, and before I had a chance to even think about it, I pulled open the door and went inside. Three desks sat empty as a coffee maker made percolating sounds on a table next to the wall. A middle-aged woman behind a fourth desk by an office door—Nick's?—was talking on the phone and tapping away at her computer. She looked up when I walked in, and gave me a smile and a nod, holding up one finger to let me know she wouldn't be a minute.

"I'll send a squad over, Darlene," she said. And then, to me, "I'll be right with you."

She picked up a microphone. "Harry," she said into it. "Darlene thinks some kids got into her shed and made off with her ladder. Will you go check it out?"

Harry responded with a quick, "Sure, Sandy," and she set down the mic. I couldn't help smiling. Small-town police.

"What can I do for you?" Sandy said to me.

"I'm wondering if Nick Stone is available," I said.

She cocked her head toward the door to her left. "He's not usually here on Saturdays, but he happens to be in his office today." She picked up the phone. "There's a woman here to see you." She looked at me. "What's your name?"

"Brynn Wilder," I said.

Nick's door opened before Sandy put down the phone.

"Hi!" he said, smiling at me. "Come on in."

I walked around Sandy's desk and into Nick's office, a warm wood-paneled room with a bookshelf on one wall and a window overlooking the street on the other. A corgi was curled up on a dog bed in the corner, eyeing me.

"That's Queenie," he said, closing the door and hopping up onto his desk as I sank into the leather chair opposite. "She's the closest we get to a K-9 unit here."

I smiled, not completely sure why I was there. Now that I was in front of the man, I didn't quite know how to ask the question that was rumbling through my mind.

"What can I do for you?" Nick said. "There's not any trouble up at LuAnn's . . ."

"No, it's nothing like that," I said. I looked at him and winced. "I'm afraid this is going to sound rather odd."

Nick chuckled. "After what I went through with Kate a couple of years back, there is literally nothing that's going to sound odd to me. So, fire away."

"I'm wondering if you've identified the woman who passed away at LuAnn's over the winter," I said.

Nick looked at me for a long moment. "That's not odd."

I gave him a small smile. "You haven't heard the rest of it."

Nick chuckled at this. "All downhill from here, is that it?"

"Something like that," I said. "I thought I'd ask the sane question first."

"To answer that sane question, we have not identified her, unfortunately," he said. "Why do you ask? Do you think you might know who she was?"

"No, I just . . ." My words trailed off into a sigh. "I think she might be haunting LuAnn's. Or me, specifically."

"Well, that's not good," he said, frowning.

"You believe me?"

"Yes," he said, simply. "I believe you."

"Is her body still here?" I asked.

"County coroner's office," he said. "I've got a guy searching missing-persons reports, but if nobody identifies her within three months, which it's nearly been now, she'll be cremated."

A shudder passed through me, and my stomach did a quick flip.

"That's standard," he said. "Her ashes will remain with the coroner for three years after that, along with all of the information we have from her. Autopsy results, photographs, just in case someone comes forward within that time."

"What did she die of? Can I ask that?"

"Natural causes," he said. "There was no foul play, nothing like that. The coroner put her at about ninety years old."

"Ninety. Wow."

"Yeah," Nick said. "Whoever she was, the lady had a good run."

"Do you still have a photo of her on file?" I asked.

He slid off the desk and turned to his laptop. After a few clicks, he turned the screen my way. I didn't even need to see it to know it was her, but the sight of her, lying there, lifeless, jarred me in a way I couldn't quite explain. It tugged at the depths of my soul. She seemed familiar somehow. Tears sprang to my eyes.

I nodded. "That's who I saw. The poor lady."

"If you see her again, ask her who she is," Nick said, a smile on his face.

I thanked him and walked out of the office and into the sunshine.

I wondered what had drawn that woman to LuAnn's. How she happened to be there during the last days of her life. Why she was sitting in front of the fire, in her nightgown and sweater, writing in a journal in a completely empty, dark hotel. Dying alone in that place, with nobody around her. Or even missing her. A profound sadness descended on me. I made my way down to the lakeshore.

I perched on a large flat rock and listened to the waves rolling into the beach. The sound of it was so rhythmic, so hypnotic—whoosh, whoosh, whoosh—it was like a meditation. My breathing slowed; my heartbeat slowed. The sadness receded, caressed away by the waves. *It's okay, Brynn,* the lake seemed to be saying to me. *It's okay. She's at peace now. She's where she wanted to be.*

There, with the lake whispering my name as it lapped at the shore, I began to feel that maybe we'd never know who she was and why she was there. And I would have to be content with the mystery remaining. *Sometimes,* I thought, *there aren't any answers. Only questions.*

CHAPTER TWENTY-SEVEN

On the spur of the moment, I bought a ticket and hopped onto the ferry. I climbed the narrow metal stairway to the top deck and stood at the railing as the ferry chugged away from the dock and into the lake. The cool breeze on my face and the sight of the tree-lined, rocky islands in the distance were restoring. It was true what people said about this lake. It was magical and comforting and healing, as though the big water embodied God Himself. Maybe it did. All I knew was a sense of peace wrapped itself around me when I was near this water. It was like nothing else I had ever felt in my life.

It was right to come here to Wharton. This place was healing my broken spirit. Since the day of my mom's diagnosis, through her treatment, and ultimately to her death, my world, my life and everything in it, had been thrown into chaos. My relationship I thought was going to last a lifetime? Gone. My mother, gone. My good, sweet dog who was by my side through it all, gone. My passion for my career, gone. I was in a state of mourning for all of it, stumbling through the days like an avatar of myself, a person encased in a shell of ice.

Only now, in these first days in Wharton, I was beginning to thaw.

Curious, I thought, the juxtaposition between the peace the lake exuded and the strangeness, even fear, that came from staying in

LuAnn's haunted inn. But then it occurred to me: Maybe it wasn't only the lake that was healing me. Maybe it was LuAnn's, too.

A shiver ran through me.

I had never been a particularly religious person. I felt more at one with . . . something . . . when I was out in nature than when I was in a church. I certainly didn't have any answers about life after death, either. When my mom got sick, I read book after book about people who had near-death experiences, who had indeed been dead for a time and came back to tell about it. I wanted to know for certain, was almost desperate to know that, somehow, she would live on. That her life force wouldn't simply extinguish. But, not being a person of strong faith who believed unequivocally that our spirits went to heaven when we died, I had my doubts about those near-death survival stories.

When my mother died, I was not only washed away in the tsunami of grief, but I was also consumed with the utter blackness and fear that descended when I thought about her simply not being there, or anywhere, any longer. That the powerful spirit that was my mother was just . . . gone. And, when my time came, would I be gone, too? Would I be nowhere?

Before my mom got sick, I had never much thought about death and had never quite understood people who had an intense fear of it. But when my mom was dying, the notion of life after death suddenly became a vital part of my psyche. The idea of being extinguished haunted my darkest thoughts.

Those were the thoughts going through my mind as the ferry pulled into the dock at Ile de Colette. Now that I was there, I didn't quite know what I was going to do with myself. It was around lunchtime, but after that massive breakfast at LuAnn's, I was still stuffed. I didn't have my car, so taking a drive was out. Maybe I'd just walk to Jimmy's for a quick glass of wine before catching the ferry back to the mainland.

When I got there, I was surprised to find Dominic and Alice sitting at a table playing checkers. Jason and Gil were nowhere in sight.

Dominic's face lit up when he saw me as I walked in. He raised his hand in greeting, waving me over.

"Great minds," he said as I sank into the chair next to him. "I thought an island getaway would be just the thing after this morning. When I didn't find you, I asked Lady Alice to be my date."

"You're terrible! It's not a date," Alice said, giggling. "Jason would be upset to hear you say that."

Dominic laughed. "You're way out of my league anyway."

I beamed at him. What a nice thing to do, taking her for a day out. For her, and for Jason and Gil. The bartender came around and took our drink orders, chardonnay for Alice and me and a gimlet for Dominic.

"I like it here on the island," I said to Alice. "It has such a laid-back vibe."

"Laid-back vibe," she said. "Yes, it does." Alice looked from Dominic to me and back again. "I like your vibe, too," she said. "Your vibe together."

I felt the heat rising to my face.

"I do, too," Dominic said.

Our drinks came, and I took a sip of my chardonnay, grateful for the distraction.

"Oh!" Dominic said to me, after taking a sip of his gimlet. "You didn't hear. You left before Simon called. They got word from the coroner about the cause of death of the woman at Harrison's House. He called to let LuAnn know, and of course she told everyone."

I wasn't sure I wanted to hear about another elderly lady dying a mysterious death in Wharton. It seemed rather like an epidemic. But I asked him to go on, anyway.

"Natural causes," he said. "Heart attack."

I furrowed my brow. "But what about the posing? The way she had her hands crossed over her chest?"

Dominic shrugged. "Only Jonathan saw that. Well, him and the EMTs. And they're not saying anything, according to Simon. He is officially going with, 'It's a sad and unfortunate event, condolences to the family, thoughts and prayers from Harrison's House,' that sort of thing. He's hoping any whispers of strange circumstances will be put to rest."

"Okay." I nodded. "But it doesn't change what Jonathan saw."

"I guess we'll never know," Dominic said.

Alice pushed back her chair and stood. "I have to go now," she said. "I need to be home before my kids get off the bus. I like to meet the bus. I don't know why every mother in the neighborhood doesn't do it. But anyway, I'm taking the girls shopping for dresses. I told them this morning before they left for school that we'd all get new dresses today."

Dominic motioned for the check and handed the server some cash. "Keep the change," he said.

"What's the occasion for the new dresses?" he asked, offering Alice his enormous biceps. She slid her thin arm around it, and he put his other hand on top of hers. "Is there something special happening?"

"We're having a party for Jason's work buddies," Alice went on. "Oh, the girls won't be there for most of it. They'll be put to bed. I know they'll stay up, though, those little devils." She laughed then, so sweetly. "But I wanted them to have some festive new dresses to mark the occasion."

"And for you, too," Dominic said. "But you don't need a new dress to show off your beauty. You could go to the party in rags and still be the most beautiful lady there."

Alice beamed. "I know you're just flattering me," she said, patting his hand. "It's nice to hear, but don't you get any funny ideas, mister. I'm a one-man woman."

"And that man is Jason," Dominic said. "Lucky bastard."

"Jason," Alice said, turning her head this way and that. "Where is he?"

"At work," Dominic said. "But he'll be home soon. Don't worry."

Alice stopped. "Will I have time to take the girls shopping before he gets home? I don't want him to come home to an empty house."

"You'll have time," he said.

He led her out of the bar so gently and lovingly I wanted to burst out crying.

His car was parked in back, and the three of us got into it. We drove to the ferry in silence, but I could feel Alice's agitation as though it were a tangible thing, hanging in the air.

"Will we get home in time?" she said finally. "I don't know where Jason is. Do you? Is he okay? Can I get out of the car?"

"No," Dominic said, his voice stern. "You know it's not safe to get out of a moving car. You've told your children that." He reached out his hand and took hers.

"Yes, you're right," she said. "Not safe. I'll stay where I am."

We all stayed in the car during the ferry ride. Dominic whispered to me that he didn't think it was safe to go onto the deck, what with Alice's apprehensiveness. I agreed. I was content to feel the swaying of the boat as it chugged along toward the mainland, and I noticed Dominic was texting. He caught my eye and nodded, and somehow I knew he had been texting Jason.

When the boat docked, we waited our turn and then pulled off. We were back at LuAnn's in no time, and the three of us climbed out of the car.

"Is Jason here?" Alice said, and just then, the man appeared, walking out the door with arms outstretched.

"There's my girl!" he said, enveloping her in a hug. "Did you have a good time?"

"The best," Alice said, smiling at Dominic and me. "I like them. They're good people."

"Yes, honey, they are," Jason said, leading her away. "Gil's waiting for us upstairs."

And just like that, all thoughts of taking the girls shopping vanished. Alice's nervousness ceased. She took Jason's arm, and at that moment, she was where her heart lived. Next to him.

Dominic and I stood in the parking lot, watching them go. All at once, I felt exhausted from the day's events.

"Up for a movie?" Dominic asked. "Really watch one all the way through this time." He smirked. "I think you're beat, and I am, too."

"That sounds great," I said.

There was no happy hour on weekends, thankfully, but we took the back stairs anyway to avoid any people who might happen to be in the restaurant. A few minutes later, I was changing into my jammies. Sure, it was still daytime, but movie watching required movie-watching attire. Dominic had agreed.

Two nights in a row with this man. That's what it was shaping up to be. I started to wonder where this was heading, but I intentionally stopped that train of thought. It didn't have to be heading anywhere. And if it was, I didn't have to monitor it. *Let it happen, girl; just let it happen.* I was done micromanaging my life. It hadn't got me too far, up to now.

I rapped softly on his door. Thankfully Jason wasn't crouching in the hallway to catch me in the act. Dominic ushered me in, and I saw he had lit a fire in his fireplace, bathing the room in a cozy glow. All at once, I felt my exhaustion and wanted nothing more than to curl into his bed. But I just stood there, hesitant.

"You've had quite the day," he said, motioning toward the bed. "Let's just relax."

He didn't have to ask me twice. I slid into the bed and rested my head on his nest of pillows.

"What would you like to watch?" he asked, curling in beside me and grabbing the remote. "It looks like we've got new-ish releases on demand on cable here."

"Anything you want," I said. And then I eyed him. "No horror."

He chuckled at this with such a look of devilish joy on his face that it brought a tear to my eye. He noticed and gently wiped it away.

"What's this?" he said.

"Tears are really close to the surface these days," I admitted to him. "You looked so joyful just then, that it reminded me of . . . joy, I'd guess you'd say. I haven't had much of it in my life lately, and just today I was thinking that I was close to rediscovering it."

He smiled at me and ran a hand through my hair, pushing it out of my eyes.

"That's what you got from today," he said to me, his voice silky. "A day in which you threw up, fainted, and for all intents and purposes saw a ghost. Yet somehow, you found the joy."

I smiled up at him. "It sounds sort of weird when you say it like that."

"No," he said. "It sounds sort of magnificent. Many people gravitate toward the negative, wrap themselves around it and define themselves by it, even when circumstances don't warrant it. They've always got something to complain about, even when the sun is shining. But you mined the positive out of a day that contained a whole lot of strangeness. That's difficult to do, and it shows what kind of person you are. It shows what your spirit is."

His words warmed me from the inside out. "That's a really nice thing, what you just said."

We gazed at each other for a moment, and I wondered if it was going to lead to more, when he broke the spell.

"All right," he said, clearing his throat as if he had been feeling it, too. "I'm going to find us something to watch."

He clicked on a drama, and I snuggled down next to him, reveling in the decadence that was having absolutely nothing to do during an afternoon other than watch a movie. I couldn't remember the last time I had felt that, and I knew that if indeed I went back to teaching in the fall, I wouldn't be able to indulge in that kind of sloth for the foreseeable future. But at that moment, I just enjoyed it. I didn't so much care about the movie. It was the supportive, wonderful man by my side who wanted to give me a distraction from a strange, upsetting, and eerie day.

We watched the movie for a while, laughing and talking together until my eyes began to feel heavy. I caught myself dozing now and then, but soon it was no use trying to stay awake. All of that intense dreaming the night before had exhausted me.

The last thing I remember before drifting off was Dominic smiling down at me, saying, "Sleep well."

CHAPTER TWENTY-EIGHT

My eyes opened with a start. I pushed myself out of my pillow nest and sat up. The television was switched off. Dominic was sitting next me, a book opened in his lap.

"You okay?" he asked. "No more upsetting dreams, I hope."

I rubbed my eyes and yawned, glancing at the clock. Not more than an hour had passed. It felt as though I had slept forever.

"No," I said. "But something occurred to me as I was waking up. You know that time when you're not quite sleeping but not quite awake?"

Dominic smiled. "The in-between time, my grandmother called it," he said, gazing off into his past. "She used to tell me it was the place where everything seen and unseen met up and danced. Present, past, and future, all at once. We who are living, and spirits of the dead. It's all right there swirling around together in that mystical in-between time."

His face softened, and his eyes began to glisten. "She told me that a few of us, a lucky few, can travel there by choice. Get out of the river of time, so to speak, and rise above it to what really is. Those are the seers, the psychics, the visionaries of this world. Or so she said."

Alice, I thought.

"She sounds like a wise lady, your grandmother," I said, imagining Dominic as a little boy listening to her tales.

"She was." He quickly wiped a tear away and cleared his throat, bringing us both back into the present. "You were mentioning that something came to you?"

"It was the oddest thing, but when I was just waking up—when I was in the in-between time—I started thinking about elephants."

He furrowed his brow at me. "Elephants?"

"There's an old legend about the elephants' graveyard," I said to him. "The way the tale goes, elephants can sense when they're going to die. When the time is near, they separate from the herd and make their last journey alone to the place where their ancestors have gone before them, the place where they will die."

"Wow, that's heavy." Dominic leaned back against the pillow nest. "Go on."

"Explorers have talked about the elephant graveyard for years. Centuries, even. Hunters have sought it out for the ivory alone. Nobody has ever found it, not that we know of."

"But the elephants know where it is," Dominic said, his voice soft.

"They say spirits of the dead are guarding it, casting a shadow over it so no man can find it. That's okay with me."

"It's a cool story. But what makes you bring it up now? The elephant graveyard isn't in Wharton. I think we can be relatively sure of that."

"I think it's related to something that happened today," I began. "Something I didn't tell you, what with Alice and everything."

"What's that?"

"I went to see Kate's husband, Nick Stone," I said.

A look of surprise, even alarm, drifted across his face and was gone just as quickly. "The chief of police? Why?"

"I wanted to know if they had identified the lady who died in room five."

"And?"

I shook my head. "They haven't. They're sort of half-heartedly checking missing-persons reports now, but she died of natural causes, and she was in her nineties, so it's not really a police matter, even though she did break in."

"You're saying they're not doing anything to find out who she was and what she was doing here?"

"That's right. That's the situation. Her body is with the county coroner, and she'll be cremated if nobody comes for her. They'll keep her remains for a few years and her information on file, just in case, someday in the future, someone comes along to identify her."

My eyes welled up with tears, and a cold breeze washed over me. "I was thinking about how lonely that sounded," I went on.

"Like the elephants, journeying off to die alone," he said, his voice reverent and soft. "That's the connection you made."

I put my hand on his arm. "Exactly," I said. "You hit on it. But there's more."

He leaned in toward me.

"Those elephants sense they're going to die, so they travel to a special place to do it," I said, the thoughts formulating in my mind as I spoke. "What if she did, too?"

"Here?" he said. "LuAnn's?"

"Yes!" I said, sitting up straighter and facing him, my legs crossed. "What if she knew she was going to die? Maybe she had been given a diagnosis, maybe she sensed it . . . I don't know. But what we do know is, she was near death. And she came here to LuAnn's, in the middle of winter, when everything was closed up tight and dark. She wasn't a resident or even a frequent visitor. Someone in town would have known her or at least recognized her from the photo that I know police showed around town. On the other side of that coin, if she knew anyone here, she would have contacted them."

He nodded. "What you're saying sounds right to me."

Energized, I went on. "We can only surmise that she journeyed here specifically last winter. She wasn't just passing by and stumbled upon the place. Nobody passes by. Wharton is a destination unto itself.

There's nothing else around. You don't pass through Wharton to get anywhere. She came here to die."

Dominic's eyes grew wide. "That's quite a theory."

"I'm not finished!" I said. "If she did indeed come here to die, the question is: Why? Why Wharton? Why LuAnn's?"

"Why room five?" Dominic added. "All of them were empty."

"Exactly!"

"What do you think?" Dominic asked.

"I think this place, and that room, meant something to her," I said. "From where I sit, that much is obvious."

He squinted at me. "How do you get to 'obvious'? It's all pretty out there, Brynn."

I shook my head. "No, it's not. Put yourself in her shoes. You're dying. You come to Wharton, to LuAnn's, to live out your last days. Alone, no less. If I'm doing that, this place means something to me. I've been here before. Spent significant, meaningful time here."

Dominic's eyes danced. "Maybe she honeymooned in room five as a young bride."

"Maybe she worked here before LuAnn bought it, when it was a boardinghouse," I offered. "Nick told me the coroner put her at around ninety years old."

"Wow," Dominic said. "That's a good run, right there."

I chuckled. "That's exactly what he said."

He smiled at me. "I think you're onto something," he said. "It just feels right, in my bones. But you know that doesn't put us any closer to finding out who this lady was."

"I know," I said, a little deflated. "Sure, LuAnn must have guest registers, but names aren't going to mean anything to us. And there are probably photos somewhere, but since LuAnn didn't recognize her, that means if the woman was here before—and I believe in my gut she was—she was here as a much younger woman. Maybe she was an employee. Maybe, I don't know, her parents owned it a century ago, and she was born here, in room five. Maybe she was a guest. But I don't think we'll ever know."

Dominic looked off, as if gathering his thoughts. "I don't see any way to find out for sure, unless someone comes forward."

I sighed. "I guess that's the end of it," I said.

"Unless you meet her in the in-between time again," Dominic said, a grin on his lips.

"Nick Stone said if I dream about her again, I should ask her who she is."

"Not a bad idea," he said.

We talked of different things then, but my mind kept drifting back to our lady. I realized that I felt okay about the mystery involving her identity and the reasons she had come here remaining just that. A mystery.

If everything I had supposed was true, if she had come back to Wharton, to LuAnn's, to die because this was a special place to her, her death seemed much less cold and lonely. Less stark. It was her choice. What she wanted. Where she wanted. And for the time being, that was enough for me.

We watched the rest of the movie and discussed going to dinner, but I was exhausted by the day's events.

"I should probably go back to my room," I said, not really meaning it.

He rolled over on his side and smiled at me. "Why in the world would you want to do that?"

I shrugged, my face reddening. "I didn't want to assume anything."

"If you want to be alone—"

"I don't," I jumped in, too quickly. "I mean," I fumbled, "I didn't mean—"

He reached over and stroked my cheek. "I know exactly what you mean. You've had a rough couple of nights. And today, too. Otherworldly shit is going on up in here. Alice spouting off about weird stuff. Gary seeing ghosts around every corner. And you're upset about the lady, too. It's a lot."

He was right. The truth was, the idea of sleeping alone had my stomach in knots. "Would you mind if I stayed?"

Dominic let out a laugh, that sense of joy returning to his handsome face. "Mind? Let me see. A beautiful woman wants to lie next to me in my bed. What to do? What to do?"

He kissed me then, gently and sweetly. I closed my eyes and let the aroma of him, a hint of cologne mixed with his own musky scent, wash over me. All at once, the mystery of the lady in room five faded. It didn't seem as important as what was happening here in Dominic's room, in the present. I looked up at his impossibly handsome face.

"You know I'm falling for you, right?" I asked him, my voice almost a whisper.

He smiled. "It's about time," he said, stroking my hair.

In the middle of the night, we were awakened by a loud banging on the door.

"Dominic!" A man's voice. More pounding. "Dominic! Wake up!"

Dominic gave me a concerned look and slipped out of bed in just his boxer briefs and a T-shirt to open the door. It was Jason.

"I'm sorry to wake you at this hour," Jason said, running a hand through his thick white hair.

"What is it?" Dominic asked.

"It's Alice."

At this, I climbed out of bed and joined them at the door. "What's happened?" I asked, a sense of panic rising inside of me, turning my stomach into knots.

"She's gone," Jason said. "I just woke up and checked on her. She's not in her bed. Gil is checking the house, but I have a very bad feeling."

"How long ago was this?" Dominic asked, pulling on his jeans.

"Just now. Moments ago."

"I'm going across the hall to get dressed," I said, hurrying to my room and jumping into my jeans and a long-sleeved shirt. I pulled on my anorak and stepped into my shoes, closing the door behind me. In and out in under thirty seconds.

The three of us raced down the stairs through the darkened restaurant, where Gil was waiting.

"Nothing?" Jason asked him.

Gil shook his head. "I've checked the house from top to bottom. She's not here."

Time stopped as we all stood there, paralyzed for an instant by the realization that washed over us.

Without a word, we all made our way out the front door, into the darkness. We stood there for a moment, not knowing whether to go up the street into town or down toward the water.

As if understanding the question before it was asked, Dominic said, "Jason, Brynn, and I will head down toward the lake. I have a feeling that's the direction she went. But just to be sure, Gil, check around the house and the neighborhood. She can't have gotten far."

Dominic took a step or two and turned back to Gil. "Did you bring your cell phone?"

Gil pulled it out of his pocket.

"Call the police," Dominic said.

As we hurried down to the lake, I saw that the town was deserted, everyone settled in their beds for the night, the shops and restaurants buttoned up tight, illuminated with the yellowish glow of the streetlights. The two ferries bobbed at the dock, their runs across to the island long since done for the day. The cabin cruisers at the town slips were dark as well.

Fog had settled in, hanging low in the air, covering everything with a swaying, living blanket of white.

"I blame myself," Jason said, looking up and down the side streets as we ran. "I know she wanders! I should have put an alarm on the front door or . . . something. This is all on me."

"Nonsense," I said. "Let's just concentrate on finding her."

Dominic trotted ahead of us and then broke into a full-on run. Jason and I exchanged a glance and followed. Dominic was headed toward the lakeside park just down the shore from the pier. Families gathered there for picnics, concerts, and to sit on a blanket and enjoy the lake on a sunny afternoon. There wasn't a beach, only a rocky shoreline with a steep drop-off a few feet away from land.

We scanned the shore, looking for Alice.

And then we saw what Dominic had seen before us.

CHAPTER TWENTY-NINE

Alice was wading into the lake, her nightgown billowing around her as she walked deeper and deeper into the water. With the fog hanging in the air around her and the streetlamps casting an eerie glow, Alice's hair loose and flowing, she looked for all the world like the Lady of the Lake descending into the mists of Avalon.

Jason and I stood there, at the water's edge, frozen for a moment by the terror of what we were seeing. Dominic was already in the lake.

"Honey!" Jason called. "Dominic is coming! Stay where you are!"

"Alice!" I tried.

But it was like she was in a trance. She didn't turn around, didn't seem to hear us. And then she disappeared, seemingly swallowed up by the lake, not even a ripple remaining on the surface where she had been.

"No!" Jason cried, lunging toward the water, but I held him back.

"He'll get her," I said. "We don't need you in the lake, too." Jason wrapped his arms around my waist and we watched for a terrible, long moment as Dominic dove under, surfaced, looked around wildly, and dove again into the dark lake, and again, finally emerging with Alice in his arms.

The red and blue lights of a police cruiser slashed through the fog, its siren growing louder as it approached.

Dominic waded back onto the shore, both of them dripping wet, Alice's head resting on Dominic's chest, her bony hands clutching his arm. She was visibly shaking. Her eyes darted back and forth as if she was frantically searching for something elusive.

"Alice, honey, are you okay?" Jason asked, his voice thin and papery.

She coughed and shivered in Dominic's arms. "Where am I?"

"You had a bad night. That's all, Alice," Dominic said as we hurried up the street toward the house. "But we've got you now."

He caught my eye. "She's ice cold," he said.

"I'll run ahead and draw a bath," Jason said, sprinting off, disappearing into the fog.

I put up my hand, waving down the squad car. It stopped, and one of the officers jumped out and opened the back door. Dominic slid onto the seat, still holding Alice in his arms. I ran around and hopped in on the other side.

"LuAnn's," Dominic said to them, and we sped off up the street.

"What happened?" one of the officers asked.

Dominic and I exchanged a glance. "She got confused and wandered off," I said.

"Does she need the hospital?" the officer asked.

"She was only underwater for a moment, but maybe as a precaution?" Dominic started.

"It's twenty minutes away," the officer said.

"She's freezing cold," I said. "She needs to get into a hot bath, not sit shivering in the car for twenty minutes."

"Agreed," Dominic said. "We'll watch her tonight."

"We'll get an ambulance if you need it."

It seemed to take forever to get back to LuAnn's.

Finally, we arrived. Dominic was out of the car with Alice in a flash and took the stairs two at a time. The upper hallway was dark, but Gil and Jason's door was open, light shining from it all the way down the hall. Gil was fretting in the living room, but Dominic carried Alice past him, directly into the bathroom, where I heard water running.

"What happened?" Gil said to me in a harsh whisper. "Jason can barely—"

"Let's get you out of that wet nightgown, honey," I heard Jason saying.

"She was in the lake," I told Gil. "Dominic went in after her."

His hands flew to his mouth. "Oh my God."

"I know. It was unreal."

Dominic emerged from the bath, where I could hear Jason talking to Alice in hushed, gentle tones. "There, now. Doesn't that feel better? I added your favorite bath soak."

Tension hung in the room like the thick layer of fog outside. Nobody knew quite what to say. So many questions swirled around us, questions nobody wanted to give life or credence to by uttering them. But we were all thinking the same thing. Was taking care of Alice a good idea? Was her safety at risk, not being in a care facility? The look on Gil's face told me he was grappling with those same questions.

Finally, I broke the silence. "You should get out of your wet clothes, too," I said to Dominic.

He nodded and turned to Gil. "I'll be right back."

A few moments later, Dominic gave the door a soft rap and came in, wearing dry sweatpants and a T-shirt, his feet in slippers.

Gil's eyes were filled with tears. "Thank you," he said, looking from one of us to the other. "I know that doesn't quite cut it."

Dominic put a hand on Gil's shoulder, pulling him into a hug. Gil dissolved into tears of relief as Dominic rubbed his back.

"It's okay, man," he said. "She's going to be just fine."

"Jason would've never forgiven himself," Gil whispered.

He pulled away from Dominic and made his way across the room to the kitchen and held up a bottle of Highland Scotch. "Anybody else need a drink?"

"Hell yes," Dominic said, chuckling a little.

Gil poured three glasses of the amber liquid, dropped a single ice cube into each one, and handed them to us in turn.

I took a sip, tasting peat and salt air as it slipped down my throat, warming me from the inside.

"I just don't . . ." Gil started, but he let his words hang there, unwilling to finish what we both knew he was thinking. He ran a hand through his hair, downed the rest of his Scotch, and poured another.

"Why don't you flip on the fireplace?" I asked. "We'll wait with you until Jason gets Alice out of the bath and into bed."

Gil sighed. "Sounds like a plan," he said. He walked over and turned on the fireplace, the gas igniting immediately and filling the room with a warm glow.

He sank into an armchair as Dominic and I took our places on the couch. None of us said anything as we watched the flickering flames. What was there to say?

I glanced at the clock. It was nearly three thirty in the morning. Gil rested his head on the back of his chair and closed his eyes, holding the ice-cooled glass to his forehead, as though it was pounding and needed relief. I could relate. As adrenaline charged as I had been just moments before, a profound fatigue had set in, and with it, a slight headache. I yawned, wishing Dominic and I could go back into bed and lie in each other's arms until morning.

But that was not to be.

"Gil!" It was Jason, calling from the bathroom.

Gil's eyes shot open. "Yes? What do you need?"

"Would you get a fresh nightgown for Alice? She's ready to come out of the tub and go to bed."

Gil closed his eyes again. "Sure, honey," he called out, the exhaustion seeping from every pore.

I reached over and put a hand on his arm. "I'll do it. Where are her nightgowns?"

He smiled at me. "You are such a dear. Bottom drawer of her dresser. The second room when you get upstairs. There should be a new pair of slippers, too."

I pushed myself up and made my way up the wide wooden staircase and down the hall to Alice's room.

I flipped on the light to see the furniture had the same Northwoods feel as the rest of the decor in the suite. A queen bed with a patchwork quilt, its headboard made of polished logs. A nightstand and dresser in the same style with black wrought-iron pulls in the shape of moose, bears, and otters. Wrought-iron lamps with shades that looked like birch bark. A woven round rug beside the bed, and a fireplace on the opposite wall.

Pictures of Alice, Jason, and their family sat in frames everywhere. I noticed one of Jason, Alice, and Gil, taken here at LuAnn's. Nice, I thought, to include Gil in Alice's family memories.

I slid open the bottom dresser drawer and found several flannel nightgowns, neatly folded, with a linen sachet cradled atop them. As Gil said, a new pair of slippers sat to the side.

I grabbed the slippers and the nightgown on top of the stack, intending to hurry back downstairs, but something I saw in the drawer stopped me.

Papers. Cream-colored sheets of paper—a child's coloring paper?— folded in half. I probably shouldn't have looked at them, but something about the sight of these papers, hidden in Alice's nightgowns, gave me a dull ache in the pit of my stomach and a chill that ran through my veins.

I set down the robe and slippers and picked up the papers gingerly, as though they were about to burst into flames, and opened them. I had to stop myself from gasping aloud.

On the first sheet was a drawing. It was Alice, in her nightgown, standing in the lake. The sky was dark, and the streetlights gave off a yellowish hue, shining down on her like a spotlight. She was smiling an awful smile, her eyes wild. The lake reflected her image, and there, in the water, another figure was floating just under the surface. But I couldn't make out quite what it was. A human? I wasn't sure. In the distance, three figures stood on the street.

This was Wharton. That was Alice wading into the lake. And the three figures were Jason, Dominic, and me.

CHAPTER THIRTY

I set the paper aside with shaking hands to reveal the second sheet. It was a drawing of Dominic, with Alice in his arms, wading out of the water toward shore.

A shaft of that same yellow light shone down on them, but in this drawing, the light was filled with faces. Some smiling, some menacing. But faces, looking down on them from above.

I folded both sheets back into each other and slipped them into my pocket as I gathered up the nightgown and slippers, grabbing Alice's robe that was hung on a hook on the back of the door as I hurried out of the room and down the stairs.

I rapped on the bathroom door. Jason opened it a crack.

I handed him the nightgown, robe, and slippers. "Thank you," he said, with both words and eyes.

I pulled the door shut and turned to Dominic and Gil, unsure whether or not to share what I had just found. I hesitated for a moment, but remembered my conversation with Gil earlier, of Alice developing what seemed to be psychic abilities. What happened tonight—Alice ending up in the water—wasn't really even about that, though. It was about Alice, and her safety. And these drawings entered into it, somehow.

I slipped the pages out of my pocket, eyeing the bathroom door, hoping Jason wouldn't emerge just then.

"I found something you two need to see," I said, unfolding the sheets.

They studied one, then the other, and then both turned their eyes to me.

"Where did you find this?" Gil asked, his voice a harsh whisper.

"In her nightgown drawer."

Gil held my gaze. "We've been encouraging her to do artwork," he said. "We've been tapping into some resources, people dealing with Alzheimer's, support groups, that kind of thing, and some families told us that artwork would be soothing. You know how nervous she gets."

I nodded. "Of course," I said. "It sounds like a perfect idea."

"She often says that, yes," Gil said. "But this—"

Just then, the bathroom door opened. I quickly folded up the sheets and slipped them back into my pocket. Gil nodded, as if he knew. Jason didn't need to see these drawings, not right now.

Jason was leading Alice, dressed in her nightgown, robe, and slippers, out of the bathroom.

"Okay, honey, let's get you back into bed," he said to her, smiling at us. His eyes radiated exhaustion. "It's just a few steps up, now."

"Just a few steps," Alice said, not seeming to register that anyone else was there.

We watched as they made it up to the second-floor landing. Then Alice snapped her head around and faced us.

"It wasn't my time," she said. "It might be coming soon. I think it's coming soon. But not today."

Dominic pushed himself to his feet. "Good night, fair lady," he called up to her. "Sleep well. We'll see you tomorrow."

"Good night, my savior knight," she called down to him. "Not today, right? I'll wake up tomorrow?"

Dominic smiled broadly, though I could not fathom how he managed it. My own throat was tight and filled with sadness.

"I'll be your date for breakfast," Dominic said to her.

Jason led her away then, to her room. After a few minutes, he opened the door and stole out, closing it gently behind him, like the parent of a fussy infant who had just fallen asleep. He padded down the stairs.

Gil met him on the landing with a glass of Scotch. They hugged for a long minute as I watched Jason's shoulders heave. He took a deep breath and pulled back, turning to Dominic and me.

"I don't know how to thank you," he said.

Dominic put up his hand. "It takes a village, man. What you're doing, it's not an easy road, and you have chosen to go down that road, despite the hardships that are in your path."

Jason stifled a sob as Gil led him to the couch.

"I don't know what to do now," Jason said after he settled into the cushions. "How can we be sure she won't wander again when we're sleeping? Lock her door from the outside? What if there's a fire?"

Dominic shook his head. "It's simpler than that, man," he said. "A locked baby gate on the top of the stairs. One with an alarm on it."

Jason narrowed his eyes at Dominic and turned to Gil. "That's not a bad idea."

"Bad?" Dominic chuckled. "It's such an easy fix to this problem. It will prevent her from getting down the stairs. And the alarm will alert you when she's trying to open it. We can order one tomorrow and get it delivered within a day or so."

Gil and Jason exchanged a glance. "Will LuAnn allow it?" Jason asked.

"I can't imagine she'd have any objections," Dominic said.

"What about tonight?" Jason asked. "I suppose I could sleep in front of the door . . ."

Dominic shook his head. "Nonsense. You two go to bed and get some sleep. You need it. I'm wide awake. I'll take the night shift. I'll stay here on the couch and make sure Alice doesn't take any more walks tonight."

"We couldn't possibly ask you to do that," Jason said.

"You're not asking. I'm offering. And you're exhausted. You'll be no good to Alice tomorrow if you're up for the rest of the night."

Gil caught Jason's eye. "He's right, you know."

"We'll install that alarmed baby gate tomorrow," Dominic said. "Maybe some cameras, too."

Jason looked at both of us. "Thank you," he said, as if at a loss for any other words. Then he turned to Dominic. "Make yourself at home."

Gil led Jason upstairs. Soon they were closing their own bedroom door. I could feel the palpable relief in the air.

I turned to Dominic. "I'll stay with you," I said.

But he shook his head. "Get some rest," he said. "I'll just be on watch duty here, and you'll fall asleep on my shoulder anyway and wake up with a stiff neck. And then complain all day about it."

I smiled. He was right.

"Okay," I said. "I'll go back to my room."

He pulled me into his arms and kissed me, taking a fistful of my hair into one hand. I wanted nothing more than to curl into bed with him and hold on to him until morning.

CHAPTER THIRTY-ONE

I stepped into the dark hallway and closed the door behind me. I heard Dominic lock the dead bolt and close the latch. All at once, it seemed like a very long journey down the entire length of the hall to my room. I nearly turned around to ask Dominic to walk with me, but then I thought better of it. He had more important things to attend to.

When I saw that the alcove leading to room five was dark, I let out a breath I hadn't realized I was holding. *Okay*, I thought to myself, *you can do this.*

It's just a hallway.

But as I took a few steps, it felt . . . alive somehow. The air around me was pulsing. A shock of cold air washed over my face and was gone in an instant. But then I felt it wrapping around me like a coil. All at once, I was freezing.

And then, the voices began. I couldn't make out any words, just the muffled sounds of people talking. As if they were in another room.

"Or another time," I heard a woman's voice say.

Just then, a light went on in one of the guest rooms, and its door opened. A man, his hair disheveled, his striped pajamas rumpled, stepped out into the hall. He visibly jumped when he saw me.

"Oh!" he said, chuckling. "You scared me. I didn't think I'd run into anyone at this hour." He smoothed down his hair as he looked up and down the hall. "Bathroom?"

"Second door on the right." I pointed to it.

"Thanks," he said, and scooted across to the bathroom. He flipped on the light and closed the door behind him.

And just like that, the spell was broken. It was a normal hallway.

I hurried the rest of the way to my room, making sure to lock and latch the door once I was inside. I hadn't known we had any short-term guests, but of course, that was what this place was. A hotel and boardinghouse. LuAnn didn't have to announce it to us when she rented a room for the night.

I hadn't been in the habit of locking my door when it was just Jason, Gil, Alice, Dominic, and me. But now . . . I realized for the first time that strangers would be coming and going, a night here, a night there. We had no idea who they were. My room had been unlocked. One of them could've been in there, rifling through my things.

I turned on my overhead light and scanned the room, poking my head into the bathroom and closet. I peered under the bed. Nobody there.

My phone was still plugged into the charger. My laptop was sitting on the table by the window, my purse next to it. I crossed the room and opened my purse, fishing out my wallet. All of my credit and debit cards were in their slots. What little cash I had on hand was still folded in its place.

I reached into the bottom of my purse and found the small black box I had been carrying with me, but hadn't had the strength to open since my mom's funeral. It was still there. I exhaled.

I opened the box.

It held a delicate gold chain with a pendant that read "SISU." It's a Finnish word that doesn't have a complete translation in English. It represents the zeitgeist of the Finnish people—strength, determination, bravery, courage, fortitude, perseverance. If you have *sisu*, it means you will not just handle but triumph over anything life throws at you.

It described my mother perfectly. She was 100 percent Finn—both of her parents were children of Finnish immigrants. When she got her stage four cancer diagnosis, she had two of those necklaces made. Gold for her. Silver for me. She knew the road ahead would be very rocky and difficult for both of us—her fighting cancer, me watching her go through it—and wanted us to remember who we were, deep inside. It was not going to be pretty; it was not going to be easy, but we could handle it, come what may.

She never took that necklace off until the day she died. I was sitting at her bedside, and she reached behind her neck, with great difficulty, unclasped it, and held it out to me, along with her wedding ring.

"These should go to you," she whispered, her voice in tatters.

I took them from her and closed my hand around them, knowing they would be a tangible connection to her that I'd have after she was gone. I nodded at her, unable to say a word. My own voice was choked into silence by the tears that were brimming in my eyes.

"This is going to be so hard for you."

"Sisu," I squeaked out.

She managed a smile and nodded. It seemed to comfort her.

Later that day, I threaded her wedding ring onto the chain. I clasped it around my own neck and wore it as we dealt with funeral arrangements. I wore it as I delivered my mother's eulogy. I wore it at the wake as I circulated around, thanking everyone for coming, accepting their condolences. And that night, I took it off and put it away and hadn't looked at it since. It was too painful a reminder.

But, as I stood in my pretty yellow room at LuAnn's, it felt like the right time to put it on again.

I plucked Alice's drawings out of my pocket, smoothed them open, and set them on the table by my computer and purse. I took another look and shuddered at the images, especially the one of Dominic carrying her, with all the faces in the shaft of light.

I crossed the room and shut off the light, peeled off my clothes, slipped into a big T-shirt, and curled under the covers of my bed. But I knew sleep wouldn't come rapidly. Too many thoughts were swirling through my mind.

What sort of otherworldly sight had taken hold of Alice? It was as though, as her brain deteriorated because of the onward death march of this horrible disease, some other part of her mind had awakened. Was it true what Dominic said? That the veil between this world and the next was gossamer thin for Alice? It made a strange kind of sense, but how would that allow her to see what she was seeing? To know what she was knowing?

I wasn't going to get any answers. There simply weren't answers to questions like these. No definitive, real-world answers at least. Just like the identity of the woman who had passed away in room five, maybe the mystery of Alice's sight was going to remain just that. A mystery. A great unknowing.

My eyes felt heavy, and I yawned, curling deeper under the covers. I smiled when I thought, *I'm slipping into the in-between time.*

And then I heard the singing. Soft and low, almost a whisper. It was my mother's voice.

I snuggled down, deeply comforted by the song my mother used to sing to me when I was a child, at night when she tucked me in.

I felt her hand stroking my hair as she used to do. I could smell her perfume.

I floated there, not yet sleeping, not quite awake, drifting off to the sound of my mother's singing as I had when I was a child. Utter and complete peace washed over me as sleep fell.

An image appeared in my mind, hazy and distant at first, but then it swam into focus. I was back in the hallway as the man who was looking for the bathroom opened his door. Had he come out of Dominic's room? No, that couldn't be. It had to have been the empty room next to his. Yes, I thought, as I was watching the scene play out, it was definitely the room next to Dominic's.

Something felt off. Wrong, somehow. My flesh crawled. But why?

I talked to the man and pointed to the bathroom, and all at once, bright light began pouring from under the doors of all the rooms, including mine, illuminating the hallway with an eerie glow.

That was when I saw that it didn't look like the hallway, not exactly. There was a runner on the floor. It was blue with tiny red flowers. Had that been there before and I just hadn't noticed it? No, I was sure the floor was bare, just wide-planked wood. And I saw wallpaper on the walls. White, with thin blue pinstripes. I was sure the walls had been painted off-white.

Gas lamps, which were lining both walls, flickered on, one by one. I watched as their flames danced. I could smell the oil.

An old mirror hung on the wall opposite Dominic's room, its pane weathered with age. I caught a glimpse of myself and realized I had on a dark-blue dress, not the jacket and jeans I had been wearing.

I stood there, staring at my own reflection, when Dominic appeared behind me. He smiled at me in the mirror before wrapping his arms around my waist. I leaned back into him and watched in the mirror as he began kissing my neck.

"This is just a dream, Brynn," he whispered, his deep voice husky and rough. "I've found my world in you. Let's go back. Just for fun."

All at once, I was in a club. A bar. Hazy smoke swirled through the air; men in suits enjoyed their cocktails. I was dressed like a flapper. A man walked toward me, smiling. Dominic. He took me into his arms. I melted into them. I realized it was the same man I had imagined when Dominic and I were sitting in my room on that rainy morning.

He led me onto the dance floor. We whirled and danced and laughed until a commotion broke the reverie. A raid! People were rushing here and there, police rounding them up. I watched Dominic wink at one of the cops as he grabbed my hand and led me through a door in the back of the room. We hurried down the back stairs and into the alley, laughing all the way.

"That was close!" I said.

He shook his head. "You're always safe with me."

But then, it all vanished. I was standing alone in the hallway. What was I doing there? Had I been sleepwalking? It was dark now, except for the moonlight shining from the window at the end of the hall. No light pouring from under the doors of the rooms. No wallpaper. The walls were painted off-white, just as they had been. No gas lamps. No mirror. No runner on the wide-planked wood floor.

I hurried back down to my room and turned on the light as I closed the door behind me. Checked in the closet and bathroom. Under the bed. Looked at my purse and computer. Checked my wallet. Took the small box out of the bottom of my purse and clasped the chain around my neck. All was quiet. I was safe.

I laid my head on the pillow and curled down under the covers.

But soon my eyes shot open, and I sat up in bed, switching on the lamp that sat on my bedside table. I took a long gulp from my water glass. I was shaking, deep in my core. That same feeling I had in my dream, my flesh crawling, still had ahold of me.

I glanced at the clock. Five thirty. Two hours had passed.

I set the glass back on my nightstand, switched off the light, curled back down, and closed my eyes, but I knew there would be no more sleep that night.

What had really happened, and what was the dream? I lay there sorting it out, retracing my steps in my mind. I had come out of Gil and Jason's suite, heard some voices, encountered the man, pointed to the bathroom, and hurried back to my suite.

My eyes shot open when it hit me: there were no bathrooms in the hallway.

CHAPTER THIRTY-TWO

I don't know how I fell asleep after that, but I must have, because I found myself opening my eyes to a bright, blue day. It was nearly nine thirty. I grabbed my towel, pulled on my robe, and padded down the hall. I needed a hot shower to wash the night away.

I passed by Dominic's room and wanted to knock but thought better of it. He'd had a long night, first rescuing Alice and then staying awake while Gil and Jason got some sleep, and I was sure he was sacked out. I wondered how everyone else was doing after last night.

I stood under the shower stream for a long time, probably too long per LuAnn's instructions to get in and get out, letting the hot water bring me back to myself. In my room, I dried my hair, scowling at it in the mirror, noting I was due for a root touch-up. Then I pulled on jeans and a T-shirt and headed downstairs. I needed some coffee and one of Gary's decadent breakfasts. I couldn't remember the last time I had eaten anything.

People were still lingering at a few of the tables, so I slipped onto a barstool. Gary appeared out of the kitchen.

"Morning, doll!" He grinned at me as he turned over the mug in front of me and poured steaming coffee into it. "What else can I getcha?"

"That same breakfast you made for me before," I said, splashing some cream into my mug and taking a sip. "The one with the hash browns and cheese."

"That'll cure what ails you. Coming right up!"

A short while later, he was back, carrying the slice of heaven that was his egg, hash browns, veggies, and cheese concoction. He set the steaming plate in front of me.

"I heard about what happened last night," he said, leaning on the counter. "Alice."

I nodded as I took my first bite. It seemed so long ago and far away, but it had happened only hours before.

"It was pretty scary."

"Word is Dominic went into the water and saved her," Gary went on, pouring himself a cup of coffee. "Like some kind of superhero."

"He did," I said. "Jason is getting an alarmed baby gate so she won't wander out of the suite again in the middle of the night."

"Never a dull moment around here," Gary said. "I hope the lady isn't too shaken up."

I took another bite and considered whether I should tell Gary about what happened in the hallway. I decided he was the one person I wanted to tell.

"I think I saw a ghost last night," I said finally. I eyed him over the rim of my coffee mug. "At least, it might have been. I'm not sure."

"The lady in room five again?"

"No," I said. "I was going back to my room after we had gotten Alice cleaned up and into bed. I saw a man in the hallway—"

"What man?" It was LuAnn, rounding the corner. She was wearing purple leggings and a black tunic, her hair tied back with a purple and black scarf. "Sorry to eavesdrop, but I heard you say you saw a man upstairs last night?"

Gary and I exchanged a glance. "I saw someone, yes."

LuAnn slid onto the stool next to mine. "What time was it?"

"Around three thirty," I said.

LuAnn shook her head. "Honey, are you sure you weren't dreaming?"

"A distinct possibility when it comes to me, but this time, no. I had just left Jason and Gil's suite and was going back to my room."

"Well, if there was a man, he shouldn't have been in the house," she said, a look of concern washing over her face. "We don't have any renters this week."

A chill ran through me. There it was, then.

"I think it might have been a ghost," I said, wincing. "He came out of one of the rooms and asked me where the bathroom was."

LuAnn let out a hoot of laughter. "There's no bathroom off the hallway upstairs," she said. "There were three of them, but not anymore. I had them turned into the shower and tub rooms when I bought the place eons ago."

"I realized that last night after I got back to my room," I said. "It gave me chills, actually."

LuAnn and Gary chuckled.

I narrowed my eyes at them and shook my head. "I can't get over you two," I said. "You take these encounters with ghosts, or whatever they are, in stride. They don't faze you in the least. You're so matter-of-fact about it."

LuAnn waved her hand. "Aw, once it happens a few times, you start to realize that most of them don't mean any harm."

"Most of them?"

LuAnn brushed some unseen lint off her shoulder. "Over the years we've had a few less-than-pleasant spirits we've had to run out of here," she said. "But for the most part, they're harmless."

"Even the lady in room five?" I wanted to know.

LuAnn narrowed her eyes and considered this. "It seems to me she's got a connection to you."

"Me? Why?"

"Honey, you're the one who keeps seeing her. She's reaching out to you. It could be as simple as the woman died in room five and her spirit is still floating around. You're the one who's here right now that she can connect to. That happens sometimes."

"A random connection?"

"Sort of. It's like you're at a party filled with people you don't know. You see one friendly face across the room and that's who you go talk to."

I nodded. I guess I could see that.

LuAnn wagged a finger at me. "But it also could be she wants to tell you something. Or ask you to do something for her. That happens, too."

My stomach knotted up at the thought of it. I remembered she handed me the book, *The Illustrated Man*, and got the feeling LuAnn was right. It was no random connection.

"How will I know what she wants?" I asked.

LuAnn chuckled at this. "For heaven's sake, honey! Next time you see her, just ask!"

Gary chuckled, too. "You're officially one of us now, Brynn," he said. "You had an encounter with a passer-through."

I narrowed my eyes at him. "A passer-through?"

Gary took another sip of his coffee as LuAnn got up and poured herself a cup. "Like I told you a few days ago, they pass through here. People who have been here before. Boarders. People who have worked here. The place draws people back somehow. Some way."

LuAnn chortled, wrapping an arm around his waist. "Gary, you and I are going to be haunting this house when our time comes, you know that, right?"

He kissed her cheek. "No place else I'd rather be."

I took in the image of the two of them for a moment, and all at once, it dawned on me. They were together. A couple. I had been so caught up in my dramas, I hadn't noticed it before.

I sat there, smiling at them.

LuAnn narrowed her eyes at me. "What?"

"Are you two a couple?"

"Twelve wonderful years with this galoot," LuAnn said, beaming at him. "He came to work for me a few years after his wife died. My husband had passed the year before."

"It took her a while to catch on to my devastating charms," he said, grinning. "Only about fifteen years. I was beginning to think she didn't have eyes to see with." He laughed his gravelly laugh.

She slapped his arm. "It was the best day of your life when I said yes."

A look of gravity came over Gary's face then. His eyes filled with admiration when he gazed at LuAnn, then back to me.

"We kid around a lot," he said. "That's the fun of it. But there's another side, too."

LuAnn nodded, knowing what he was going to say.

"Both Lu and I were married before. Me for thirty-four years, her for—what, honey?"

"Twenty-nine," she said, gazing off into the past. "Two months shy of thirty."

"You're damn lucky if you can find love once in this lifetime," Gary went on. "We found it twice."

"That's right," LuAnn said. "That's exactly right. I thought I'd never marry again. Never find anyone. That I'd grow old alone. And then this old coot came along and stole my heart."

"Not many people can say they've had two great loves in their lives," Gary said. "We both know how rare it is. How lucky we are."

I took another sip of my coffee and smiled at them, even as tears were stinging the backs of my eyes. LuAnn and Gary had found love the second time around, and a happy, playful love at that. I thought of my parents, the great loves of each other's lives for sixty-three years. Kate and Nick. Simon and Jonathan. Jason and Gil. All of them had the kind of love that had eluded me.

I had reached this stage of life without finding it. It made me wonder what I was doing wrong. If *I* was wrong somehow.

Yes, Dominic and I were in the throes of a blossoming romance, there was no doubt about it. But was he my true love? I had no idea. It was too new for me to be thinking in those terms. There was still plenty of time for it to fall apart.

As if sensing what was going through my mind, LuAnn reached over and took my hand. "Love comes along when you least expect it, but when you need it most," she said. "Sometimes, if you're lucky, the right people come into your life at just the right time. People ask me if I believe in destiny. Hell no, I used to say. But now? I'm not so sure."

"Destiny?" I asked.

"Gary toddled into my life when I was grieving the loss of my husband. I thought I was going to lose this place, too. I didn't think I could run it alone."

"You certainly could have," Gary broke in.

She shook her head. "Not then, I couldn't. And here he came. He stepped in, ran the kitchen and did the maintenance and everything else. Helped me remodel. At first, I was just grateful for his friendship, companionship, and partnership."

"Then she finally opened her eyes," Gary said, laughing. "But the lady has a point about the right person at the right time. When I walked into LuAnn's, I had lost my wife a few years prior. Then I was the one who got lost."

I leaned my elbow on the counter, resting my chin in my palm. "How so?"

Gary poured himself another shot of coffee. "I had been a career Coast Guard man," he said.

"A sea dog," LuAnn piped up, chuckling.

"Inland seas, if you please. I served on the Great Lakes. Superior, mostly."

"Wow," I said. "I'll bet you saw your share of adventure when the gales of November hit every year."

Gary shook his head and whistled, long and low. "I could tell you stories. Anyway, I had been retired for a few years before my wife passed. Cancer."

The very sound of the word burned my ears.

"I had been taking care of her during her last years," he said.

Tears pricked at the backs of my eyes, and I involuntarily fingered the chain around my neck. "Oh, Gary. I know how hard that is."

He waved his hand. "It was hard, but it was a privilege."

I knew exactly what he meant. I hoped I could come to that realization myself one day, after the grief had lessened.

"But when she was gone, I had no idea what to do with myself," he said. "I watched a lot of meaningless television. Found myself at the bottom of a whiskey bottle more times than I care to admit. Stopped reaching out to friends. I was never a churchgoer, so I found no comfort there. I was an old, retired seaman who was rudderless. Can you imagine that? Some days, I didn't care if I lived or died. I was just beginning to think dying would be a blessing. Then I came to Wharton, walked by LuAnn's, and saw her 'Help Wanted' sign in the window."

"And the rest is history." LuAnn smiled at him.

"I found purpose in life again," he said. "LuAnn needed help, and so did I. All of a sudden, I had a reason to get up in the morning. So, I might have come along just when she needed me, but she came along just when I needed her."

"Two people, walking through life, gasping for air, slowly dying because we desperately needed what the other could provide," LuAnn said. "And somehow, we found our way to each other."

"How wild is that?" Gary piped up. "What are the chances?"

"That's why I believe there are forces at work out there," LuAnn said, raising her eyebrows. "Strange and mystical forces. I didn't do anything to bring Gary to me but put out a 'Help Wanted' sign. He didn't do anything to find me but walk by my place on a weekend trip to Wharton. So random, all of it. And yet, those small, random acts led us to the next chapter for both of us."

"Destiny brought me here to meet you," Gary said.

"Well, let's thank destiny, then," LuAnn said, kissing his cheek.

I sipped my coffee, wondering if, like Gary, destiny—or something else—had a hand in bringing me to Wharton.

CHAPTER THIRTY-THREE

After breakfast, I took the mystery I was reading and sat out on the deck in the sunshine. When I had come back upstairs, I noticed the door to the suite was closed. I wanted to check on Alice—on all of them—but I didn't want to intrude if they were sleeping. I wouldn't blame them if they were sacked out for most of the day.

It was peaceful, reading on my own for a couple of hours. I hadn't had much solo time since I'd arrived—not that I really needed it—and it was nice to be alone with my own thoughts, getting immersed in a mystery that did not involve me being pursued by ghosts, the lady in room five, or even Alice. I was off the clock, and it felt good.

I was in the middle of a chapter when my phone buzzed. I glanced at the time—almost two o'clock already.

"Hey, you!" Kate chirped. "How's your day going?"

"Entirely uneventful," I said, exhaling. "Thank the gods above. I've done nothing all day but eat Gary's famous breakfast and sit on the deck reading."

"After last night, you deserve a day of rest," she said.

This stopped me. "You heard what happened?"

"This is Wharton, and I'm married to the police chief," she said. But then her voice turned serious. "Is Alice okay? Are you?"

"I'm assuming she is," I said. "I would've heard about it if she had taken a turn for the worse. I haven't seen any of them today. I'm sure they're wiped."

"I heard your man was the hero of the night. It's all over town."

I chuckled at this. "Word travels fast. And yes, he was. He dove into the water and got her out of there."

"You can tell me all about it when you come for dinner tonight," Kate said. "Are you free? I know it's really last minute but Simon has been pestering me to invite you."

"Let me check my ever-full social calendar." I laughed. "I'd love to come. What time do you want me there?"

"We have a tradition around here of an early Sunday dinner. More like a linner. Lunch-dinner." She laughed.

"Linner. I love it."

"So, how about four o'clock? We'll have drinks and appetizers to start. Chef is roasting a couple of chickens and we also have a light pasta tonight that will make you weep."

"I'll be there. Can I bring anything?"

"How about the Illustrated Man? His name is on everyone's lips these days, and I'd love to get to know him."

"I'll ask him," I said, but my stomach did a quick flip at the thought of it. She was inviting us as a couple. "We're not dating, you know."

"Oh, stop," she said, laughing. "The whole town knows he somehow managed to catch the eye of the most incredible single woman in Wharton. Lucky man."

What a lovely thing to say. I could feel my face redden, but I was warmed from the inside out.

I hung up with Kate and pushed myself up from the Adirondack chair where I had been sitting. Back inside the house, I knocked softly on Dominic's door. Not too loudly to wake him if he was sleeping, but enough to let him know someone was there if he wasn't. I waited for a moment. No answer. I walked down the hall to Jason and Gil's and rapped softly. No answer there, either.

I made my way back down to the restaurant, where I found Dominic sitting at the counter, a beer bubbling in a tall glass in front of him. He smiled when he saw me.

"There she is," he said, grinning.

"I was just knocking on your door." I slid onto the stool beside him. "How was last night? With Alice, I mean."

He took a sip of his beer. "All was quiet on the Alice front," he said. "It was really peaceful, actually, sitting in front of the fire with everyone else asleep. I had a lot of time to think. Gil woke up about seven o'clock and relieved me."

"Did you get some sleep after that?" I asked.

"I conked out for a few hours," he said, nodding. "I'm good."

"I talked to Kate earlier," I said. "She invited us to Harrison's House for dinner. Do you feel up to it? I can tell them no if you're too tired."

Dominic smiled. "Sounds like fun. I've been wanting to see the inside of that place. Police chief going to be there, too?" He gave me a sidelong glance.

"Don't do anything shifty, and you should be fine," I said, but immediately I wished I could take back the words. I hadn't thought of it before, but it occurred to me that, given Dominic's situation growing up, he likely hadn't had too many positive interactions with the men and women in blue. And Kate had told me her husband had looked into Dominic as a suspect for a suspicious death in the Twin Cities. Maybe this wasn't such a good idea after all. "I didn't mean—"

His grin stopped my words. "I will endeavor to keep anything shifty out of sight," he said. "But you never know. I tend to shift. You'll have to dive in and pull me back if I do."

I grinned at him. "They want us there at four."

The look on his face made me burst into laughter. It was a mixture of revulsion and surprise.

"Four?" he said. "The early-bird special? What are we, senior citizens?"

"There's nothing wrong with senior citizens, mister." It was Gary's voice, coming from the kitchen. "Some of us are pretty hot."

"Some hotter than others," LuAnn's voice piped up.

Dominic and I both dissolved into laughter.

"They like to do an early main meal on Sundays," I said. "Lunch-dinner. Linner."

He grinned. "Linner. First the fish boil and now this. What's next with you Great Lakes people?"

"You could also call it lupper."

Dominic shook his head. "I'll meet you down here at three forty-five," he said, pushing himself up from his stool. "I'm going to take a shower and clean up for the good of humanity at large, but especially for you and our hosts."

"It's a date," I said, smiling up at him.

He stroked my hair and leaned down, kissing me lightly on the cheek. "See you then."

I watched him disappear up the stairs, and LuAnn emerged from the kitchen carrying a martini, her eyebrows raised.

"Well, well, well," she said, grinning at me. "I haven't seen you look so happy since you've been here. What's that we said this morning about people coming into your life at the right place and the right time?"

My face was growing hot, and I knew I was blushing. "We're just getting to know each other," I tried.

LuAnn chortled. "'Just getting to know each other,' my ever-widening behind. From where I sit, it looks like you've known each other forever. Stop fighting it, girl. What's the worst that could happen? You'll have a fun summer fling and then dump him when the next Greek god comes along. But I think it's a lot more than a fling." She stopped and looked into my eyes deeply. "And so do the two of you."

I changed into a black ankle-length cotton T-shirt dress and slid my feet into my go-to black flats. I wound a necklace with blue and silver beads around my neck and chose my favorite earrings, silver with blue glass drops.

I dug my makeup case out of the vanity drawer and tried to work a little magic. Moisturizer, a hint of bronzer, concealer under my eyes, and a dash of cream blush on my cheeks. Eye pencil and mascara.

I grabbed my jean jacket from the closet and slipped it on before taking one last look in the mirror. *Not too bad,* I thought as I scooped up my purse and went out the door, careful to close and lock it behind me.

Dominic was waiting downstairs when I came through the door. He was leaning against the wall wearing jeans and a formfitting black T-shirt under a casual black blazer, black boots on his feet. Diamond studs adorned his earlobes and two heavy gold chains wound around his neck, one a jeweled crucifix, the other an intricately woven chain.

He smiled at me when I came into the room, and it took my breath away.

"Look at you," he said, raising his eyebrows. "Nice."

I blushed. "You clean up nice, too," I managed to say.

As we walked out the door, I looked back over my shoulder and saw LuAnn and Gary standing behind the counter, each with a martini in their hand. They raised their glasses to me with a knowing look.

Outside, Dominic fished his keys out of his pocket. "We could walk up to the house, but . . ."

"Oh, let's drive, absolutely," I said. "I've been sitting on the deck all day and have burned zero calories. Why ruin that streak? If we have a couple of drinks and want to walk home—"

"The police chief will be watching our alcohol intake," Dominic broke in, chuckling.

"Exactly. And it's all downhill from there."

We walked around to the back of the house, hopped into his car, and drove slowly through town. It was just before four o'clock, but the bustle of the day already seemed to be winding down. We passed Just Read It and saw Beth outside, taking in the chalkboard placard that sat on the sidewalk. I rolled down my window and waved.

"Hey, lady!" she called to me. "Stop in tomorrow!"

"I will!" I called back to her.

I turned back to Dominic, and as he drove up the hill, he was smiling from ear to ear.

"What?" I asked him.

"You've been here less time than I have, and yet everyone in town seems to know you," he said. "LuAnn and Gary adore you, to say nothing of Jason and Gil. You've got these friends at Harrison's House, and now Beth at the bookstore."

I shrugged. "I guess so."

"It's because you give off a good vibe," he said. "You make people feel safe around you. Me included. It's a gift, what you have. An openness that invites people into your world."

Did I really do that? It warmed me to think that was what he thought of me.

He pulled into the parking lot at Harrison's House, and only then did I realize the home's grandeur. It was an enormous dark-purple and cream Victorian-style home sitting on the highest hill in town overlooking the harbor. It had a turret on the third floor and a porch that wrapped around the entire front of the house. Baskets filled with colorful flowers hung from the porch's ceiling, and armchairs and sofas were clustered in groups here and there.

A man and a woman I assumed were guests sat on one of the sofas on the far end of the porch, a bottle of wine in an ice bucket on a coffee table in front them. Both were reading books, snuggled into each other. It reminded me of my afternoon on the beach with Dominic.

He caught my eye and smiled, and I knew he was thinking the same.

As Dominic and I walked up the steps to the front door, Kate opened it and came out to greet us, followed by Simon and Jonathan, who were carrying trays of appetizers. Nick came last and stood in the doorway, his arms crossed, leaning against the frame.

"Welcome!" Kate said, enveloping me in a hug. "So glad to see you!"

"You, too," I said, kissing her on the cheek. I turned to my date. "Everyone, this is Dominic."

Kate took a step forward and gave him a quick hug. "So nice to meet you!" she said. "I'm Kate."

"Thank you for including me," Dominic said, turning on that movie-star smile. "I'm not the type of guy who gets invited to grand homes like these," Dominic went on. "I hope I don't use the wrong fork and ruin the evening."

"Nonsense," Kate said, squeezing his arm.

"Darling, you could eat with your hands, and it wouldn't ruin the evening," Simon piped up. "I'm Simon. This is my husband, Jonathan." He pointed to Nick. "And that's Kate's husband, Nick. He tends to glower. Don't mind him."

I smiled at Nick but didn't catch his eye. His eyes were trained on Dominic in a way that made me shudder.

"Who wants drinks?" Nick said. "I'm the designated bartender."

And our linner began.

CHAPTER THIRTY-FOUR

We enjoyed our appetizers—a plate of gourmet cheeses and crackers, figs stuffed with cream cheese, various nuts, prosciutto-wrapped grilled asparagus bites—and drinks on the porch, taking in the spectacular, expansive view of the harbor and town. Sailboats floated lazily between the islands; cabin cruisers bobbed in their slips at the dock. The ferries chugged along toward Ile de Colette, and tourists strolled through town. Flowers lined the paths in the park by the lake. And we were looking down on it all. It truly was the shining house on the hill.

I noticed a group of kayakers set off toward the island, and only then did I realize I hadn't been paddling yet.

"I've got to get out and do some kayaking this week," I said, taking a sip of wine.

Jonathan gave Simon a look and burst out laughing.

I looked from one of them to the other. "What? Something about kayaking?"

Simon rolled his eyes. "I stay away from kayaks. Not my thing."

"When we first moved here, we took lessons," Jonathan said, wiping his eyes. "Let's just say they did not go well."

Kate laughed. "Tell her about the wet suit."

Even Simon was laughing now. "All right, all right," he said, turning to me. "Casey's is the kayak rental business, but they won't rent to you unless you get certified. And to get certified, they take you out and teach you how to kayak, what to do if you flip over, how to deal with the waves, that kind of thing."

"That makes sense," I said.

"It's Lake Superior," Jonathan piped up. "They can't send people out there who don't know what they're doing."

"So, what about the wet suit?"

"You need to wear one if you're kayaking because the lake is so cold," Simon said. "Let's just say mine was a bit . . . snug."

Jonathan snorted.

"Every ounce of baby fat on display for all to see!" Simon wailed. "It was mortifying. I looked like a sausage. Anyway, I got past that, and out we went into the water. The first thing they teach you is how to capsize your kayak and swim out when you're upside down."

I shuddered. I wasn't so sure I wanted to kayak after all.

"I went first," Simon said, taking a sip of his drink. "The capsizing went fine. I unsnapped the skirt from the kayak and swam out of it, no problem. I was thinking: I'm a pro! I'm great at this! I'll bet the teacher has never seen anyone so naturally adept in his first lesson!"

Jonathan put his face in his hands and shook his head. Kate was in tears, and even Nick was laughing.

"Then you need to get back into the kayak. In open water. You have to flop on top of it, on your belly, and somehow maneuver yourself back into that *little hole* so you can sit down. Kayaks are tippy! They are not at all stable. And you're trying to twist around like you're suddenly in Lake Superior Cirque du Soleil."

"Whoever thought this up is a total barbarian," Jonathan added.

"In that wet suit, I was a walrus trying to flop onto an ice floe," Simon said. "And it was my birthday! Total humiliation on my birthday."

"Now we have champagne and play croquet on birthdays instead," Jonathan said.

Dominic was wiping his eyes. My stomach hurt from laughing.

Then Jonathan began to regale us with stories about their recent antiquing trip, and Simon had us in stitches again, complaining about his latest bridezilla.

"Whoever thought it would be a good idea to open up the ballroom for weddings should be impaled with a poison boutonniere," Simon declared.

"That would be you, dear," Jonathan said.

Dominic caught my eye and mouthed, "Ballroom?"

I nodded. "Simon inherited the house from their grandmother, who grew up here," I said to him. Then, turning to Simon, I asked, "Isn't that right?"

"Exactly," Simon said. "I lived here with Grandma Hadley and took care of her for the last years of her life."

Tears threatened although I tried to hold them at bay. They were always ready to make an appearance lately. Dominic must've sensed it because he took a couple of steps toward me from his spot leaning against the porch railing, and put a hand on my shoulder. Nick took notice of this in a way I didn't quite appreciate.

"Brynn knows a little something about how difficult that is," Dominic said to Simon, his voice filled with gentleness and understanding. "You did a good thing, taking care of your grandmother."

"No trouble at all. She was a sweet old girl," Simon said. "Funny, too. Wasn't she, Kate?"

Kate chuckled. "She always cheated at cribbage."

Simon hooted. "I had forgotten that!"

I smiled at them, marveling at the joy that had found its way in to temper their grief at losing such a big part of their lives. I wondered when, or if, I would ever get to that place. Dominic's hand was still on my shoulder. I put my own hand on top of his and looked up at him. I knew he knew exactly what I was thinking. Out of the corner of my eye, I saw Nick watching us. Yet again.

He and Kate exchanged a wary glance. I wondered what that meant.

I broke that silence.

"After your grandma passed, you decided to turn the house into an inn?" I asked.

"Oh, long before that," Simon said. "Gram, Kate, and I had been talking about it for a while."

"I wasn't too involved at that stage just after Grandma died," Kate said. "I was caught up in my own . . . drama."

"Divorce from Hellboy," Simon said in a loud stage whisper, eliciting another rare laugh from Nick.

"I think you mentioned you recently completed the renovations in the house?" I asked Simon.

He nodded, taking a sip of wine. "We did the whole house, floor by floor. Everything needed work, from the plumbing to the electrical to the decor. The whole thing was Jonathan's brainchild."

"The ballroom was the last project," Jonathan said. "We thought when it was finished it would be a hot ticket for weddings and other types of events. Little did we know. Kate does most of the heavy lifting with that part of the business now, thank goodness, leaving us free to tend to the other guests."

Nick was busy refreshing everyone's drinks. He caught my eye and smiled. I couldn't quite figure him out.

I watched him, remembering Simon's comment about Nick being like Eeyore. It wasn't right, the characterization. I found Nick to be friendly and welcoming, but extremely wary. Even tonight. Overly so. But he had a right to be, I thought, with all he had seen as a cop. Still, I noticed him glancing at Dominic over and over again. What was that about? It was starting to pool in my consciousness, and not in a good way.

"We were all upset to hear about what happened with Alice last night," Simon said, leaning in toward me. "Is she okay? Are you?"

"She's okay," I said, squeezing Dominic's arm. "This guy was the hero."

Did Nick just roll his eyes? Or did I imagine it? A flare of irritation rose within me, and after what we had all been through the night before, it got the better of me. I was well and truly tired of what I perceived to be this man's attitude toward Dominic.

"She disappeared into the lake, Nick, unless you didn't get the full report from your guys," I said, with more than a little irritation in my voice. "She went under. It was pitch black outside. Dominic raced into that dark water after her without giving it a second thought. He dove several times before finding her and carrying her out of there. He saved her life."

"Really," Nick said. "Good job there, man." But the look on his face didn't match his words. And I didn't much like what I was seeing.

I stared at him, aghast. "Your squad got there several minutes too late," I pressed on. "We were already walking back up to LuAnn's. Dominic was carrying Alice. If we had waited for your people, she would have drowned. Lucky for Alice and her family, Dominic was there."

"So we heard," Simon broke in—was he trying to break the tension? He raised his eyebrows and turned to Dominic. "Gil told me that, after you all got Alice into bed, you stayed the night in their suite so he and Jason could get some sleep."

"It was no trouble," Dominic said.

"We invited them to join us tonight, but Gil said another time would be best," Simon said. "I guess she was still pretty shaken up today. Fearful. Not quite herself. Apparently, she's been sleeping a lot."

The image of Alice's drawings floated into my mind and sent a chill through me. It was as though she had known what was going to happen to her, where she'd end up that night, and who would save her, all long before it occurred. I thought about bringing it up, eliciting another discussion about Dominic's theory about the veil. Maybe Simon had experienced the same sort of thing when his grandmother was declining? But in the end, I kept it to myself. I had already talked a bit to Simon and Kate about it. Nobody else needed to know.

"They're getting an alarmed baby gate installed at the top of the stairs in the suite to prevent it from happening again," I said.

"We installed it today," Dominic said. That was news to me. "And yeah, the lady was in no condition to pay a social call. I'm wondering . . ." He sighed and let the thought lie there unspoken.

"If it's wise to care for her here?" I said, my voice a whisper. "I hate to even say it."

"Gil's wondering the same thing," Simon said, exchanging a glance with Jonathan. "But Jason won't even entertain the discussion."

Just then, a man who appeared to be the chef opened the door and popped his head out. "We're ready when you are," he said.

"Excellent, Charles!" Simon said as he and Jonathan piled up the trays and napkins. "Everybody, take your drinks!"

CHAPTER THIRTY-FIVE

We walked through the door, and I took a quick breath in. Both Dominic and I had been wanting to see the inside of this place, and it did not disappoint.

Dark wood paneling covered the walls; there were high, beamed ceilings and a fire roaring in the fireplace; overstuffed sofas, armchairs, and ottomans were arranged in groups; antique Oriental rugs lay on the gleaming wood floors. There were heavy antique tables, Tiffany lamps, and framed black-and-white photographs lining the walls.

The whole effect was warm, welcoming, and homey, while at the same time opulent.

I looked from Kate to Simon and back again. "This is gorgeous," I said.

Simon grinned and squeezed Jonathan's hand. "I want to take all the credit, of course, but it was Jonathan's eye that put this all together. If he hadn't come into my life, I would've been living in this dusty house alone, rattling around like a crazy person."

"Just you and a family of raccoons," Jonathan offered. "That might have been nice in its own way."

Simon leaned his head on Jonathan's shoulder and laughed. *The right person at the right time,* I thought.

"Then I would've come here after my divorce, run off the raccoons, and the two of us would've gone quietly insane while the house crumbled around us, like our own version of *Grey Gardens*," Kate said.

"There's still time for that," Simon said.

I liked these people. So much laughter, so much good-natured teasing. I got the sense that they would go to the ends of the earth for each other. What a nice thing to have in life.

We made our way into the dining room, which had windows on three sides. A round table in the back was set for six. I saw our "linner" was already on the table, served family style. Two chickens, roasted with rosemary and lemon; pasta with fresh basil, tomatoes, lemon, parmesan cheese, and pine nuts; a mixed-greens salad; a basket of hot bread.

Bottles of white and red wine stood uncorked on the table, and crystal glasses were beside every plate. Looking closer, I saw it was china, a cream-colored background with a delicate pattern of roses and green leaves.

"This is beautiful," I said to Kate. "The china."

"You noticed." She beamed. "It's our grandparents' wedding china," she said. "We use it on special occasions with special people."

I clasped her hand. I had my parents' wedding china in boxes in a storage facility. Awaiting the day I'd figure out where to live and what to do with my life. All at once, I wished those decisions were made. That I knew where I'd be in a year. And with whom. And doing what. I was tired of all this uncertainty. For the first time since my mother's diagnosis, I wanted clarity about me. All because of china? But sometimes the smallest of things can incite the biggest of revelations.

We all took our seats. Jonathan carved and served the chicken, and we all passed the side dishes around as a server filled our wineglasses.

"So, Brynn," Nick began. "Rescuing Alice last night aside, how are you liking Wharton?"

I finished a bite of my chicken and smiled at him, thinking of my visit to him in his office. He had been so helpful, so welcoming. Not like tonight. I decided then and there that I was going to let it go. Everyone had their moods, their bad sides. Their inner Eeyore.

"I love it," I said. "Spending the summer here is just what I needed after a stressful few years."

"I'm sorry about your mother," he said.

Before I even had a chance to thank him, he turned to Dominic. "And you? Why did you decide to summer in Wharton?"

Simon and Jonathan seemed to be holding their breath. Simon was glowering at Nick.

"Nick," Kate said softly. "Let's just have a nice dinner."

A tangible tension grew in the room. Why wouldn't that question lead to a nice dinner? Everyone asked summer residents that same question.

All at once, my senses were on high alert. I saw Nick's eyes trained on Dominic. Intense. Focused. What was this about? Anger started bubbling up in the pit of my stomach.

"I thought it might be fun," Dominic said, nonchalantly. "Why?"

"It's no big deal," Nick went on, taking a bite of his chicken, a benign smile on his face. "We're always curious when people come to stay awhile. You know Whartonians. We're busybodies."

"So I've heard," Dominic said, chuckling. "Happy hour is one big gossip fest."

I caught Dominic's eye and smiled at him. I wanted him to know I was behind him.

But then Nick said something that wiped the smile off my face.

"It's just that we don't get many visitors like you here," he went on. "People are wondering about you."

"What people?" Kate said, a bit too loudly.

Simon's eyes narrowed. "Are you kidding me?" he said to Nick. "*We don't get many visitors like you here*? What are you, in *Deliverance*?"

"I was just saying—"

"Saying what?" Simon pressed. "Just curious."

I knew Nick was suspicious because he'd had his eye on Dominic when he first got into town. But this felt like it was crossing a line. Why did they invite us here? To interrogate him?

Kate looked aghast.

But Dominic chuckled, looking around at everyone at the table.

"I don't mind, really. The man's just curious about a new man in town."

He smiled at Nick, who wasn't returning the goodwill.

"Nick," Kate said in a harsh whisper. "That's enough. I mean it."

Hostility hung in the air. The sound of silverware scraping against the plates was palpable.

"What do you do for a living, Dominic? Do you have your own business?" Nick kept on. "A website or something like that?"

"No," Dominic said, calmly taking a bite of chicken. "My business mainly comes from word of mouth."

"I get that," Nick said. "I did an internet search on you and couldn't find anything."

Dominic smiled. "Oh, looking me up?"

Nick smiled back at him. "I'm a cop. It's what we do."

"You do internet searches on everyone who comes to Wharton?" Dominic wanted to know. "I suppose you need something to keep your guys busy."

This was a dance of rivals, and I didn't like it one little bit. I was going to shut it down.

"What brought you to Wharton, Nick?" I interjected, breaking the silence.

Evidently, I had broken his focus as well. Nick snapped his head around to look at me, surprised. "I'm sorry?"

"You're asking everyone what brought them to Wharton and grilling them about why. I'm curious about your story. How you ended up here. And exactly why." I smiled broadly at him. "Don't leave out any detail, no matter how small. I have all night."

Simon put an elbow on the table and rested his chin in his palm, raising his eyebrows. "Do tell, Nick."

"Kate brought me here," he said.

"Really?" I asked him, deliberately not looking at Kate. "That's not entirely true."

"What?"

"I heard all about it. You were an up-and-coming police officer in the Twin Cities. You didn't know Kate before you came here. Hers was the first case you investigated in Wharton, and you were brought here to do that, but Kate herself didn't bring you here. Although it might be convenient for you to say so."

Simon stifled a laugh and poured another glass of wine for himself and Jonathan.

"I guess I'm not the only one searching on the internet," Nick said. He held my gaze for a long moment. "I was reassigned here."

I smiled, taking another sip of wine. "Why were you reassigned to this small, sleepy town?"

Nick narrowed his eyes at me, his look tinged with anger. "What are you implying?"

"I'm not implying anything," I said, not letting up. "But I see you'd rather not get into it."

Everyone at the table was staring at me.

I looked over at Dominic. "You ready to go?"

He pushed himself up from the table. "Whenever you are."

I held Kate's gaze for a long minute. "I'm sorry," I said.

Kate put her hand up. "I'm the one who's sorry."

She glared at her husband. Nick pushed his chair back from the table and stalked out of the room.

Kate turned to Dominic. "I did not invite you here for this. I have no idea what got into him, and frankly, I'm mortified. Please accept my sincere apologies."

Dominic smiled at her and turned that warmth to everyone else at the table. "I wouldn't want to be that guy tonight." He grinned. "He is going to need a serious 'I'm in the doghouse' bouquet of roses to smooth this thing over."

It broke the tension.

"Are you sure you have to go?" Simon asked. "We could have a nightcap and gossip."

I exchanged a glance with Dominic. "I'd love that, but I think we'll take a rain check," I said, pushing my chair away from the table.

Kate stood up and held her arms out. "I am so sorry," she said, hugging me. "I have no idea what got into him. He's really not that guy."

"I'm sorry I got so defensive, but I wasn't about to let him talk to Dominic like that," I said. "No matter what Nick thinks, he's a really good man."

Kate, Jonathan, and Simon walked us through the salon to the front door. Dominic took my hand, and we walked through it, down the steps to the path leading to the parking lot.

Simon, Kate, and Jonathan stood on the porch. "Promise me you'll come back," Simon called out to us. "I will personally sit Eeyore down and give him a PowerPoint presentation on how to treat a dinner guest. Better than that, I won't invite him."

Kate shook her head. "I don't know what to say," she said.

As Dominic and I walked to the car, hand in hand, I felt his anger course through his veins and into mine. In the car, he sat looking straight ahead for a moment.

I reached over and took his hand.

"What was that about?" Dominic asked me. "Why does he have such a chip on his shoulder?"

"No idea," I said.

A more familiar expression crept onto his face. He grinned at me. "Heads on stakes."

I smiled at this. It completely defused my anger. "I didn't like his tone," I said.

"You were a lioness back there," he said. "Defending me." He reached out and took my hand. "I haven't had a whole lot of defenders in my life. Thank you."

My phone buzzed before we got out of the parking lot. I fished it out of my purse and saw it was a text from Kate.

"I am completely mortified. Please say you don't hate me."

I texted her back. "Of course not. I'm sorry I went off on Nick like that. No idea what his problem with Dominic is, but whatever it is, it's wrong."

I dropped my phone back into my purse, wondering why Nick had been so hostile. All of that badgering about why Dominic had come to Wharton. What did he care? It was none of his business.

I gazed at Dominic's profile as he drove us back to LuAnn's. Against my will, my stomach did a flip when I realized I didn't know why he had come to Wharton, either.

CHAPTER THIRTY-SIX

All was dark at LuAnn's when we got back. We quietly made our way through the restaurant and upstairs to Dominic's room. There wasn't even a question this time; we simply went inside together.

I closed the door behind us, and he backed me into it, kissing me with an urgency that made me lose myself in his touch. Without a word, we tumbled onto the bed, our arms and legs entwined.

Later, after a jumble of curious dreams, my eyes fluttered open. Moonlight was streaming in through the window, falling on his chest. I lay there next to him, lightly tracing his illustrations with my finger. Always something new to find. A face that hadn't been there before. Or a new position for an illustration I had seen, or thought I had seen.

Who was this man? Mystery swirled around him and wrapped me up in it. I wanted to know, and yet I didn't want to know. Something deep within my heart told me to just let it be.

As I was drifting off, I heard a voice, soft and low in my ear. "Savor every moment with him," a woman whispered. I curled in closer, and soon we began breathing in and out slowly in tandem, our hearts beating together as one. *This is exactly where I belong,* I thought, before sleep overtook me.

The next morning, after showering the night off my skin, I met Dominic downstairs for breakfast. We chatted with Gary a bit, neither of us wanting to bring up the ugliness with Nick the night before. As we were finishing our omelets, Dominic looked at his watch.

"I have a few things to take care of this morning, but I'll be back this afternoon," he said, pushing his chair back. "I'll come find you." He leaned down and kissed me on the forehead and then was gone.

I didn't ask him where he was going. He did this often, disappearing on mysterious errands. I thought of the night before and vowed to just let it be. Yet another great unknowing. It was becoming a pattern this summer.

On my way back to my room, I noticed Jason and Gil's door was open. I poked my head inside and rapped on the frame.

"Knock, knock," I said.

Gil was sitting at the table engrossed in some paperwork but looked up when he heard me.

"Morning!" he said. "Come on in."

I slipped through the doorway and took a couple of steps into the room. "I don't want to bother you all, but I'm wondering about Alice. How's she doing?"

He shook his head slightly and glanced up to the second floor. I noticed the new baby gate at the top of the stairs.

"Not great, I'm afraid," he said, his voice low. "She was in bed all day yesterday. Jason's up there with her now. He hasn't left her side."

I pulled out a chair and sat down next to him. "Is it exhaustion?"

"I'm not sure," Gil said. "Yes and no. It's like the disease has advanced several stages all in one night. Whatever made her go down to the lake really took it out of her."

"Have you called her doctor?"

"He was here yesterday," Gil said, holding my gaze.

"And?"

"He said it's best to just let her rest. Her vitals are fine. Her heart is strong. She just needs to get her strength back, and at this stage of the game, it might take a while. That's what the doctor said, anyway."

"Did you tell Jason about the drawings?" I said, dropping my voice to nearly a whisper.

Gil shook his head. "He's been in a state himself," he said. "Yesterday he called the girls, Bec and Jane, to tell them what happened. They're on their way here with their families."

I let that sink in for a moment.

"I apologize in advance for the onslaught of kids."

I reached over and took his hand. "I'll bet it will be good for Alice to see them," I said. "The kids, the grandkids. Where are they all staying?"

"LuAnn found them a house a couple of blocks away," he said. "We'll be there with them, mostly. They'll be in town for only a few days, but we thought it best to have them in a house they can retreat to rather than the kids running around through the hallways here the whole time."

"That would have been fine with everyone, you know," I said. "But I get it. It will be more comfortable for the kids to have a house and a yard. When are they getting in?"

Gil glanced at his watch. "Later today. Before dinner, I think. Bec is going to call me, and I'll meet them at the house with the keys."

Jason emerged from Alice's room and closed the door quietly. When he saw me, he smiled an exhausted smile and trotted down the stairs after locking the baby gate behind him.

His normally impeccable appearance was showing the cracks of stress. His hair was rumpled and looked as though it needed a cut and a shampoo. Bags, with dark circles, ringed his eyes. He hadn't shaved yet today. My heart squeezed when I noticed his T-shirt was on inside out.

I pushed back my chair and rose to envelop him in a hug. We stood like that for a long time.

"What can I do to help?" I asked him.

He sighed. I was searching my mind for anything I could do, and then I had a delicious idea.

"You both are exhausted and need some rejuvenation," I said, looking from one to the other. "Why not take a couple of hours and go to the spa at Harrison's House? I'll stay here with Alice, and I'll find Dominic to stay with me. You could get massages or at least a decadent shave and haircut, and be refreshed by the time your daughters arrive."

Jason shook his head. "We couldn't possibly."

But Gil reached out and took his hand. "Yes, we can. I think it's a wonderful idea. You need it."

I reached into my purse and found my phone. "I'll call Simon right now and make the arrangements if you say the word."

Both of us looked at Jason. "You are an angel," he said to me.

I keyed in Simon's number, and he picked up on the first ring.

"Are you calling to say you hate us?" he said, clearly chagrined.

"Yes," I said, "and also to make spa appointments for Jason and Gil."

"Oh!" he said. "I happen to know we have nobody booked in the spa today. What is it with these guests? Our aestheticians are sitting around eating bonbons. Anyway, when do they want to come?"

I looked from Gil to Jason. "Now?" They both nodded. Gil hurried off to get his keys and wallet.

I heard Simon exhale a long breath. "Seriously, darling, I don't know what got into Wyatt Earp last night, but Kate nearly died of mortification. Me, too."

I smiled. "It's okay."

"No, it isn't," he said, "but Jonathan and I are still laughing about how you beat him at his own game."

I laughed. "Hey, you come after one of my own, that's what you get."

"Ohhhh," Simon said, drawing out the word. "So, he's 'one of your own' now?"

"I hope so," I said.

"He's a lucky man, if he is," Simon said. "You send Jason and Gil up to the house. Tell them I'll have mimosas waiting."

I hung up and only then realized the two of them were staring at me.

"What happened last night?" Jason asked. "What did we miss?"

I told them about the interrogation, how Nick just wouldn't let up on Dominic.

"He actually said something to the effect of, 'We don't get too many visitors like you here.'"

"Are you kidding me?" Gil said, his eyes wide. "That's totally uncalled for."

Jason's mouth was a tight line. "Dominic is family at this point, as far as I'm concerned. Is he upset?"

"No," I said. "A little confused, maybe, but he took it all in stride. I got the idea that it wasn't the first time he had been . . . I don't want to say *profiled*, but it felt like that's what it was."

Jason shook his head. "I will give that man a talking-to if I see him today. What in the world was he thinking? It's outrageous."

"Speaking of Dominic, let me quickly find him before you guys go," I said. "I know he was doing some errands, but maybe he's back by now. I'll just run to his room and see if he's there."

I hurried out the door and down the hallway. I knocked a few times, but no answer. I walked back to the suite.

"No luck," I said.

"I tried him on his cell, and it went straight to voice mail," Jason said. He exchanged a glance with Gil. "We could cancel."

I shook my head. "Don't be silly. I'm perfectly happy to stay with Alice on my own."

"She hasn't been out of bed all day today or yesterday," Jason said. "She's in a deep sleep. I don't expect that she'll get up anytime soon."

"It's okay if she does," I said. "Not a problem."

Jason looked at me for a long moment. "I'll keep my phone on. If anything happens, call me, and I'll be here in five minutes."

"Foil papers wrapped in his hair and all," Gil added.

Jason smirked at him and pinched his arm. "Only my hairdresser knows for sure." He turned to me then. "Obviously, anything in the fridge is yours. On the way out, we'll let Gary and LuAnn know you're here with Alice and to send Dominic up if he gets back while we're gone."

As they closed the door behind them, I glanced up the stairs at Alice's closed door.

I was looking through the bookshelf for something interesting to read when my phone buzzed. It was Kate.

"Can you meet me at the coffee shop?" she asked. "I talked to Nick about last night."

"I can't," I said. "Jason and Gil are actually on their way up to Harrison's House to get massages. I'm staying with Alice."

Kate was silent for a minute. "Can I come over to you then? I just want to talk with you about something, and I think it's best to do it in person."

I gave her the room number, and we hung up. I padded up the stairs and opened Alice's door a crack to check on her. She looked like an angel, sleeping so peacefully. Her blonde hair fanned out on her pillow, framing her face. She had a slight smile. Whatever she was dreaming about, I left her to it, closing her door as quietly as I could.

About fifteen minutes later, I heard a soft rap at the door. I opened it to find Kate standing there, wincing. She pulled me into a hug.

"That's not how our dinner parties usually go," she said.

"Come on in," I said. "Alice is asleep upstairs. Would you like some tea?"

She shook her head, pulling out one of the chairs at the table and sinking down into it. "Thanks, but I won't stay long."

All at once, a growing dread settled around me. "What's up?"

She sighed. "There's no easy way to say this," she said. "How well do you know Dominic?"

CHAPTER THIRTY-SEVEN

The moment seemed to freeze in time. I became aware of all the atoms buzzing with life around me. It was as though I was experiencing the moment and watching myself experience it at the same time.

There was Kate, my good friend, looking at me with loving concern in her eyes.

"What do you mean?"

"I mean, how much do you know about him?"

"Quite a lot, actually," I said, but even as I said the words, I felt them falling apart in thin air.

When it came right down to it, I didn't know much. I knew how his face looked and what he whispered in my ear when he was in the throes of passion. I knew how easily he made me laugh. I knew the timeless connection we seemed to have. I knew he had a rough upbringing and was now trying to help others. That was what he had told me, anyway.

I didn't know why he was in Wharton. I didn't know where he was at that moment. There was so much I didn't know.

"So, tell me about him."

I shook my head, anger mixed with dread and fear bubbling up inside me. "No, I don't think I will. What are you getting at, Kate?"

She didn't respond for a moment, holding my gaze. "Nick is really suspicious of him," she said finally. "After the woman died at the inn, it was too much of a coincidence. First the lady in the hospital in Minneapolis, then the one here at LuAnn's, now Harrison's House. The common denominator is Dominic."

"But he wasn't here at LuAnn's when the woman died," I said, feeling defensive.

"He came shortly afterward," she said. "Who knows when he really arrived in Wharton."

A chill ran through me.

"But they all died of natural causes, right?" I asked.

"Nick decided to check him out. Like he alluded to last night, he can't find any information on him. Nothing. No internet presence whatsoever. Not so much as one tweet."

"So what?" I said, a bit louder than I intended. "Now it's a crime if you don't post on social media?"

Kate shook her head. "Nick ran his prints this morning."

"Prints? You have got to be kidding. Are you telling me Nick took his prints off a glass he touched last night?"

She winced. "I'm afraid not. At happy hour."

"Is that why you asked us to dinner? To confront Dominic?"

"No!" she said quickly. "I had no idea about his growing suspicions until this morning."

The world seemed to be getting smaller, contracting around me. It was like there was nothing else, except for Kate and me, sitting at this table.

"He's been in prison, Brynn. He has a record a mile long. Assault, grand theft. Juvenile stuff."

All at once, I wanted to shake her. A violent anger bubbled up inside me.

"How dare you violate his privacy like that," I hissed at her. "And mine! Who does Nick think he is?"

She gave a strangled laugh. "The chief of police."

"For your information, Dominic grew up in very rough circumstances. I'm not surprised he ended up on the wrong side of the law when he was younger. It's what he dedicates his life to now, if you must know, helping people transform their own lives, to rise above the cards they were dealt."

"That's what he told you," she pressed on. "But what if it's not true? What proof do you have of it? What if Nick's right? What if Dominic is the common denominator in all of those deaths?"

A great silence fell over the room then. "Are you saying your husband thinks Dominic is a serial killer?"

Kate reached over and took my hand. I pulled it away.

"I'm not saying that," she said, her voice soft, pleading. "But he is watching him. Be careful, Brynn. Please."

"I think you should leave," I said.

She looked at me for a long moment and shook her head. "I'm sorry," she said. "I had to let you know."

After she left, I sat at the table silently sobbing tears of frustration, anger, even rage, my head in my hands.

I felt a small hand on my shoulder. I looked up to see Alice standing there, a little wisp of a woman in a floral nightgown, her hair wild. But her eyes were comforting.

"Alice!" I said. Some babysitter I was. I hadn't even heard her come down the stairs. Wasn't that baby gate supposed to have an alarm on it?

"He is not a serial killer," Alice said, her voice faraway and thin. "How silly. Don't believe that for a minute."

All at once, I opened my eyes. I looked around wildly. No Alice. What had just happened? I couldn't have been asleep, could I?

I pushed myself up from the table and hurried up the stairs, unlocking the gate and padding over to Alice's door. I opened it a crack, and there she was, in a deep sleep, just as she had been when I checked on her earlier.

What in the world?

I went back downstairs, shaking my head. I poured myself a glass of water and realized my entire body was shaking. I drank it down in a gulp and poured another, resting the cool glass against my forehead. It was pounding.

I crossed the room and sank onto the sofa, staring out of the window, not thinking of anything at all, until Jason and Gil returned, refreshed and looking like themselves again.

"How's Alice?" Jason said, peeling off his jacket and hanging it on a hook by the door.

"No change," I reported. "I checked on her a few times. She's been sleeping peacefully. I don't think she's even moved."

I didn't tell them about my strange vision, or whatever it was. And I certainly wasn't going to tell them about Kate's visit.

Jason and Gil exchanged a glance. "Do you think we should get the doctor back here?" Gil asked.

Jason nodded. "Just what I was thinking. That's a lot of sleeping. I don't know quite what to make of it." He glanced up the stairs toward her room. "I'm going to check on her. Will you make the call?"

As Gil pulled his phone out of his pocket, Jason trotted up the stairs and unlocked the gate. A feeling of dread wrapped around me then, and I didn't quite know why. I wished he wouldn't go into her room. *Please don't go in there, Jason.*

A moment later, we heard the scream.

CHAPTER THIRTY-EIGHT

Gil and I rushed up the stairs and burst into Alice's room to find Jason cradling her lifeless body.

She was gone.

The next few hours were a blur of sirens, EMTs bustling in and out, the coroner arriving, assessing, and leaving. LuAnn and Gary were there in an instant, offering comfort and support. Just their presence helped. I longed for Dominic's broad shoulders, wishing he would come.

Alice's body was taken away. Natural causes, the coroner suspected, especially after the incident in the lake.

"Sometimes a thing like that is all it takes to push someone who is already fragile, already close to the end, over the edge," she said.

Jason was slumped on the couch, Gil holding him while he wept, when Kate, Nick, Simon, and Jonathan came through the door.

Simon and Jonathan flew to Jason's side, and Simon gathered him into his arms. The four of them wept together.

"The girls are on their way," Jason sobbed. "We were going to spend a few days together. We thought the grandkids would . . ."

Kate and Nick were standing in the kitchen, stricken looks on their faces. I wasn't going to make a scene, not now.

A moment later, Dominic appeared, and I flew into his arms, sobbing on his shoulder. He whispered into my ear and rubbed my back.

"There, there, honey. There, there now." The words were meaningless, but the very sound of his voice quieted my cries. I held on to him as tightly as I could.

Two nights later, we gathered downstairs in the restaurant for a private happy hour: Dominic and me, Jason and Gil, Rebecca, Jane, and their families, LuAnn and Gary, Simon and Jonathan, and even Kate and Nick. In light of what had happened, I softened toward him. Dominic had no hard feelings. If he wasn't holding any grudges, neither would I.

That night, we ate, we drank, and we shared stories about Alice. There were a lot of tears but a lot of laughter, too. I learned more about her that I hadn't known. Stories about her childhood growing up in a small town, more tales of her early life with Jason. Funny stories from the childhoods of her kids. Alice had had a life well lived, despite the heartbreak. It was just too short. Too terribly short.

As the evening was winding down, and Bec and Jane took their children back to the house they were renting, I found myself standing with Dominic, Gil, and Jason.

"Have you made plans yet for any kind of service?" I asked.

Jason nodded. "There's so much to do after someone you love passes away," he said. "I think it's just to keep you busy, to force you to put one foot in front of the other."

I could completely relate to that. The service would be in two weeks' time, in the church where Alice and Jason had been married, and where their children and grandchildren had been baptized.

"We wouldn't miss it for the world," I said, putting a hand on Jason's shoulder.

On the day, Dominic, Gary, LuAnn, and I drove to the small-town church where Alice would be laid to rest. The service was beautiful and heartfelt, filled with loving tributes, music, laughter, and tears. A fitting send-off for a lovely woman who had touched so many lives. Including mine.

"She was a woman well loved," Dominic said as he hugged Jason on the church steps. "I was honored to have known her."

"Me, too," Jason choked out, his voice strangled into a sob. "Thank you for all you did for her. For us."

I hugged Gil, and we held each other for a long time.

"You're not coming back to Wharton for the rest of the summer," I said. It wasn't a question. I knew somehow.

Gil shook his head. "We think it's best to stay here with Jason's family," he said.

I wondered if they'd ever go back to LuAnn's, with the memory of Alice haunting its halls. I wondered if Alice would become a passer-through.

Jason enveloped me in his arms. "Don't be a stranger," he said. "You'll be in the Cities after the summer, and I want to hear all about how much your students are annoying you."

"You've got a deal," I said.

After Alice's funeral, something changed for Dominic and me. Even though we'd known each other only a short time, we felt as if we had lived a lifetime together, and we both simply dropped the pretense that we hadn't. Life was too short for artifice.

When we got back to LuAnn's, I moved into his room, freeing up the Yellow Lady for rental, and we got down to the business of living and loving, appreciating every moment together.

The rest of the summer passed gently, quietly. Dominic and I kayaked around the islands, Simon's hilarious story about his experience ringing in our ears.

"It happened on his birthday!" Dominic called out to me as we paddled, laughing about it. "Insult to injury!"

We had dinners with Simon, Jonathan, Kate, and even Nick, the rift between him and Dominic, if not healed, then sufficiently smoothed over. We helped out with the Friday fish boils, with Dominic becoming master of the boil over, much to Gary's delight. We came to view LuAnn's ever-eccentric outfits as a little treat for us every morning, a funny way to start the day. We grew to love happy hour, feeling a part of this warm community of wonderful people.

But mostly, it was about "we." Just being together. Reading on the beach, taking lazy walks around town hand in hand, simply living where our hearts and souls had always resided—within each other.

It was like we were suspended out of time, given an impossible gift, a dream summer, one I knew would come to an end. We would leave LuAnn's and drive out of Wharton, leaving its glorious peace behind us. I would go back to my students; he would go back to his clients. Our "real lives," the worlds we had created for ourselves outside Wharton, were waiting for us. I tried not to think about that day, but I knew it was coming. I hoped we could live those real lives together.

One night, I awoke, hearing a voice whispering my name.

"Brynn. Brynnnnn."

I noticed a warm glow under the door, coming from the hallway. I slipped out of bed, Dominic sleeping deeply next to me, and opened the door. It was Alice. She was wearing her signature sweater set and pearls and was smiling. She took my hands.

"You are stronger than you know," she said. "Love never dies, Brynn. Love is all there is." And then she disappeared, fading from view little by little until she was gone. And I knew, in that moment, a part of me was gone, too.

CHAPTER THIRTY-NINE

Dominic and I were standing on the deck of the ferry, crossing to the island. It was a bright, blue day, and we brought a picnic lunch and a bottle of wine with us, along with our blankets and paperbacks.

We settled into our favorite spot on the beach for the afternoon. We floated in the water, our arms and legs entwined, and soaked up the sun. As the day wound down, we found ourselves at Jimmy's, dancing the evening away, just as we had that first time. On the dance floor, we lost ourselves in each other's eyes, seeing eternity in that one moment.

It was perfect. A great gift. One I would cling to for the rest of my life, although I didn't know it then.

As often happened on Lake Superior, the weather turned in an instant. Clouds rolled in, making our blue day into a potentially stormy night. We hurried to the ferry and stood on the deck, watching lightning sizzle through the darkening sky as the ferry chugged away from the dock. Thunder rumbled in the distance.

When we were about halfway across, a young man who had been standing on the other side of the deck began to climb over the rail.

"What are you doing?" someone called out. "Get off there!"

Everyone on the deck froze in horror. I reached for Dominic, but he was already rushing across the deck. When he neared the man, he slowed down and put his hands up.

"Listen, brother," he said, his voice calm and low. "You don't want to do this. Whatever it is, we can figure it out."

The man turned to Dominic. I'd never forget the look on his face. Utterly vacant. As though there was no spark behind his eyes at all, as though his soul had already left, and he was an empty shell.

"Come on, brother," Dominic said, holding out his hand. "Give me your hand."

As everyone on the deck held their collective breath, the man simply fell backward, hitting the water with a terrifying splash.

What was more terrifying came next. Time slowed to a crawl. I watched as Dominic climbed over the rail. He turned back to me, nodded slightly, mouthed, "I love you," and jumped in after him.

The skies opened up, and rain poured down as lightning crackled and thunder roared, as though the very lake and all the heavens were crying out in anguish.

I didn't know what happened next. All I remembered was a jumble of images. Floodlights. Coast Guard ships. A lot of yelling. At one point, I tried to go over the side after the man I loved, and somebody wrestled me away from the rail and got me out of the rain. Somehow, I ended up at the ferry dock in Wharton. Kate and Nick were there—who called them, I don't know.

They tried to get me to go back to LuAnn's, but I wouldn't leave the water's edge. The rain poured down, stinging my face and eyes, but I didn't care. I wanted to be with him.

"Come on, Brynn," Kate said, pulling me away from the lakeshore. "You'll catch your death out here."

Oh, how I wished that were true.

I stood there, watching the lights of the Coast Guard ships as they searched for Dominic. I stood there as the sun came up and divers went down into the water. It had become a recovery. Not a rescue. I stood there until the divers came back to shore, shaking their heads.

His body was never found. Lake Superior doesn't give up its dead.

I had no idea how I got back to LuAnn's, but I collapsed into our bed, which still smelled of him. I did not leave that bed for days.

Kate and Simon hovered. Gary and LuAnn, worried, called Jason and Gil, who rushed back to Wharton. Beth read to me as I tossed and turned. Together, the force of all that love got me out of bed and helped me put one foot in front of the other.

When I did, I walked back into my old life. I called the head of my department and made arrangements to come back, midyear.

I didn't want to talk about Dominic, or to have any kind of service for him. I fended off people's well-meaning words of sympathy. I'd be living his funeral every day for the rest of my life, and I didn't want to share that pain with anyone.

The day I packed up and left, taking Dominic's clothes with me, LuAnn and Gary saw me off.

"This place is a part of you now," LuAnn said. "It'll be waiting for you to come back."

"Everyone comes back," Gary said. "We'll be seeing you."

CHAPTER FORTY

A lifetime has passed. I am sitting here by the fire, remembering it all, the strange and otherworldly summer of my Illustrated Man, a summer of incredible love wrapped up in heartbreak and loss.

It was the summer I learned to go on living after unspeakable grief, the summer I learned there is more in this world than we can imagine with our expanded minds, or experience with our five (or, as dear Alice taught me, more) senses.

It was the summer I learned I had more questions than answers, and that I could be okay with the great unknowing. I had to be, to go on living for the life that began growing inside of me.

I named him for his father, and for me. Dominic James Jr. was now a grown man, a wickedly funny, gentle, intelligent man, with a wife and children of his own. They were my reasons for staying alive this long. Like the woman in Cornwall, the widow of the Widow's Cottage, who has stayed in my heart all these years, I needed to put one foot in front of the other and move forward for my—our—child despite losing the love of my life.

But now my time is here. It is my turn. I exhale at the thought of it. I came back here, to the boardinghouse, to room five. We had a date. And I intended to keep it. I wonder if he'll remember.

I'm holding the sheet of paper in my lap. It had fluttered out of my copy of *The Illustrated Man* when I unpacked it, all those years ago.

"Meet me in room five," it said. "You'll know when the time is right."

Now the time is right. I fold it and tuck it back into my copy of the book. My stomach is in knots at the idea of seeing him again.

Snow is lightly falling outside. I push myself out of my armchair to put another log on the fire, and I groan. These old bones. Aging is not for sissies.

As I sink back down into my chair, I realize I am tired, deeply tired. I have been for days. The end is near, now. I can sense it. That's why I am here. But I am not afraid. How could I be, after all I have seen?

I take another sip of my tea—it has gone cold, but I have no energy to turn on the kettle for hot water—and lean my head back. I close my eyes, listening to the crackling of the flames. And I begin to drift into the in-between time. My body feels like it's floating on a gently undulating sea.

The room had been dark except for the firelight, but all at once, a warm shaft of light appears, shining down from the ceiling.

A young woman walks into the room. She is watching me, afraid. I am amused by this. What does she think I am, a ghost? And what is she to me, if not that?

I look closer, and recognition flows through me. She is no ghost. She is me. Time has doubled back on itself, and back again. I am the woman in room five.

I must tell her to cherish him. To hold him as long as she can. To not get on the ferry that fateful day. To not let him go. I try, but I can't speak to her. I'm not sure why. The book is sitting in my lap, and I hold it out for her to see.

Ah, yes. She sees it. I see it. She will love him. I can feel it.

I wish, with all my might, that I could change what happened. Influence her. But I don't think it works that way. And besides, I have something more important to do. Something more immediate.

He is coming.

After she leaves my room, I see him. Hazy at first, and then swimming into focus. He is walking toward me from . . . where? I don't know where. Out there. Elsewhere.

But he is smiling. That movie-star smile. Wearing a black T-shirt and jeans. The love of my life.

He is just the same as he had been the last time I laid eyes on him. Strong, broad-shouldered. Devastatingly, devilishly handsome. Time has not aged him a day.

Now that he is standing right in front of me, I cannot speak. I can barely breathe. He is here. My heart seizes up at the sight of him. My love. My true love is here. I want to run to him, to throw my arms around him and hold him close, finally, after a lifetime, but I can't move. My body won't let me.

He is Dominic, but he is also something else. My stomach seizes up, as though I am in danger.

"There she is," he says, his voice like velvet. "You remembered our date. I wondered if you would."

"I've missed you," I squeak out.

The sight of him is too much, after all this time. I have thought of nothing else, no one else, all these years, when I've allowed my mind to drift.

When I haven't been feeding a toddler or watching baseball practice or crying at his graduation or dancing at his wedding. For my—our—son's life, I was fully present, and I was grateful for every moment of it. I forced myself to be. What I did, who I thought of and cried about during my alone time, was my business.

"I've missed you, too," Dominic says, tears welling up in his eyes. "More than you realize. But it's just a minute in time."

It didn't seem like that to me. It seemed like—it was—an entire lifetime.

"He's a good boy," Dominic says. "Man. You were the best mother to him."

He peels off his shirt, and I gasp at the sight of him. I never did get used to his beauty, those mystical tattoos. They are shimmering, moving, filled with color and life. I see the image of myself, there, over his heart. So that's what it is, then. The images are of the people he helps cross over.

"Are you ready to step out of that shell, honey?" he asks. "You've had a really good run with it. Now it's time to let it go."

I know what he's asking of me. I nod. "I can do without the aches and pains," I say. "The incontinence, too. Nobody tells you about that, and yet one day, there it is."

He laughs, and the music of it lights up the room. I feel my years start to fall away. They are disintegrating into dust.

I see wings appear behind his back. The scarab wings from his tattoo, in all of their intricate, colorful glory. I gasp at the sight of them. They're like Tiffany stained glass. I can barely stand to look at the intense, awful, fierce beauty.

And then it hits me what he is. Life coach, indeed.

"Are you an angel, Dominic?" I ask him.

He grins. "It sounds sort of dramatic when you say it like that."

"No," I say, unable to stop staring at him. "It sounds sort of magnificent. Fallen, I assume?"

"Hey, now." He gives me a mock scowl. He flaps his wings petulantly, and a whoosh of air flies over me.

"A scarab, then? You know they're also called dung beetles, right?"

The look on his face, aghast, disgusted, causes me to laugh. Oh, how I have missed that look. The laughter makes me feel young. No, not *feel* young. Become young. The years are melting away. I glance down at my hands. Not the gnarled hands of an old woman. Not anymore.

"Listen now," he says. "Get serious. I'm trying to show you the majesty of this thing."

I'm drinking in the easy conversation we always used to have. It is life to me. Oh, how I have missed this man.

"Stop your missing," he says, as if hearing my thoughts, a wide smile on his face. "I'm here. Right here. I've always been here. So have you. Are you going to take my hands again or what?"

I reach out my hands, but don't clasp his, not yet. "So, this is how this works?"

He exhales an exasperated sigh. "This is how it works. For you, it's a little different because, like it or not, you're my love. My partner. You get the special treatment."

"Not everyone gets to see the wings?"

"I swear, lady," he says, shaking his head. But he can't help smiling from ear to ear.

All at once, I don't feel like teasing anymore. The gravity of what is about to happen begins to settle around me, like a shroud.

"Will Dom be okay?"

"He'll be okay. You've seen to that. And I'll see to him. Just like I've always done."

"Will it hurt?"

"Okay, this is why not everyone gets the special treatment. All of this yakking. Take my hands, already. It will not hurt. I promise. But I might pinch the heck out of you when you get over to this side."

I lock eyes with him and place my hands in his. I step out. Just as easy as that.

"I thought it would be painful," I say to him.

"Nah," he says. "Nothing to it."

"So, what now?" I ask him. "It's sort of anticlimactic. I mean, I thought there might be a choir or something."

He shakes his head and smirks at me. But then he grows reverent, gazing at the body slumped in the chair by the fire. He leans down and cradles her in his arms, carrying her from the chair to the bed. He lays her down gently, and tenderly folds her hands together, smoothing her hair. He kisses her forehead and makes the sign of the cross.

"I don't like to leave them slumped over," he says. "They deserve some dignity. Especially her."

Then he reaches out and twirls me around, and I see that the shroud of old age is gone. I am young again, vibrant, healthy, just like I was that summer. He takes me into his arms, finally, after a lifetime, and I drink in the aroma of him. He puts his lips on mine, and I want to stay like that forever.

And all at once, I know. We *will* stay like this forever. I pull back and look him in the face, and I see it all. I see the timeless connection of our two souls.

"What do you say?" he says, low in my ear. "Do you want to do it all again?"

"Yes," I whisper. "Yes, I want to do it again."

"I thought you might. It's about love, baby, and we do that right."

"Our son, too? Will we see him again?"

Dominic smiles. "You're getting how this works. Finally, if I may say so. Yes, we'll see Dom again."

"We had a daughter, too. From another time. I dreamed about it."

"She'll be along. Don't worry about that."

"Were there any others? Other children from other times?"

"Only those two souls," he says. "They'll always be with us, honey. That's how it works for us."

"Can I pick the place this time?"

His amused face makes me laugh. "Now you want to pick the place. Where?"

"Cornwall?" I ask. "In a little cottage where we were happy before. Can we do that?"

"We'll see."

"We need to have longer together this time around," I say. "It was way too short last time."

"We'll do that, honey. But right now, some people are waiting for you," he says, leading me out of room five. We walk down the dark hallway and to the stairs. Under the closed door below there is light. We descend the stairs arm and arm, and he opens the door for me, smiling from ear to ear.

The room is filled with people, my people. Everyone who has gone before.

They are all smiling at me, clapping and cheering. There are my mom, dad, and grandma, vibrant and healthy and young. And my brothers. LuAnn and Gary, holding martinis aloft. Jason and Gil and dear Alice, free of the disease. She waves at me. Relatives, friends, students, everyone who has ever loved me during this life is here.

The force of the love in this room nearly knocks me over. I realize, that's everything. Love. That's all there is. I look up at Dominic's beautiful face, his dancing eyes, his devilish grin.

It's happy hour.

ACKNOWLEDGMENTS

What a joy to come back to Wharton! I was so delighted to find myself poking my nose into what was happening across town from Harrison's House. When I told my editors I was setting another tale in this otherworldly town where I had set *Daughters of the Lake*, they immediately said, "Ooooh! Is Simon in it?" Back by popular demand, one of the most beloved of my characters lights up the pages of this story, too. My friend Ken Anderson, the inspiration for Simon, was thrilled. I was, too.

To my agent, Jennifer Weltz, I feel profoundly blessed to have you in my life. Your friendship, support, guidance, and all of the laughter you bring into my world mean more than you know. You and everyone at the Jean V. Naggar Literary Agency have my never-ending gratitude for all you do for me.

To my team at Lake Union: Danielle Marshall, Faith Black Ross, Alicia Clancy, Ashley Vanicek, my eagle-eyed copy editors, and everyone else who works on my books, I am so lucky to have each one of you in my corner. Some authors dread the editing process. I love it! Faith and Alicia, I love reading your comments. Your insights are spot-on, you make me laugh, and you make the story stronger. And, Ashley, you are an absolute joy. All of you at Lake Union are not only stellar pros, but you make my life more fun, too.

To the independent booksellers and librarians who champion my books—thank you from the bottom of my heart. Anytime you'd like me to bring my dog-and-pony show to your place, I'm happy to come. (I might just bring my dog, FYI.) I love meeting readers, hearing their thoughts, and telling a ghost story or two.

As people who follow me on Facebook or Instagram know, some of the inspiration for this book came from my real life. Here's just one example.

One summer a few years ago, something unusual happened at the house next door to mine. A lovely, beautiful, graceful, funny, gentle woman in her sixties, who had early-onset Alzheimer's disease, came to live with my neighbors, who happened to be her former husband and his partner. Rather than this woman having to spend her last months in a nursing home, they took her in. It was one of the most breathtaking acts of love I had ever seen.

I spent a lot of time with her that summer. We'd sit outside under the shade of my crab-apple tree and talk about her past, her life, their children. It was a privilege to know that great lady. She passed at summer's end.

They were, obviously, the inspiration for the Alice-Jason-Gil story. Not the paranormal stuff. That all came from me. But she was just as gentle and lovely as Alice, and they were (and are) just as loving and funny and dear as Jason and Gil.

Just before I sent this manuscript to my editors, we shared a bottle of wine and talked about that summer. If you're so inclined, please give to the Alzheimer's Foundation of America so we can put an end to this cruel, heartless disease.

THE HAUNTING OF BRYNN WILDER DISCUSSION QUESTIONS

1. What is it about Wharton that has the power to heal? What draws people there after their lives have fallen apart?

2. What is your impression of LuAnn's? Is it just a hotel and restaurant, or something else?

3. Why are some places more haunted than others?

4. When did you know Dominic wasn't exactly earthly? Did you figure it out before the end?

5. If you were Brynn, would you have fallen for him?

6. Who is your favorite character, and why?

7. Have you ever cared for a loved one with dementia or Alzheimer's disease?

8. Many different kinds of love are explored in this book. Who do you think showed the most love, and why?

9. How could Brynn be in room five in the past and in the present at the same time?

10. Have you ever had something odd happen to you in the "in-between time"?

11. Was this an emotional book for you to read? Why or why not?

12. Wharton is based on a real place, Bayfield, Wisconsin. Would you ever want to visit? (Hint: LuAnn's is Gruenke's First Street Inn & Dining, and they really do a fish boil on Fridays in the summer. Harrison's House is Le Chateau Boutin. Ile de Colette is Madeline Island. The beach with the eerily temperate waters is Big Bay Town Park, and if you go there, you will pass by Tom's Burned Down Café, shirt and shoes not required.)

ABOUT THE AUTHOR

Wendy Webb is the #1 Amazon Charts bestselling, multiple-award-winning author of five novels of gothic suspense, including *Daughters of the Lake*, *The Vanishing*, *The Fate of Mercy Alban*, *The Tale of Halcyon Crane*, and *The End of Temperance Dare*, which has been optioned for both TV and film. Her books are sold worldwide and have been translated into seven languages. Dubbed Queen of the Northern Gothic by reviewers, Wendy sets her stories on the windswept, rocky shores of the Great Lakes. Wendy lives with a good dog in Minneapolis, where she is at work on her next novel. For more information visit http://wendykwebb.com.